Praise

"Laura Olson has succeeded in capturing ... rebellious cohort as well as our living spirit. What a blessing she has given her readers by reminding us that it ain't over."
— MARK RUDD, POLITICAL ORGANIZER, ANTI-WAR ACTIVIST, LECTURER, AND AUTHOR

"In this poignant narrative of three men and three women, now eighty years old, Olson deftly captures not only their ongoing commitment, struggles and setbacks as they reach retirement and old age but the power of abiding friendship to heal each other's tired spirits."
— JO FREEMAN, CIVIL RIGHTS ACTIVIST, A FOUNDING MEMBER OF THE FEMINIST MOVEMENT, AUTHOR

"Capture[s] many of the personal nuances and life complications confronting those who sought so urgently to save the world."
— PAUL BUHLE, FOUNDING EDITOR OF THE SDS JOURNAL *RADICAL AMERICA*, RETIRED SENIOR LECTURER, BROWN UNIVERSITY

"These badass activists reject the temptation to wallow in recitations of an old despond, or any nostalgia for a ship that's already left the shore."
— BILL AYERS, POLITICAL ORGANIZER, ANTI-WAR ACTIVIST, AUTHOR OF *FUGITIVE DAYS: MEMOIRS OF AN ANTI-WAR ACTIVIST*

"A beautifully crafted work of art. Lovingly constructed characters captivated me from page one. Embedded in this novel is a micro history of the 1960s."
— GEORGE KATSIAFICAS, POLITICAL ACTIVIST, AUTHOR OF *THE GLOBAL IMAGINATION OF 1968: REVOLUTION AND COUNTERREVOLUTION*

"For those who want to learn about the momentous years of social struggle in the 1960s—the civil rights movement; the anti-Vietnam war movement; the women's liberation movement—Olson gives an engaging and lively flavor of these events through six different relatable characters."
NANCY ROSENSTOCK, AUTHOR OF *INSIDE THE SECOND WAVE OF FEMINISM: BOSTON FEMALE LIBERATION 1968-1972 AN ACCOUNT BY PARTICIPANTS*

"A warm-hearted, engaging novel of the life-shaping force of '60s activism and its enduring aftermath; a rare treat for those who were there and for those who wish they were."
DAVID FARBER, AUTHOR OF
THE AGE OF GREAT DREAMS: AMERICAN IN THE 1960S

"If you lived through the '60s, you'll know these characters, remember the events and issues. If you didn't—start here. This is the novel to savor: enjoy the ride!"
TERRY H. ANDERSON, AUTHOR OF *THE MOVEMENT AND THE SIXTIES*

About the Author

Laura Katz Olson, AGF Distinguished Professor of Political Science, has taught at Lehigh University since 1974. To date, she has published nine nonfiction books, focusing on aging and healthcare. Her latest, *Ethically Challenged: Private Equity Storms US Health Care* has been awarded several gold medals, including the Independent Book Publishers Association (IBPA) and the Benjamin Franklin Awards. *Elder Care Journey: A View from the Front Lines*, which relates her personal experiences as a caregiver for her mother, won a gold medal in the Ninth Annual Living Now Book Awards. She is also a recipient of the Charles A. McCoy Lifetime Achievement Award. *Wrinkled Rebels* is her second novel.

wrinkledrebels-olson.com

Wrinkled Rebels

Laura Katz Olson

Wrinkled Rebels
Copyright © 2024 Laura Katz Olson
All rights reserved.

Print Edition
ISBN: 978-3-98832-075-9
Published by Vine Leaves Press 2024

No parts of this publication may be reproduced, stored in a retrieval system, or transmitted in any form or by any means, electronic, mechanical, photocopying, recording, or otherwise, without the prior written permission of the copyright owner.

This book is sold subject to the condition that it shall not, by way of trade or otherwise, be lent, resold, hired out, or otherwise circulated without the publisher's prior consent in any form of binding or cover other than that in which it is published and without a similar condition including this condition being imposed on the subsequent purchaser. Under no circumstances may any part of this book be photocopied for resale.

This is a work of fiction. Any similarity between the characters and situations within its pages and places or persons, living or dead, is unintentional and coincidental.

Cover design by Jessica Bell
Interior design by Amie McCracken

This book is dedicated to progressive political activists, young and old, seeking social justice and a better world.

PART I
The Invitation: December 2024

1
Deanna

DEANNA EYES the purple envelope peeking out from among the usual bills and advertisements that she grabbed from the mailbox. She has a sense of foreboding. Did one of her college friends die? It's long past the time when they visited each other, and these days they mostly communicate by annual holiday cards, usually a UNICEF variation of multi-colored children waving peace signs. Rebecca's envelopes are invariably purple, like this one, to remind them of their City College alma mater.

Deanna hobbles slowly up her long, rocky driveway, clutching the mail tightly in one hand as she navigates a cane with the other. She winces. The pain in her knee has been worsening over the past few years. She shakes her head sadly. You would never know that she was the athlete among their group. The five of them had cheered her on when she ran her first marathon those so many years ago. When was it? Probably 1964, their second year of college. She mimics them now as she wills herself forward: "Go, Deanna, go!"

Her body tightens as a slight breeze filters through the thin sweater she's thrown on. Damn, it's up to sixty degrees and she's shivering. Imagine if she still lived in New York, where the weather is so bitter in December. She'd reveled in California's climate when she arrived in Stanford nearly fifty years ago. But nowadays she always feels cold.

She looks up at the spacious Victorian house she and Sam bought when they finally paid off their medical school loans. Deanna knows she should sell it. An elderly widow doesn't need five bedrooms, she chides herself. They should have dumped the place long ago when the three kids Sam wanted never materialized. Their adopted daughter and two grandchildren rarely venture west from New Jersey, though she surely has coaxed them.

Early on, she took up gardening for a break from her arduous medical routines and the grounds of their home, depending on the season, smelled of lavender, jasmine, gardenias, and lilies of the valley. Their splashes of color enlivened her spirits. She especially prided herself on the lavish rose garden she carefully tended for decades, nurturing the flowers with the same care she gave the poverty-stricken pregnant women who had no place else to go for an abortion. But recently, when she found that just bending over took monumental effort, she hired a gardener.

Deanna trudges on, forcing herself up the last two steps leading into the house like a truck shifting into low gear. Exhausted, she plops into a nearby chair, throws the mail onto the glass coffee table, and seizes a nearly empty bottle of Tylenol. As she waits for the medicine to take effect, she stares at the purple envelope. It's probably about Russell, she decides. Her charming Russ, long dark curls falling over his forehead. He had called her after his second heart attack five years ago. He was frightened and yearned for a soothing voice. "The stents will keep you going just fine, Russ," she reassured him. "But you must stop drinking. That will kill you." She was sure he wouldn't take the advice, but he seemed comforted by her medical opinion even though she was a gynecologist.

She had met Russell at a Congress of Racial Equality meeting when they were both still in high school. At the time, CORE—as it was known—was organizing Freedom Rides through the Deep South with the aim of disrupting segregated interstate bus services. Several of the CORE volunteers, nearly all of whom were in college, had joined in the struggle but their parents had forbidden them from participating. "Deanna, Deanna," her mother had said, shaking her head. "If you get thrown in jail, you'll risk being rejected by City College. A good education for free. And for what? Who are they to you?" Mom had accentuated *they*, staring straight at her with a frozen smile. Deanna simply turned her back and walked away, cringing in disgust.

Russell's parents were equally vehement and dismissive of his arguments. "Do you want to throw away everything we've dreamed of for you, all the sacrifices we've made?" his father had barked, his face turning red. "City College will toss out your application if you have a police record." He hesitated, then added almost as an afterthought, "And you can't even vote yet yourself."

Both Deanna and Russell would have eagerly taken part in the Freedom Rides, despite the risks, arrests, and beatings that college students were encountering in the South.

Deanna had been willing to defy her parents. "Let's take our chances," she said. "Our parents don't own us."

Russell gave a half-hearted shrug and stared at the floor. "I can't. Dad has sacrificed too much for me. It would crush him."

"And you are crushing me. I want to go." She lifted his face up to her pleading eyes.

Russell had been torn but he knew he couldn't challenge his parents at this point in his life. He touched her arm lightly. "Not yet, Deanna. For now, we can work together at the CORE office. Help the cause in that way."

She swallowed hard, holding back tears. At least they would be beside one another. "For now," she repeated.

Deanna had been immediately beguiled by the ruggedly handsome boy with intense, dark brown eyes and an infectious smile. The round, horn-rimmed glasses gave him an intellectual look that complemented his love of books. He carried around at least two volumes in an olive-green satchel that he toted everywhere, tossed over his shoulder like a mail carrier's bag. He read incessantly, mostly about philosophy and politics. His two favorites, David Riesman's *The Lonely Crowd* and William Whyte's *The Organization Man*, spoke to the sense of alienation he had felt since junior high school. A few novels captured his imagination as well, especially *Animal Farm* and *Lord of the Flies*. Russell could spend hours talking about his latest theoretical discoveries and debating them with anyone who would listen. She always did.

Deanna was more action-oriented, though she read her share of books as well. She had been particularly moved by Michael Harrington's *The Other America*. How could such poverty exist in this land of plenty? Her parents and neighbors had rejoiced in the modern inventions taking over their homes—washing machines, dryers, dishwashers. They shined their new cars with a religious fervor and escaped the summer heat by heading to bungalows in the countryside or at the seashore. Yet Harrington made clear that others, mostly minorities, were struggling to pay rent and feed their children.

It had forced her to look at her own all-white, middle-class Irish neighborhood in the Bronx with a critical eye. She had rarely ventured elsewhere during her adolescence, wary of the ethnic and racial strongholds across the borough, not to mention the entire city. "Stick to your own kind" had been her mother's mantra. The invisible boundaries that divided the Italians, Irish, Jews, Germans, Asians, and other nationalities residing in the northern section of the borough were stark. She'd been warned against the dangers of the South Bronx, where Black and Puerto Rican residents clustered in their separate enclaves confronted gangs, crime, and a breakdown of essential services. Until high school, she had turned a blind eye to their suffering.

Deanna felt an even greater sense of moral outrage after witnessing televised police brutality against minorities who were struggling to integrate the South through peaceful sit-ins. Seeing those images was the first time she had been exposed to legal segregation and the consuming wrath driving the perpetrators. The inequality stung at her core, and a deep sense of injustice swelled within her. She was ready to join the battle. Charging ahead, in her junior year she signed up with CORE.

♀

She and Russell had begun their liaison several months after they met. It was challenging to get together since he lived in Brooklyn, far from her family's apartment. They were too young to drive and it would have taken hours to rendezvous by subway. But they saw each other three times a week at CORE headquarters at Park Row and regularly sneaked off to an older volunteer's apartment nearby.

He was her first lover. She had never gone beyond necking and petting in the back of a car, guardedly pushing previous boyfriends away. With Russell, her approach had been different; she longed for his touch. They were awkward and clumsy at first, not quite sure how to proceed. He kissed her urgently, slipping his tongue into her mouth, and gently fondled her breasts, arousing her entire being. When he pressed between her legs, however, it hurt, and the excitement dissipated. Oblivious, Russell entered her, eager and hard, thrusting until he ejaculated with an ecstatic moan. Uncertain as to what was wrong and not wanting to disappoint him, she had pretended to have an orgasm. He lay back on the bed, his arm around her, sweaty and pleased with himself.

It went on like that for over a year. When they made love, Deanna fell into a dreamy state, Russell's caresses tugging at her heart. But sexually she felt stiff, still incapable of letting herself go, of achieving the big O. She decided to experiment more on herself, discovering the precise places of pleasure. Stimulating her clitoris, she had learned, gave her far more pleasure than the opening in her vagina. She read, too; other women admitted to faking their climax. And she found an obscure essay by radical feminist Anne Koedt, "The Myth of the Vaginal Orgasm," suggesting that the clitoris is the main source of a woman's sexual climax.

Eventually, Deanna had gathered up the courage to educate Russell about female anatomy, mindful of his fragile male ego. Every so often, when he disregarded her needs, she gently moved his hands to her erogenous zones. In the end, they developed a relatively satisfying intimate relationship, though she still sensed there could be more.

At the CORE office, they both had been assigned drudgery work—printing leaflets, folding and mailing them, and fetching coffee for the college students who were directing the activities. Her body relaxes as she mentally replays their time with the group. That was not actually true, Deanna reminds herself. She had brought the coffee and accommodated the everyday needs of the college boys while Russell had been tapped to help write pamphlets and provide input on strategies.

She wrinkles her nose. What girls put up with in those days. They eventually had figured things out. . .yes, they did. She leans back on the sofa, her lips twisting into a smug smile. There had been six of them in their circle of friends when the three women connected with a consciousness-raising group. That had been eye-opening. The men at first had scoffed at the Women's Movement. Russell told her that there were more pressing issues. "Our civil rights work is about racial injustice," he had said, "and that should be the priority."

"Women's lib?" Max had snorted, with a cocky grin. "What a bunch of malarky."

"Are you chicks going to burn your bras?" Keith chimed in, rolling his eyes.

It wasn't easy, but the guys were steadily nudged into the Women's Movement several years later when it became fashionable for New Left men to rally around the cause. Or at least they claimed to be feminists, even if they didn't always act accordingly. Russell had been the most resistant while she, Rebecca, and Malaika increasingly gobbled up books on radical feminism: Robin Morgan, Kate Millett, Shulamith Firestone, Germaine Greer. They had read them all, consuming them like chocoholics indulging in overflowing baskets of sweet, gourmet treats. Deanna constantly had to remind Russell that he was behaving like a male chauvinist pig, which never failed to irk him. Only Keith mostly abandoned his sexist attitudes, which endeared him to the women.

♀

Deanna gazes at the modest living room furniture, clearly out of place in a Victorian house. What an eclectic potpourri, she laughs to herself. She and Sam had picked out most of it at flea markets, yard sales, and antique shops. The gang would have approved, she is sure.

Her eyes land on the purple envelope. She's still afraid to open it. She loves her entire college clan and can't bear the thought that one of them is most likely gone.

Deanna closes her eyes. She smiles slightly as she looks back on how they had first connected. She and Russell had met Max and Rebecca on the bus to the March on Washington for Jobs and Freedom in August 1963.

Rebecca had approached Deanna first. "This is going to be a long, lonely ride for me," Rebecca had said. She rolled her eyes at Max, who was absorbed in a book. "He's reading about a major, major, major, major," she had chuckled.

"Hmm," Deanna murmured. "It's *Catch-22* and I just finished it." She pointed to Russell. "And he's reading it now."

Rebecca tapped Max on the shoulder. "The guy seated next to us seems to be buried in the same book as you."

Both men had looked up. "It's a good read so far," Max had called out. "Great satire." He introduced himself to Russell and Deanna.

"And I'm Rebecca," she told them.

They spent the next four hours on the bus swapping political stories and then hung out together at the National Mall, listening to the speeches. They had so much in common, starting with the fact that all four of them would be entering City College in a few weeks. Their bond had been cemented as they listened, misty-eyed, to Martin Luther King Jr.'s "I Have a Dream" speech. Their attachment only grew deeper the next day as they joined hands, singing "We Shall Overcome" along with Joan Baez, surrounded by well over two hundred thousand marchers.

It had been an awe-inspiring experience for the four high schoolers, like an adrenaline rush from a first-time sky dive. They had felt the energy, strength, and power of numbers as they witnessed masses of people standing up for what they believed in. The historical event was indelibly etched in their minds.

At college they had gathered daily in the South Cafeteria, where they exchanged ideas, discussed books, planned joint political actions, and generally amused each other with stories and word games. By the end of the first month, they were joined by Keith, whom Max had met in his "Introduction to Philosophy" course. They linked up with Malaika shortly thereafter. She had been wandering around the cafeteria, coffee cup in hand, seeking an empty table. "Hey! Why don't you sit with us?" Russell said almost as a command. She never left them.

In warmer weather, they had sat on the college's South Lawn, where Keith would strum his guitar to the latest folk songs. He began writing his own music. Deanna sang with the rest of them, mostly off-key, her waist-long flaxen hair tossing every which way as she bobbed her head to the music. Their times together soon expanded to include weekend movies, lectures, folk concerts, and coffee houses in Greenwich Village.

On Sunday afternoons, they often met at the fountain in Washington Square Park. The place had been bursting with a patchwork of folk singers, poets, beatniks, families, and political gurus. Old men played chess; children ran amok. One could smell marijuana in the air, and Deanna suspected that harder drugs were available as well. She had loved looking at the bizarre, colorful apparel including men and women running around in bathing suits, even in winter. Keith would bring his guitar and open the case for coins. They usually ended the afternoon with coffee at a nearby café, paid for with Keith's earnings.

One morning, sitting together prior to classes, Max had suggested they take the subway out to Coney Island. "Let's play hooky," he said. "All work and no play are not good for the soul."

Malaika had stirred uncomfortably in her seat and said pointedly, "Unlike the rest of you I would be conspicuously absent from class. I don't exactly blend in." She furrowed her brow, adding, "I must maintain my grades for the scholarship."

"Touché," Deanna had whispered, stumbling for words.

"Sunday then," Max piped up, without missing a beat. "Instead of Washington Square."

The outing had turned out to be one of the more intoxicating days of their early friendship. Deanna calls to mind the agreeable mix of aromas as soon as they had stepped onto the boardwalk—cotton candy, caramel, cinnamon, onion rings, fried clams. Before long they caught whiffs of beer, margaritas, and then, suddenly, the ineluctable scent of Nathan's hot dogs, sauerkraut, chili, mustard, ketchup, and crinkle-cut French fries, all insisting on being devoured.

The companions had pooled their meager resources and indulged themselves. Rebecca dropped a $20 bill into the pot, a huge sum at the time. Her daddy had slipped her the money and told her to treat her new buddies. Rebecca's family was generous and doted on their only child. When Malaika hesitated, reluctant to let anybody pay her way, Rebecca waved aside her concerns, saying "From each according to his ability, to each according to his needs." They spent the rest of the day splurging on rides.

When they ventured toward the Cyclone roller coaster with its drops, curves, and plunges of up to sixty miles an hour, Rebecca had put her foot down. "Not me," she said. Max attempted to convince her, but she was adamant. "These two feet stay firmly on the ground." She resisted the 150-foot-tall Wonder Wheel as well. She had sat on a bench, contentedly munching on a funnel cake that dusted her T-shirt with sugary white powder. Whenever her friends spun past her, she waved.

Deanna remembers how the feisty Rebecca had been wheedled into a bumper car, and everyone had aimed directly at her. That raised her hackles, and she returned their crashes with a vengeance. She also joined them on the merry-go-round, sitting on the outside row of horses, eager to grab the brass ring. The uncoordinated Rebecca never had a chance and was furious when Max seized an iron one, which he offered to her.

Deanna leans back on the sofa, conjuring up the comingled smells, screeches of delight from the daring rides, images of grainy sand and gently rolling waves, and the cloying tang of sweets. They are a snapshot in time as though captured by an instant camera. She is wistful, remembering how they had headed home, drained but blissfully filled with each other.

The six of them had become a community unto themselves, reveling in each other's company. Cautiously, they began sharing personal histories and concerns. Initially, the boys had been guarded; they weren't the touchy-feely types. Deanna, unfailingly the facilitator, slowly drew them in. It was the first time they had ever revealed their innermost thoughts to anyone, and the disclosures had brought the gang even closer.

2
Russell

RUSSELL DESCENDS the spiral staircase of his New York City condo, eager for another cup of coffee. As usual, the place is unbearably hot, almost like a steam bath despite the 35° temperature outside. No matter how many times he warns Beth about the oil bill, his wife quietly turns up the thermostat. He's been writing all afternoon in his study, re-working an article on the precarious state of progressive politics for *CounterPunch* magazine. The subject depresses him, and the muggy air is giving him a headache.

He walks into the kitchen. "What happened?" he asks. There is lavender glitter scattered on the table, spilling onto the floor.

"We're invited to a reunion," Beth says, crossing her arms. "With *them*." She spits out "them" with a snort.

He sees the purple envelope that had contained the offending glitter, sits down, and reaches for the card his wife threw on top of the mess. His heart pounds as he reads the note from Rebecca. The message is terse. "The six of us will reunite at The Mountain House near New Paltz, New York, for the weekend of June 5, 2025. Please do not bring your significant other, children, grandchildren, dogs, cats, or pet snakes. The gathering will be just us." A command performance. Typical Rebecca, he thinks.

Russell fingers his wedding band as his wife glares at him, fists clenched. Their relationship has been particularly rocky these past few years and the reunion will no doubt be yet another flashpoint. The glitter twinkles ominously in the December mid-afternoon light shining through the large window. An unbearable silence falls, sucking the oxygen out of the room. He can't breathe. At length he gets up, walks toward the door, and says, "You're not invited, Beth. You already know that."

He steps into the elevator, rides eleven stories down to the ground floor, and struts outside into nippy gusts of wind. He pulls his wool cap over his ears, turns up the fleece collar on his down jacket, and tightens his scarf. As he roams the streets of New York's Upper West Side, slightly stooped over, the Christmas sounds, scents, and sights put him in better spirits. He takes in the savory aromas of roasting chestnuts, fresh pretzels, sizzling hotdogs, and sweet knishes in corner carts. Large gold and silver bells and red-and-green-striped candy canes sway from iron railings. Brightly lit Douglas firs, blue spruces, and Scotch pines covered in assorted ornaments and fairy lights are blinking everywhere. Storefront windows with dazzling displays, many featuring mechanical forms jumping every which way, beckon pedestrians.

The clanging bells of Salvation Army Santas reverberate throughout the city as do honking horns and sirens of ambulances and fire trucks, screeching and wailing. A man pulling his bundled-up toddler on a wooden sled with wheels smiles at Russell, and he gestures back with a slight wave. Lightly falling snow is twinkling everywhere like the lavender glitter on his table. Should he go to the reunion?

Russell walks into a pub, sits at the bar, and takes off his hat. He brushes melting snow from his beard.

"What can I get for you, old man?" the bartender says.

Russell rubs his balding scalp as if to confirm the affront. Old man indeed, he mutters to himself. "Martini," he says. "Dry. With a twist."

Should he go? Perhaps it would be best not to trample on the memories of his youth, which soothe him like a warm bubble bath. For him, the six of them had been a legion of committed activists, devoted to social causes and each other. They had become his reinvented family with no pretensions between them; they accepted one another as-is.

Yet perhaps the lens of time has distorted the truth of their friendship, allowing him to twist reality into a fantasy world of his own making. His whole life is in shambles at the moment, like a topsy-turvy playroom scattered with broken toys, and he's not sure he's up to facing a potential flood of disappointment. Maybe he should leave his recollections, even if illusory, intact.

Russell envisions Deanna's tall, lean body strutting along in a miniskirt and an embroidered, gauzy peasant blouse on top that afforded hints of her ample breasts. He had loved her long, silky, blonde hair that she sometimes tied into a long braid streaming down her back. She wore dangling beaded earrings of various sizes, shapes, and colors. Her steely blue eyes were somewhat incongruous with the straight-edged nose, tipped up at the end, sprinkled with freckles. She certainly had turned a few heads.

When they made love, he would undress her with urgency, as if it would be the last time. In his mind's eye, he pictures stripping her naked like he used to. He then circled her nipples with his tongue, feeling them become erect, alive. His fingers had stroked her milky skin, steadily reaching down for the sweet spot between her legs. As his dick became increasingly hard, he tried to distract himself, fearful that he would come prematurely. But her voluptuous body had always called him back, and he would thrust into her, succumbing to his seemingly irrepressible lust.

His mother had called her his "shiksa." Neither of their parents had been pleased with the relationship. Her family did their best to sabotage it from the start. He didn't know which offended them more: the fact that he was Jewish or his politics. They had blamed him for Deanna's atheism and growing radicalism. They obviously didn't know their headstrong daughter very well. She had long abandoned the Catholic Church by high school. "My religion is social justice," she would say to anyone who asked about her faith.

Alone at the bar, he takes a sip of his martini. The cocktail is comforting. She and the others had been so sure that they could make a difference in the world. The six of them were steadfast in their commitment to social change. They had spent hours in the City College cafeteria debating the major issues of the day. By early 1964, they were weighing the pros and cons of Malcolm X's call for more militant action in the fight for civil rights. Deanna had turned out to be the most hardline of their group, pushing everyone to confront head-on whatever controversies emerged. She was the one who pushed the six of them to participate in CORE's Freedom Summer Project to register Black voters in Mississippi.

The friends had helped mimeograph the brochures for the undertaking, and in March they applied to join the campaign. They were giddy with anticipation when they received their acceptance letters and, shortly thereafter, left for two weeks of training in Oxford, Ohio. Their eagerness had been somewhat dampened when they learned about the "disappearance" of three college activists—James Chaney, Andrew Goodman, and Michael Schwerner—who were presumed dead. They recognized that they could meet the same fate. After a long discussion and much trepidation, they had resolved to keep going.

At the end of June, they left on a Freedom bus to the Deep South, joining over 700 other civil rights activists from other organizations—The Students Nonviolent Coordinating Committee (SNCC), Southern Christian Leadership Conference (SCLC), and even the National Association for the Advancement of Colored People (NAACP). They had anticipated harassment and some danger but were truly shaken almost immediately by the shootings, beatings, bombings, and murders they witnessed. The state and local police forces had been reinforced with additional officers, riot gear, and weapons, ready to take the northern "outside agitators" head on. After a few close encounters with out-of-control white supremacists and their law enforcement allies, a few following the six friends in pickup trucks, the guys decided that Rebecca, Malaika, and Deanna should go home.

The women had stood firm even though they were terrified. Malaika, who was most at risk, was particularly offended by their pressure to leave and told them, hands on hips, "We make our own decisions." She had even suggested at the end of their stay in the South that they head to Atlantic City to protest the seating of the all-white Mississippi delegation at the Democratic National Convention. Demonstrators were striving to install the Mississippi Freedom Democratic Party's alterative biracial contingent. Russell recalls that they had been tempted to go but were too burnt out. Instead, they returned straight to college, physically unscathed but emotionally traumatized. In addition to their own ordeal, they had observed firsthand how Black citizens who attempted to exercise their right to vote were subjected to arrest, beatings, shootings, and possibly death. Many also faced losing their home or their job. The horrors they had encountered were forever burned into their psyches and left them even more determined to fight on.

Russell recoils as he remembers the mayhem of the 1960s. There certainly had been much to struggle against. Yet, even the most peaceful marches and demonstrations against dilapidated housing, poverty, poorly funded schools, bias in the workplace, and sorely deficient public services had been met with clubs, tear gas, and guns. More civil rights activists died. Police brutality against Black people, endemic in northern as well as southern cities, had incited greater militancy among demonstrators. In August 1965, the Watts Uprising broke out near Los Angeles, culminating in massive property damage and the loss of thirty-four lives. This had been followed by uprisings in major cities throughout the nation for several years thereafter. The country was a tinderbox.

Until they had become caught up in the Anti-War Movement, the six friends continued their work against racial injustice. They maintained their support of sit-ins, voter registration drives, and marches in the South. They were particularly active in recruiting City College students to the Civil Rights Movement by disseminating fliers about the atrocities. They had stoked outrage through weekly articles in *The Campus*, the college's student-run newspaper.

Russell wrote most of the initial drafts but overall, the pieces were a collaborative effort. His best commentary had been on the 1965 march from Selma to Montgomery, Alabama, led by Hosea Williams of SCLC and SNCC chairman John Lewis. Six hundred people, including women and children, had been attacked at the Edmund Pettus Bridge by state troopers and local law enforcement agents with Billy clubs, tear gas, and bullwhips in what became known as "Bloody Sunday." His article had inflamed the student body.

Russell gives a satisfied sigh and lifts his cocktail glass to toast himself. Should he go? he asks himself again. He orders another martini, savoring the question along with his drink. What has he accomplished over the last decades? He would have to justify his career to them. To her. He tallies up the books he has published. Fifteen in all, if you count the edited volumes. Every one of them by high-ranking presses. Hundreds of articles in popular magazines, refereed journals, blogs, and online sites. He is a highly accomplished scholar, having won lifetime achievement awards from the Association for Critical Sociology and eventually—but reluctantly—from the more traditional American Sociology Association. He has climbed the ladder of academic success as a radical sociologist with his original pieces on class, gender, race, and social movements. He is a distinguished professor. Emeritus, he grudgingly reminds himself.

As a graduate student at Columbia University, he had led the charge of the Sociology Liberation Movement that demanded resolutions by the American Sociology Association to condemn the renewed bombing of Hanoi, had censured Nixon for covering up his role in the Watergate break-in, and supported radical sociologists whose tenure was in jeopardy. Later, he had chaired the Association for Critical Sociology and was selected as editor for three top left journals, *Critical Sociology*, *Monthly*

Review, and *Capital and Class.* By retirement last year, he was what his young colleagues and graduate students would call a superstar in his field.

But his five college friends would not be impressed. "Exactly what have you achieved?" Deanna would demand. "Really achieved over the decades to make this a better world." He has no appropriate answer. He has written so many words consumed only by other academics. He had led organizations that simply challenged mainstream professors. The main impact of his work had been to advance his career. He was a star in the isolated ivory tower. He would be held to account by the entire gang. He's haunted by their guiding principle: "Philosophers have hitherto only interpreted the world in various ways; the point is to change it." They had constantly reminded each other of its significance during their time together. He orders a third martini.

3
Malaika

MALAIKA MULLS over the reunion yet again. The invitation simply surfaced one day like a bottle on the sand with a message from across the ocean. She rarely saw any of them after graduating from law school and moving to DC.

The gang had provided Malaika a solid footing in college through their fierce, binding friendship along with imbuing her with political know-how and a sense of activist engagement. She would have been alone and lost at City College, a Black woman from the ghetto amidst a sea of white middle-class kids. Until she met them, she had felt like an illegal immigrant breaching the US border. Later, Rebecca and Deanna pushed her even harder, firing up and sustaining her ambitions.

Malaika walks across the cozy living room and switches on the CD stereo player at high volume. As "California Dreamin'" booms from the oversized amplifier, she sits in her leather recliner, leaning back as far as possible. She breathes slowly, her eyes brimming with tears.

So much has happened in the long years since then. She has raised children who have kids of their own. And she's had her share of life's hiccups, including a short separation from her husband. He had become fed up with the late hours and weekends at the office, claiming that her work seemed more important than him and the family. Now, at ninety-two years old, Darryl is fighting Stage 4 prostate cancer; he has opted for active surveillance rather than radiation therapy, which is worrisome for Malaika.

Relationships with her siblings are complicated; one has been in and out of jail. A bout with uterine cancer set her back for a while as well. But she had been strong-willed and indefatigable. Resilient. That's how they knew her. Not so much at present. Malaika is anxious about exposing the raw insecurities and uncertainties tormenting her. She feels as though her days are churning in nothingness.

Her eldest daughter, a psychologist, has been hounding her to get help. "There are so many medications out there for depression—Paxil, Prozac, Zoloft. Drugs will help you bounce back."

"I'm not depressed," she retorted in a flat, even voice. "And I don't want to become one of those old biddies popping a handful of pills every night. I already take too many."

Like Malaika, her headstrong daughter didn't take "no" easily. "I'll get you the names of a few psychiatrists. Just try one session. For me. And Dad." Laila became exasperated. "These are supposed to be your golden years, Mom. You've had a long, successful career, and it's time to relax."

Malaika thinks about her first position in the Civil Rights Division at the US Department of Justice. The bureaucratic hurdles had been frustrating, like finding your way through an elaborate maze. She felt hemmed in, powerless to choose which cases to engage in, forever having to obtain authorization from multiple levels of supervisors. None of them had the same criteria as she did—at the top ranks, they factored in the cost of litigation, political advantage, and the odds of winning. Malaika's singular concern was to represent the downtrodden, people who had nowhere else to turn, even if it would be a Herculean struggle. But she had plugged along, winning several noteworthy racial and gender discrimination lawsuits in federal court.

Ten years later, when she started her own law firm, she had attained her dream job. Racism in housing and unwarranted evictions. Educational and workplace inequities. Disability and women's rights. Sexual harassment. Her firm aggressively pursued anything that smacked of injustice. Darryl had given her the go-ahead; they had made a pact that he would earn the big bucks while she was free to dedicate herself to worthy causes irrespective of financial considerations.

Her career had given her great satisfaction, a sense of purpose. For Malaika it had been a calling. The drive to combat societal wrongs was baked into her DNA. Over the years, she had gained a reputation as one of the finest lawyers in DC, aggressive and sharp-witted. She was regularly offered far more lucrative positions and even had been wooed by partners from large corporate practices. But defending rich clients didn't appeal to her. Malaika viewed herself as having a solid moral compass, like the rest of her college friends. A piece of her identity depended on her legal skills, especially for the poor whom she took on pro bono. The unremitting work had been a labor of love.

She relished her accomplishments and would have stayed on at the firm, but at seventy-eight, she could no longer keep up the pace or her share of the caseload. And her hearing had deteriorated to the point that even the hearing aids were insufficient. "What'd you say? What'd you say?" she heard herself continuously asking clients. She had known it was time to leave.

Malaika walks into the bathroom and stares intently into the mirror. When did she first become herself, she wonders. Or at least this version of herself. She knew that lives transform as people grow old. Hers certainly has. But how much has she changed? She pushes a spiral lock of hair from her face. Perhaps this latest version of herself is just a recycled form of her young one but more wrinkled, with considerably fewer brain cells, and certainly far fewer expectations for the future. Her voice quivers as she tells the contorted facial image, "I had wanted to change the world. Now I'm through."

Even her to-do lists have disappeared, those scraps of paper that assured her that there was something demanding her attention. They were a sign of optimism, a sense of moving forward as she crossed out completed obligations. Since new ones promptly replaced the old, her life was always in motion. Or so it had seemed. Malaika even feels the absence of the jarring sound of her alarm clock, its unvarying buzz that begrudged her sleep but announced the opening of a new, wondrous day. Nowadays, it is silent.

She's not taking retirement well and is feeling at loose ends. The law firm had been a guardrail. Without the everyday challenges, she is plunging downward into an abyss. Darryl has been urging her to go to the reunion, as have her four children. They seem to agree that the group might raise her spirits and even light a fire under her to search for a new meaning in life. Malaika's not so sure. Her husband, who retired from the law school faculty twenty years ago, has leisurely pursued model boat building, baking, photography, and refurbishing items around the house—even when they're perfectly fine, in her opinion.

He has taken to proposing pastimes for her to try, writing them on a small pad placed on her dresser each morning. This tender gesture irks her; she rips out the paper, crumples it into a ball, and pitches the wad toward the waste basket across the room, usually short of the mark. She remains unmotivated. . .hobbies are just not for her.

♀

Darryl sidles up and puts his arms around her waist. She looks at him and a flicker of a smile crosses her lips. "I was a good lawyer, really good, wasn't I?" she murmurs, more a statement than a question. "Who would have thought a Black female attorney from the ghetto could win so many civil rights cases." There is an unaccustomed pride in her voice.

She had been a curiosity, even among her African American schoolmates in Brownsville. Beginning in her earliest years, she had harbored ambitions that were so unlikely to materialize that she never confided them to anyone. Not even to her best friend, Issa, who lived in the apartment next door. Since she was twelve, Malaika had avidly consumed every TV show about the legal system. *The Verdict Is Yours, Accused, Divorce Court, Perry Mason,* and *Lock-Up* were fodder for her longing to become a lawyer. At the time, of course, any career for her was unthinkable.

She had lived with her mother and four younger siblings in a deteriorating public housing complex surrounded by poverty and crime. There were few police and those who patrolled the neighborhood were brutal, crooked, or both. A deep distrust had developed between the locals and the officers who engaged in racial profiling and other oppressive tactics. Back then, they were imposing figures, towering white men dressed in navy blue shirts and pants with holstered revolvers at their hips. Although the residents were not well-disposed toward them, Malaika had been ambivalent; their presence both frightened her and gave reassurance. Gangs roamed the neighborhood, triggering a sense of trepidation whenever she stepped outside her building. She had felt caught between their lawlessness and the intimidation of the cops.

Gunshots were common as she worked on her homework at the kitchen table. Few of her classmates even bothered to do the assignments. Her grades were excellent, generally As, even though she had to care for her siblings every day after school. As the eldest, her responsibilities also included shopping and preparing meals. There was no supermarket within walking distance, so she had to shop at the high-priced local grocery with her siblings by her side. She regularly passed jeering, jobless men on the way. "Hey, darkie," they would say, "Wanna come home with me?" She would wrap her arms around her already well-covered breasts as though wishing them away.

Malaika's dark-skinned complexion contrasted sharply with that of her family. Aiysha, Julene, Maya, and Frederick were light-skinned. She especially envied Aiysha, whose face was flawless, like a polished stone. Her momma would tell Malaika with a sly laugh, "We know there's no slave-owning daddies in your genes." She would look at her mother, whose own skin resembled her siblings', and wonder who her daddy was. Momma wouldn't tell. Perhaps she didn't know.

In high school, she caught the eye of a guidance counselor, Mrs. Levy, who lavished her with encouragement and advice. "You are college material," she had told Malaika in her sophomore year. "And your marks are high enough for City College, which is tuition-free." She had paused, wrinkling her forehead. "That is if you keep them up," she added, not unkindly.

Malaika was taken aback. Yes, she had private dreams of college but never thought she'd actually go. What was expected of her had been to finish high school and obtain a job, maybe becoming a hairstylist like her mother. She had long been reconciled to a working-class future, a labor-intensive life with long hours and low wages. She would follow orders, be under the thumb of a boss or supervisor, and take home a meager paycheck. At best, in due course, she could advance herself by obtaining training and certification as a paraprofessional, working as an LPN or administrative assistant.

She remembers gasping and trembling at Mrs. Levy's assertion that she could possibly attend college. After an awkward silence, Malaika stumbled to fill the void. She met her teacher's gaze and in a hushed, tiny voice, like a child whose hand was caught in the cookie jar, affirmed her readiness to work hard. Malaika had not asked any follow-up questions.

Over the next three years, she embarked on a grueling regimen to catch up with students at more affluent high schools. She steadily improved her reading and writing skills on her own, practicing every day along with the usual homework and chores. Mrs. Levy chased down resources from New York's Board of Education to cover the costs of a private tutor, who coached Malaika weekly for the SATs and assigned her stacks of pricey practice books. At times, when juggling academics along with her family responsibilities had become almost unbearable, she verged on giving up. But she plowed on like the Energizer Bunny.

In September of Malaika's high school senior year, Mrs. Levy obtained the City College application and helped her complete it. Over the next several months, she paced, picked at her food, broke out in rashes, turned snappish, scolded herself for uppity aspirations, and even stole a few Xanax tablets from her mother's cache.

The notification ultimately had arrived. She sank down in a chair and fingered the purple-and-gray City College seal on the return address. She sniffed the envelope as if she could ascertain its contents by scent. Malaika closed her eyes, letting herself go numb as a buffer against bad news. After summoning up the courage, she ripped it open, tearing a corner of the letter. She had been accepted.

Elation morphed into relief and then uncertainty as she dreaded her mother's reaction, a dark cloud hanging over her dreams. Malaika approached her one evening after dinner, her face muscles tense. "Tuition is only fifteen dollars a semester," she had said. She felt as if she couldn't breathe.

Momma looked at her intently, without saying a word. "It won't be easy for me," she finally said, avoiding Malaika's pleading eyes. "But college could be your ticket out of here. I haven't been able to accomplish that for you, have I? Or your siblings." Momma had set her jaw firmly. "Aiysha and Julene are old enough to take over at least some of your chores."

♀

Momma had tried her best to lift up the family. She cleaned homes in Flatbush for years, taking two long bus rides to get there. Charlie had moved in when Malaika was six, but in her view, the only things he contributed to the household were three babies, one after another. For her, he was just another mouth to feed. He worked periodically, but as far as she could tell, he kept most of his earnings for himself. Malaika quietly resented him, especially when he demanded that she iron his fancy shirts. He didn't seem to spare anything when it came to his own wardrobe. The rest of them had to make do with second-hand clothes, most of them from Momma's clients.

Malaika knew he cheated on her mother. His conduct particularly irked her when he made passes at other women during their rare Sunday outings together, humiliating the family. On one occasion, Malaika found him in bed with a neighbor when school let out early for a teacher's conference. Shaken, she had glared at the two of them; he just sniggered. His womanizing infuriated her and fed her barely concealed contempt for him. She once asked her mother why she put up with his philandering. Momma had replied, in a resigned voice, "Someday you'll understand, honey. It's the lot in life for Black women."

Malaika had vowed, then and there, that she would never marry anyone who treated her badly. She had been relieved when Charlie left, several years after Fred was born. She was thirteen by then.

After he departed, Momma worked her way through beauty school in the evenings, eventually obtaining a hairstylist license. She had proudly hung it, framed, in the kitchen. Malaika had been a guinea pig along the way, her hair subjected to sundry chemicals and flat irons. Her tresses were straightened so often she almost forgot what its natural texture felt like.

She recollects how anxious she had been about paying for textbooks, supplies, transportation, and other necessities for college. Her mother had made clear that Malaika was on her own monetarily, though she could continue to live at home. A few weeks before the semester began, Momma slipped her money for a new outfit and suitable shoes.

Malaika had toyed around with waitressing in the evenings or even flipping hamburgers at McDonalds. She was accustomed to tight schedules, juggling household chores, childcare, and schoolwork. Nevertheless, she indulged herself in a moment of self-pity—just a minute or two—with a craving to pursue her academic years without financial worries like her carefree college peers.

Then, as though a fairy godmother had tapped her shoulders with a magic wand, she received a notice from Governor Nelson Rockefeller's office informing her that she was eligible for a Regent's Scholarship, amounting to more than seven hundred dollars a year. The letter stipulated that she had to maintain at least a B average. It felt as though she had won a million-dollar lottery.

Nevertheless, her enthusiasm was soon muted when she had stepped off the subway near the college, adrift among throngs of students. Everything about City College rattled her. She felt dwarfed by the Great Arches at the entrance of North Campus and the huge Gothic buildings. For registration, she had timidly entered Shepard Hall, a dominating cathedral-like structure, and walked its long stretch of polished floors to the enormous Great Hall, where tens of folding tables were set up with card files. Lines of students were waiting at each one to request a course, only to find that it was already closed. She took her place, and like an automaton moved from one queue to another until she finalized the requisite credits for the semester. There was no one to advise her, so she could only assume that her course load was in order.

Two weeks into the semester, Malaika had embarked on her usual route from North to South Campus, leaving behind the engineering undergraduates with their slide rules conspicuously poking out of their back pockets. Negotiating the stream of students coming and going, she passed the tennis courts that she knew she'd never use and the massive library that intimidated her. It was a beautiful fall day, and she leisurely headed for her next class in Wagner Hall. The course was in political science, "Introduction to American Government," taught by the popular Professor Feingold. His students seemed to lap up his every word, like thirsty cats at their milk dish. Malaika had found the course enlightening but held back during discussions—everyone else seemed so knowledgeable, so sure of themselves.

With two hours to spare before class would begin, she had sat down on a bench, watching the flood of students come and go. The sky suddenly darkened and it started pouring. Malaika ran straight for the South Campus's cafeteria, vainly trying to protect her hair with the heavy books she was carrying. The place was downstairs in the cellar, tucked away in the shadows of the college. Drenched and chilled, she grabbed one of the thick buff-colored mugs lined up in neat rows and poured herself a cup of steaming coffee. No cream or sugar.

She had looked around. The cafeteria was dingy. No windows and dimly lit. The walls, painted seafoam green like an asylum, lacked pictures or posters. Only the colorful graffiti, sprayed randomly, brightened the room. The floors were a dull gray and felt sticky from splatters of soda, coffee, ketchup, and mustard mixed with scraps of food; the custodians could never quite scrub them sufficiently. Yet the place was alive with students. Several tables were jam-packed, undergraduates crowded together laughing, chatting, debating. She observed couples engaged in earnest conversations, a few holding hands. There were individuals diligently studying alone, their notebooks monopolizing the entire table as if to warn against any intrusion. Nearly everyone was white. Malaika felt intimidated, almost in tears.

She had looked prim in her new cream-colored blouse and black high-waisted skirt that fell just below her knees. On her feet were black vinyl pumps with low heels, quite different from her usual ragged penny loafers. She clasped a small black purse and two books in one hand and the coffee mug in the other. Her soggy hair, newly straightened by her mother, hung limply on her shoulders.

There were no empty places, and she was about to leave when she heard an imposing male voice inviting her to sit down. She looked around in case he was talking to someone else. But his wide, welcoming grin convinced Malaika, despite some hesitancy, to join the group. There were five of them at the table, looking like a bunch of hippies. The boys had various lengths of longish hair and two of them sported beards. The girls wore no lipstick, in contrast to her brightly painted pink mouth. As usual, she had felt like an outsider. But they were amiable enough and seemed not to notice, or care, about her appearance.

Malaika had been drawn to their conversation immediately. They talked about ideas she had never heard of but, in her own way, had sensed. Though never officially addressed in the public schools she had attended, racial inequality, unemployment, and poverty were ubiquitous in her everyday life. She did not require formal theories to know that her family, neighbors, and former classmates lived in deteriorating housing, suffered food injustice, and experienced acute deficiencies in their education. Her own schooling had, of course, been sorely lacking. Although Malaika felt these wrongs in her gut, she relished hearing them put into words.

Over the months they fed her books, which she devoured almost as fast as they came in. She gorged on the classics and the latest thinkers, novels and nonfiction alike. She began questioning materialism and consumerism as well as exploring the roots of racism. Over her college years, Malaika progressed to Black Power and feminist authors. She labored over Karl Marx, Malcolm X, Frantz Fanon, Betty Friedan, Sylvia Plath, Gloria Steinem, and Virginia Woolf. She delighted most in sharing her emerging views with her new friends. None of them ever discounted her opinion, even when they disagreed. She was shy at first, but as her comprehension deepened, she became more confident. And more militant.

The daily grind of travel to City College wore on her, though she used the hour-and-a-half subway ride to read and think. She had to trudge long blocks to the station, which was especially taxing in the winter snow. By the spring of her first year, much to her surprise—and relief—Rebecca's family invited her to move in with them.

Momma was far less pleased. She had become increasingly wary of Malaika's steady estrangement from the family along with her developing political radicalism. "Look what college has done to you!" she would spit out, shaking her head. "No good will come of this. I warn you." Malaika packed her bags and lived in her friend's West Village brownstone, only a block from the subway station, for the rest of her college years. Rebecca was an only child, and Malaika had reveled in the unaccustomed quiet.

Now, gripping Rebecca's purple note, Malaika peers again at the shriveled, white-haired old lady in the mirror. Rebecca had played such a momentous role in her early adult life. Each and every one of them did. They even had emboldened her to go to law school despite the complications and burdensome loans. Maybe they would inspire her again like they used to. Perhaps they could help her sort out who she had been, what she has become, where she is heading. Malaika hungers for a shot in the arm to keep going, like an addict craving drugs. Her tightened muscles slowly relax as she decides to go to the reunion.

4
Keith

THE INVITATION is balanced on the arm of his recliner, certain to fall off as soon as he switches on the power lift. Sara, his companion of over forty years, insisted that they buy what he calls "the monster" to aid him in rising to his feet. "Keith," she pleaded, "I'd do anything to help you cope with this awful disease. But it's just too hard on me to keep pulling you up. I'm not as strong as I used to be."

He avoids the chair as often as possible because its padded arms make it difficult to maneuver his guitar. Not that he often plays these days. Even with the Parkinson's medication his fingers sometimes tremble, and he must snatch limited "on" times, when the Levodopa is controlling his symptoms. Besides, he can't concentrate for long periods anymore.

Keith questions how much longer he can stay in the house, in any place, without outside assistance. It is becoming unduly challenging for Sara though she rarely complains. But he's watched her struggle to keep up with the ongoing chores around the house while caring for him. A few years ago, they downsized and moved to the outskirts of Boston, hoping upkeep would be easier. They installed a ramp for the wheelchair that most likely will appear sooner rather than later. Perhaps he should move to an assisted living facility and free Sara, despite her protests that she is managing just fine, that she chooses to attend to him. "I would never dump you in an institution," is how she had put it.

He glances around the living room at the furniture, tired looking, like him. The space is sparsely furnished, as he prefers, and "the monster" seems to dwarf everything. The chair faces a 32-inch TV, not like the humongous screens that generally dominate such areas. Keith watches the news regularly but seldom much else. He prefers to read, although that too is getting taxing lately. Perhaps he should make an appointment with an ophthalmologist.

The well-worn wood floor is scratched, sections are eroding, and loose boards render it precarious, in places, to walk—especially with a cane. Sara painted the walls burnt orange, a color he finds obtrusive but has learned to live with. There are photographs displayed everywhere, like a retrospective gallery exhibit: pictures of their daughter, Emma, sequencing her coming-of-age moments and achievements, and doubly so of granddaughter Jenna, the apple of Keith's eye.

But the preponderance of prints depicts Keith performing in various venues around the country or him with prominent activists engaged in their ecological endeavors to save the earth and its endangered animals. Rescue the whales. Protect the Arctic. Sara is displayed as well, although mainly with him. The framed snapshots, like frozen moments in time, have found themselves on walls, bookshelves, benches, and end tables. She is obsessed with preserving their former life.

♀

In 1982, Keith had linked up with Canadian Greenpeace in its sea action against industrial whalers. That's where he met Sara, the hazel-eyed, scrappy fighter with a huge heart. He had been drawn to her straightaway. Not only was she courageous and spirited but also stunning. She had full lips, a dimpled smile, a strong, straight nose, and thick, chestnut hair, usually worn in braids or tied into a bouncy ponytail.

The following year, he joined Greenpeace USA shortly after the organization was formed. He had held many positions over the decades—research specialist, senior political strategist, campaigns director. But he loved the direct action most, the confrontations for environmental justice. Sara eventually moved to the States to marry him. Side by side, they had fought one environmental battle after another, like two people singing in perfect harmony. She still participates in Greenpeace campaigns nearby, when feasible.

Keith has moved on. He's tired of protesting, trying to wring concessions from self-interested, bullheaded corporate and political leaders, some of whom don't even believe in climate change. He has let go of that. For him, Trump and his cronies had been the flashpoint. Keith had gone postal as they dismantled, reversed, and weakened hundreds of hard-fought eco-friendly measures. Years, even decades, of campaigns to safeguard threatened species, wetlands, waterways, and the atmosphere from toxic wastes—all wiped out in what felt like a nanosecond. Over Trump's four years as president, Keith's rage had turned to stony silence as he witnessed their intensifying, misguided disregard for Mother Earth.

"I'm leaving the battle for the next generation and their kids," he had informed Sara in an impassive voice. "I've done my share." He had touched her arm affectionately. "I'm old, sapped, and sick."

Now his eyes dart to the invitation that has somehow managed to keep its equilibrium on the armrest. Keith ponders what it would be like seeing the gang after so many decades. As always, he yearns to sort his feelings out through music. It's been a while since he's written songs for them, about them. In the early years, he had created little ditties about their antics that amused them. The girls appreciated his limericks the most, especially later when he made fun of the guys for their macho attitudes. But they mostly valued his protest songs. He had begun with social justice and civil rights lyrics but by 1965 had concentrated on the Vietnam War. They nearly always embodied his sardonic sense of humor and biting wit.

♀

Music had been a part of his life from the earliest age on. Both his parents were amateur musicians. His mother was an expert pianist who taught him the keyboard when he was four. His father would often accompany her on the violin. His parents had assumed that each of the three siblings would learn an instrument, though Mom was the arbiter of which one. His eldest brother took cello lessons, and his sister, next in line, was assigned the viola. Much to his parents' delight, Keith had proved to be the most gifted and became a virtuoso violinist, completing their longed-for piano quintet. At times, the family performed for friends on special occasions, such as weddings or bar mitzvahs, but they mostly played for themselves in their small living room in Queens. For his siblings, the recitals had felt like a forced march, but Keith reveled in them.

After returning from the war, his father attended night school on the G.I. Bill, majoring in finance. He later joined an accounting firm, which provided a middle-class lifestyle for his growing family. The work was mundane, but he had stayed there for nearly forty years until he died on the job.

Keith's mother had quit her position as an elementary school music teacher directly after her first son was born. Any dreams about becoming a concert pianist had long been forsaken but not the bitterness. When questioned years later about her abandoned career, she would intone, "That's the way things were done then. Girls became mothers and homemakers." She would pinch her lips together with a detached look and add, "I followed the rules." Keith knew that his father, too, had discarded his musical aspirations for the family. He also understood that his parents intended their youngest child to fulfill those ambitions for them. Keith was expected to become a classical violinist.

He had entered the High School of Music & Art in 1963, the magical castle on a hill in Harlem. His siblings had previously been turned down, much to his parents' chagrin. Even among the finest young musicians, Keith had stood out. By his sophomore year, he was playing first violin at the school's highest orchestra level. The following year, he had been chosen as a soloist for Beethoven's Romance No. 2 in F major, and then as the violinist for the school's end-of-the-year play, *Fiddler on the Roof*. It had been a heady time for him.

But it was the students' hall music that had stirred his soul. Doo-wop harmonies, with their pulsing beats, had reverberated in every part of the five-story building in between classes. Dion and the Belmonts, The Platters, The Temptations. The highly talented high schoolers sang tune after tune, and he joined in. At that time, Keith discovered his voice. His smooth, resonant tenor had blended effortlessly with the others. In his junior year, he signed up for voice lessons.

At Music & Art he also had encountered the richness of the guitar. Stairwells echoed with folk music as well as doo-wop. Scattered students jammed before school, after school, and every time in between. For Keith, the guitar was love at first sight, a sentiment not shared by his parents. They had been ecstatic at his musical achievements. "You must concentrate on the violin if you want to be a virtuoso," his father said. "You can't join the New York Philharmonic strumming a guitar."

But Keith had been determined to follow his own dreams. He spent weekends teaching young kids in his neighborhood to play the violin, children of his parents' friends. He didn't mind too much even though his pupils were mostly indifferent and inept. Few practiced in between lessons. But their parents insisted and they paid him. Finally, he reached his goal and purchased his first guitar, a Gibson J-50. The two of them became inseparable, like a boy and his dog.

His high school years had been eye-opening in other ways. M&A introduced him to the art world. The walls were lined with student-created woodcut prints, thickly painted, vibrant oils, delicate pastels, dreamy watercolors, pencil sketches. The ever-changing displays showcased every style—from landscapes, still lifes, and nudes to Impressionism and Surrealism. Keith had appreciated the required art history classes that expanded his horizons even further. At museums, his peers patiently explained why deceptively simple blocks of color, like Piet Mondrian's *Broadway Boogie Woogie* or Jackson Pollock's splashes and drips of paint on canvas, were considered great works of art. He developed a particular affinity for the abstract techniques of Klee and Kandinsky.

But it had been music and books that affected him the most. The middle-class neighborhood bubble enfolding him had burst as he was bombarded with disquieting ideas. Many of his fellow students were questioning the world around them, goaded by critical literature along with the developing folk music scene. Woody Guthrie. Bob Dylan. Joan Baez. Pete Seeger. Dave Van Ronk. For the first time, he grappled with income inequality, racial discrimination, and capitalism itself. Herbert Marcuse's *One Dimensional-Man*, assigned by his favorite teacher, had forced him to wrestle with notions of social repression, conformity, consumerism, mass culture, and even the very meaning of human existence. His brain swirled with unconventional thoughts and he put them into song.

When he had met Russell in college, and then his small circle of friends, he connected with them immediately. They became family during his emergent adulthood, galvanizing him to explore his embryonic politics even further. He particularly admired Malaika's quick mind as he fed her book after book from his high school years. Soon the group relied on her uncanny ability to weave theoretical constructs with streetwise know-how. And she, along with Deanna, were almost always the first to prod them into the thicket of political action.

His newfound comrades had been instrumental in his growth as a musician too, serving as both advocates and critics. After listening to a Bob Dylan album, Rebecca had egged him to take up the harmonica. It didn't take him long to master the instrument and, using a neck brace, coordinate with the guitar. He loved playing for his five friends, his greatest fans, especially when they gathered on City College's South Lawn.

♀

Sara has gone shopping and Keith is alone, sitting listlessly in his chair. He eyes the TV but can't stomach the thought of the news, listening to Republican maneuvers to destroy the country and even the world. Every broadcast seems to ring with hate, meanness, duplicity, and corruption.

He reaches, instead, for his guitar, toppling the purple note, and perches the instrument awkwardly across his lap. He has long ago switched to his beloved Martin D-28, a gift from Sara when he turned sixty-five. He refuses to play anything electric. Keith lifts the instrument and strums while composing verses about their forthcoming reunion.

He is consumed with concerns about the get-together, not the least of which is how he will negotiate the trip given his unsteady gait. Much to his surprise, Keith is eager to see them. It's been nearly fifty years since their last rendezvous. They had met for a two-day camping trip in Canada, where Max had fled after burning his draft card. Deanna had just returned from a stint in the Peace Corps. They had sung their old protest songs and talked late into the night by the campfire while they took turns fueling both the blaze and each other. It was as if they had never left one another; their bond had remained solid, like blood kin.

All the same, beneath the waves of camaraderie, there was an undertow that was pulling them out to sea in different directions. Keith had noticed that Deanna would give Russell a brief, glassy stare whenever he called her, Malaika, and Rebecca "girls" or tried to boss them around in his imposing voice. There were other visible signs of discord. Malaika had become more strident about Black Power and her identity as a woman of color. Rebecca was now a vegetarian and periodically looked cross-eyed at their barbequed hamburgers and hot dogs. Russell seemed distracted and would steer the conversation to Columbia University politics, where he was writing his dissertation on social movements. Max was a bit aloof, as though his flight to Canada had cut him off from everything American. And he, himself, would conspicuously separate the recyclables from the trash, annoyed at their insensitivity to the environment.

Still, the camaraderie had remained deep as they canoed, took long hikes, and swam together that charmed weekend in Canada. In those days, he didn't have to worry about limbs that didn't quite work. Or relentless exhaustion. Or problems with balance. Or Parkinson-induced "on" and "off" times. Keith stares at the newly purchased walker, standing idle in the corner of the room, that he refuses to use. Sara had coerced him into buying that as well. How could he possibly manage the trip? Perhaps he'll have to grit his teeth and take the walker, at least as a standby.

5
Max

MAX IS watching his grandson's hockey game, admiring his grace and skill on the ice. He reaches out to his son, who is seated next to him. They are both wearing down vests and scarves to ward off the damp, wintry chill pervading the arena. Max has taken off his wool cap, exposing a recessed hairline, wisps of white hair covering the top of his scalp, and a long, sparse ponytail drooping down his back. He is still a fine-looking man despite small buff-colored age spots sprinkled across his face like dim stars in the overhead Canadian sky, and creases under his eyes. The deepened lines defining his cheekbones and trimmed white beard impart a distinguished appearance.

The stands are full of cheering family members, and Max hardily joins in. He repositions his body periodically in a futile attempt to get comfortable on the hard benches that lack back support. "These are not made for the geriatric crowd," he whispers to his son, grimacing. "I would have designed the entire stadium more effectively." He rubs his hands together. "And the place would be far less drafty."

His son, Noah, a mirror image of himself in his youth, indulges him, as usual. "Yes, Pop, I know. You were one hell of an architect."

Max is sorry he said anything about the place. He dislikes it when Noah or his daughter, Johanna, patronize him. Their constant determination to reassure him started shortly after he began forgetting. Little things at first. Sometimes he is confused about his whereabouts when heading home from his daily walk on the Seawall, which circles the magnificent Stanley Park. The nearly six-mile trip, with its snowcapped view of the northern mountains and surrounding rippling blue waters of Vancouver Harbor and English Bay, invigorates him, but he's become a bit apprehensive about getting lost. He's misplaced his hat, coat, umbrella, car keys, and once even the car itself, which somehow disappeared in the mall parking lot. He takes a shopping list to the supermarket after failing to bring home the main ingredient for his favorite dinner, Pacific Northwest salmon. It's the words that concern him most, the tip-of-the-tongue terms that elude him. He stumbles, scours his brain, leaves embarrassing pauses. Max has always had a first-rate memory and while the forgetfulness unsettles him, it disturbs his offspring even more.

Johanna had insisted that he seek medical help, and Max dutifully made the rounds of primary care doctors, neurologists, and psychologists accompanied by his daughter. They probed his mind and body—attention span, memory, orientation, reasoning, judgment, language skills, problem solving, movement, senses, balance, reflexes. An MRI indicated no signs of a stroke or anything else for that matter. Diagnosis—mild cognitive issues that will most likely progress. "There's no cure for dementia," the neurologist told him. "But you can slow its progress with memory training, social interaction, and physical exercise."

Next came the onslaught of brainteasers, riddles, math quizzes, and crossword puzzles his children regard as essential to his well-being. He doesn't like being humored and tried to make that clear to them. He's not sure how fast the disease will advance but at present is content to simply take pleasure in his walks and five grandkids.

He hasn't told Noah or Johanna yet about the invitation because he is wary about opening himself up to questions about his youthful exploits, things he does not want to discuss with them. It's not that he's self-conscious about his prior activism; quite the contrary. But he has split his life into two distinct parts, what he calls "before" and "after." The demarcation was the only way he could move on in his adopted country, an unfamiliar place, after leaving everything and everyone he cared for behind. For years he had felt as though he were on a raft, floating down the river, throwing overboard anything he didn't need at the moment.

He had stuffed the purple envelope in his vest pocket and, as he watches the hockey game, fingers it gingerly. The invitation takes him back to a place he had left behind long ago. Can it be over fifty years since he abandoned the States, nearly that long from the time the six comrades were together? When you're young, he ruminates, the clock ticks slowly, as if every day is a lifetime. As you age, time quickens, like stepping up a metronome.

His college friends have always had a place in his affections, and he regrets the distance, both emotionally and geographically. But it was never on his radar to return to the US, even to see them. He had not gone back when President Carter issued a pardon to draft dodgers in 1977. Nor did he attend his parents' funeral, much to the fury of his siblings. He had skipped their burials as well; his brothers had died, one after the other, from the Coronavirus, four years ago. Rabid Trump supporters, they had adamantly refused the vaccine despite their individual vulnerabilities. So stupid, he had muttered to himself at the time. It only verified how dysfunctional his family was and why he could forsake them so remorselessly.

♀

He glances at his son and releases an appreciative sigh. He has his own family now, which has grown to seven including the grandkids. That should be sufficient to fill his need for love, tenderness, and dependability. They have become his world, even if his daughter tends to be overbearing, like a lioness protecting her cubs.

Nonetheless, the invitation tapped into a deeply buried longing for his five pals that catches him off guard. They had been so intertwined during his young adult years that he felt lost when he first bolted to Canada. Over the decades, he became more self-contained, not part of a clique of fiercely loyal stalwarts. But he can feel them now tugging at his heartstrings, like a demanding child at his mother's sleeve. He supposes that nostalgia, too, intensifies as you grow old. Max is grateful that his long-term memory is fully intact.

Perhaps socializing with them for a weekend would be just what the doctor ordered for his deteriorating brain. Certainly better than puzzles. The idea grows on him, especially the chance to spend time with Rebecca. He had always been putty in her hands. All of them had been susceptible to her bidding, like this summons to meet in New Paltz. As an only child, the pugnacious Rebecca had been accustomed to getting her way. Yet she had been there, without fail, when he or any of the others needed anything. She was kind, generous, and reliable, almost to a fault.

Rebecca had been his first love, and although the intensity mellowed over the decades, he has never quite gotten over her. In high school, everyone had viewed them as an improbable match, and his feelings for her, as they strengthened, surprised even him. Surrounded by girls wearing bouffant hairdos, thick eye makeup and lipstick, soft flowing skirts, and clinging sweaters, Rebecca had dressed in ill-fitting shirtwaist dresses at school; pants were not allowed. But at other times she wore jeans, usually with an oversized, plaid button-down shirt. She was short, about five feet three, heavy set, and her medium-length frizzy hair gave her a bedraggled look. No lipstick, ever. No eye makeup. But she had penetrating green-brown eyes that flashed with intelligence and, at times, stubbornness. Her face seemed to be set in a perpetual solemn expression.

Much to Max's dismay, their intense connection had not developed into a romantic relationship. Not that he didn't try, at least in subtle ways. He knew she cared deeply about him, but there was some indefinable barrier between them, a spark that never quite ignited. But they had embraced often, cuddled together, held hands. He loved stroking her face, which almost always elicited a reluctant smile. Most people at the high school, though puzzled, had viewed them as a couple.

His affection for Rebecca extended to her family, especially her father. Despite his rough and tough demeanor, Izzie was a cultured man who eagerly shared his love of theater, opera, and music with his daughter and Max. He purchased tickets for *Camelot, Bye Bye Birdie, Carnival, Oliver,* and other spectacular Broadway musicals. He and Rebecca were treated to Balanchine's *Midsummer Night's Dream,* the NYC Opera's premiere of Poulenc's *Dialogues of the Carmelites,* and to Bob Dylan, Patsy Cline, and Johnny Cash at Carnegie Hall. These excursions were accompanied by lunch or dinner at one of the finer restaurants in the city. Although they lived nearby, in Chelsea, Rebecca's parents and his were worlds apart in mindset and temperament; Max preferred hers.

In their senior year, Izzie offered both of them jobs at Local 1199. The work itself had been somewhat tedious, but the excitement around them was intense and inspiring. The office buzzed with talk of the egregious conditions suffered by hospital workers. Fliers were everywhere. Social justice posters lined the walls. Max felt as though he were part of something important for the first time in his life. It was Izzie who had suggested that they take the bus to the Jobs and Freedom March on Washington at the end of that summer. He offered to pay for the trip. Max eagerly accepted.

In the fall, the two of them had entered City College and joined with Deanna, Russell, Malaika, and Keith in a commitment to the Civil Rights Movement. In the spring semester of their sophomore year—1965—they had assembled around the television in Buttenweiser Lounge, inside the Finley Student Center, to watch the peaceful March 7 protest walk from Selma, Alabama to the state capital in Montgomery. Horrified, they witnessed an attack on the six hundred marchers, including women and children, by state troopers and local law enforcement officials at the Edmund Pettus Bridge. Billy clubs. Tear gas. Bullwhips.

A huge crowd steadily gathered in the bustling college room, everyone aghast at the unprovoked violence perpetrated on the demonstrators. "Pigs," one undergraduate had shouted at the officers who were hitting individuals with their night sticks. "What kind of country do we live in?" another yelled, as they continued the assaults. "Stop it! Stop it!" several female voices screamed as blood spewed every which way on the televised scene. The cold-blooded massacre, viewed worldwide, fomented such anger that the students were ready-made fodder for political mobilization. Max had sensed this immediately and passed around a notebook requesting names and telephone numbers for recruitment to the activist organization he and his buddies had recently joined.

Earlier that spring, Max had walked by a small table in Finley Hall set up by Students for a Democratic Society, an incipient group of New Left activists. He stopped, leafed through the materials, and chatted with the SDS representative at the stand. He had been intrigued with the group's vision of participatory democracy. He took a few pamphlets and a copy of the *Port Huron Statement*, SDS's founding document, to his friends. They perused the information and discussed the organization's positions and goals. The perspectives were a good fit for them; they felt aligned with its determination to confront social and economic injustices in the North as well as an in southern states. They signed up and began the recruitment of other students at City College. With the help of Max's list, by summertime the year-old local SDS chapter had become a respectably sized group.

They had been particularly impressed with SDS's Economic Research and Action Project (ERAP), initiated by Tom Hayden, that had just begun putting together interracial community organizing projects in nine cities. Max and his friends initially volunteered to assist in the development of the ERAP venture in Newark but instead became involved in preparations for a march on Washington to protest the escalating Vietnam War. SDS leaders were enraged at the Gulf of Tonkin Resolution, enacted earlier by Congress, seemingly giving President

Johnson carte blanche to increase US military presence in the small, beleaguered Asian nation. They had become even more alarmed as the administration began bombing the northern parts of the country. Although reluctant to shift their focus from the Newark project, Max and the others agreed to help with local plans for the rally, set for April 17.

For Max, the DC anti-war demonstration was reminiscent of his first experience at the Jobs and Freedom March two years earlier. In some ways, it was equally significant to him. At this event, he and his friends were exposed to the full horrors of the Vietnam War and what their country was inflicting on innocent civilians. And much to Max's surprise—and that of SDS— nearly twenty-five thousand people, mostly college students, showed up. At the time, it was the largest peace protest in US history.

At the demonstration, they had first picketed the White House, demanding withdrawal from Vietnam from an absent President Johnson, who had earlier left DC. Nonetheless, a hungry national press was devouring the massive, colorful event. Max experienced great satisfaction that SDS had grown in prominence.

Later, the six friends sat crowded together on the grounds of the Washington Monument. It was a warm spring day, and they breathed in the sweet fragrance of the cherry blossom trees surrounding the area. Periodically, they exchanged satisfied smiles at the apparent success of the rally.

They listened to impassioned speeches but the one that inspired Max the most was given by Paul Booth, one of the main SDS national organizers. It had been an aha! moment for him as Booth highlighted the inextricable link between the Anti-War Movement and the domestic civil rights and anti-poverty campaigns. Max finally understood the importance of prioritizing the Vietnam War.

His gang had been further energized by Joan Baez, Judy Collins, and Max's favorite folksinger, Phil Ochs, who performed moving, piercing songs portraying the inhumanity of the conflict. Then and there, the six friends decided to throw themselves fully into the Anti-War Movement.

♀

Max's parents had dutifully supported President Johnson and refused to accept their son's anti-war activism. "You would look so handsome in a uniform," his mother had said one evening at dinner. She typically closed her eyes to anything that distressed her, including his anti-war activities. Sharing a look with her husband, she added, "We would be so proud to have all of our boys serve this great country of ours." His father nodded, but Max could sense some hesitation. Perhaps he was thinking about the risks. Both of his older brothers had enlisted and needled him relentlessly when they returned from active duty in Vietnam. "Get a haircut, bro," the eldest had demanded. "And ditch those anti-American friends of yours. They're a bunch of commies."

"Love it or leave it," his other brother chimed in, with his usual mechanical adoption of the patriotic buzzwords of the day.

Max had drawn a low lottery number in the draft and couldn't fathom the idea of killing people who he had no quarrel with, in a land on the other side of the world. Much to his family's shock and chagrin, he ultimately left.

6

Rebecca

"I'M EIGHTY years old today and finally retired," Rebecca whispers, her words hanging in the empty bedroom. She had promised herself she would step down on her eightieth birthday, and now the act was done. For the first time in thirty years, she craves a cigarette. She breathes in slowly and, rounding her lips, exhales a smokeless breath. She does it again. . .and again. It's not as satisfying as a Marlboro, but it had been so challenging to shake the habit that she is afraid to light up, even once. But she's tempted. At her age, Rebecca reflects, she'll probably die of something else before lung cancer can set in and anyway, who would care?

She sits down on the cushioned seat in the small alcove overlooking the association's manicured gardens. Its bay window is covered with opaque shades. She canvasses the darkened room, which seems as forlorn as she is. The king-size bed, with its sagging mattress, dominates the space. The headboard is topped by wide shelves brimming with books and stacks of magazines, mostly unread. On each side of the bed is a nightstand, one of whose drawers are bare. There are two matching mahogany dressers on the opposite wall, one crammed with assorted clothing, the other also empty. Rebecca stares at the sole snapshot of a beaming Susan, incongruous with the gloomy atmosphere of the room. She has stored the rest of their framed photos in a box at the back of a closet. The wooden floor is partially covered with an intricate oriental rug that she and Susan had bought in Turkey on one of their rare vacations.

Over the years, she had held back on personal pleasures because of tomorrow's promises of what she could achieve in the world. Her job with SIEU had taken her from city to city as she tirelessly attempted to unionize underpaid and overworked healthcare staff across the nation. She had her share of failures, especially with nurse's aides and homecare workers, but the achievements vastly outweighed the disappointments, giving her immense satisfaction. Periodically, she contended with formidable, complex racial politics in the local unions that she had managed with a hard-nosed approach tempered with pragmatism. At those times, she had to move through precarious situations like a soldier clearing landmines. In her estimation, she had learned from the best, her daddy.

Nonetheless, prior to Susan's death, she had looked forward to retirement, to slow down from their hectic existence. The two of them had longed to be together for more than a few weeks at a time. Susan often complained about her companion's consuming dedication to the union and the long hours she kept, even when she was at home.

They had compiled a bucket list of places they would explore abroad when Rebecca stepped down from her job. Paris was at the top of the agenda, a city of Susan's dreams, followed by a tour of Europe and Asia. What had they been thinking? Did they really expect to globetrot as geriatrics?

Rebecca had also agreed that, after retirement, she would socialize to a greater extent. Over the decades, Susan had turned down invitations from colleagues and neighbors because Rebecca was absent or too busy. When Susan attended alone, she was disconsolate for days.

Rebecca rises from the alcove and heads over to the photo. Stroking the image gingerly, she conjures up Susan's expressions of disappointment, the slumped shoulders, watery eyes, weak smile. It's too late to undo the past, Rebecca softly moans, or atone for the transgressions that brought her partner to tears. Empty promises, as it turned out.

Now that Susan is gone and she has given up her life's work, Rebecca no longer has tomorrow's possibilities but can't seem to indulge in the moment. In truth, she has never been one for immediate gratification except for food. Nowadays, she can stuff herself with a package of chocolate-chip cookies and still feel empty. Her life is unraveling like a wool scarf whose knitter has missed a stitch or two.

♀

Susan had been the steady one, always there when Rebecca returned from her union-related travels. As a professor of LGBTQ Studies at the University of Pennsylvania, she had flexible hours and most of her research, class preparations, and grading were accomplished at home. They had set up two large desks in the study, and when Rebecca was not on the road, they sat on opposite sides of the room, each engrossed in her own world but aware of the other's presence. Occasionally, Susan would share an insightful article or ask Rebecca's opinion about a paper she was writing. Rebecca had appreciated those moments. She disliked, however, engaging in academic politics; she found it boring and would listen to the ongoing sagas impatiently.

Susan had assumed most of the household responsibilities, Rebecca having abdicated them bit by bit over their years together. She was too busy, or so she claimed at the time. Susan had been good with money, paid their bills, and unfailingly squeezed a bit of savings out at the end of the month. Rebecca had liked that about her, the frugality. Their plants, scattered throughout the rooms, survived only because of Susan's loving attention to them. Nowadays, there are none left; they steadily wilted away after her death. The whole condo is grungy. Unlike Susan, Rebecca has a slapdash approach to housework.

She must admit that organizing from city to city had been overly consuming, to the detriment of Susan's well-being. But in the end, that turned out to be her saving grace, Rebecca reminds herself. What would otherwise have held her life together when her partner was diagnosed with lung cancer? That had been the most devastating year of Rebecca's life. Susan's dull pain had escalated over time, along with the dosage of oxycodone. There were other medicines for nausea, to help with breathing, anxiety, loss of appetite. Susan became confused and eventually semi-conscious. Rebecca had tried to take care of her, curtailing her travels. She hired a full-time hospice nurse from one of the agencies she had helped to unionize. Medicare paid only a fraction of the huge tab, and the bills kept piling up.

The loss of Susan shattered her. She had been her soulmate. At the time, Rebecca rolled the reality of her lover's death around and around in her mouth. It had left a bitter taste on her tongue that lingered for months. She experienced recurring terror every evening that mercifully receded somewhat in the morning. She had felt like an orphan after Daddy and Mom died. No children. No siblings. Too busy for friends. For so many years, their world had been just the two of them.

After the funeral, Malaika came to stay for a week. She fed Rebecca, drank wine with her, cried with her. Her commiseration and compassion had been fortifying, but the tough love worked best. "You have work to do," Malaika had said. "Millions of health workers desperately require your help. Nurses. Nursing aides. Technicians. Medical assistants. Maintenance staff. These oppressed women of color are in dire need of a union." She had reached over and gripped Rebecca's hand. "And you are the best organizer around."

Their other friends sent letters, lengthy affectionate notes, and then periodic emails. Deanna had called frequently. Rebecca must have talked to Max at least once a week for months. Keith sent her a DVD, alive with union songs for inspiration, including one he composed especially for her. Rebecca had emerged from her grief, if not fully intact then at least not totally broken. And she was ready to continue her work.

♀

The five of them had been a source of strength for her since college. She had previously been a loner, estranged from her young classmates for as long as she can remember. The disjunction between her education and home life often confused her, like facing unmarked forks in the road. Throughout grade school, Rebecca had been forced to dive under her desk and cover her head to protect herself against a hypothetical atomic attack and nuclear annihilation by the Soviet Union. The Cold War generated anxiety against communism that was reinforced by the books and teachers in her public schools. She had learned that labor unions were infiltrated by communists—they were everywhere, trying to take over the country. The situation was "us against them." She and her schoolmates had said the Pledge of Allegiance every morning, right hands over their hearts.

With her parents and their friends, she had encountered diametrically opposed viewpoints. Her father was a communist sympathizer, an outlook he had embraced shortly after his arrival in the US. He never actually joined the party but was deeply affected by the execution of Julius and Ethel Rosenberg. By then, he had joined Local 1199, Martin Luther King's favored union. In 1959, her father helped spearhead its drive to organize the mostly Black and Latino healthcare workers at the city's top hospitals. These nonprofit institutions had been exempted from labor laws, and the wages and working conditions were deplorable. After a bitter forty-six-day strike against staggering odds, they had won. Daddy was her hero.

In the beginning, attempting to comprehend the dichotomy, she peppered her teachers with questions. But that only isolated her more from them and her peers. At least home had been a haven. She revered her father who, in turn, adored her. She looked forward to their lively exchanges at the dinner table, where Daddy, a natural raconteur, regaled Rebecca and her mother with stories about the Labor Movement, David-and-Goliath battles for workers' rights. He talked about 1199 and their drives against segregation. He had been particularly proud of one of its earliest campaigns in 1937 that forced drug stores to hire Black pharmacists in Harlem. And the family invariably deliberated about the day's political events.

By the time she reached junior high, she encountered segregation to such an extent that the Black, White, and Latino kids carved themselves into separate worlds, just like the discrete communities in which they lived. Tensions among the groups were combustible, ready to ignite in a flash. They taunted each other at their invisibly partitioned lunch tables, calling each other vile names. Spontaneous fights flared up regularly. The teachers, nearly all Caucasian, seemed incapable or uninterested in drawing them together.

She had probed her father about the divisions at her school. He patiently explained that there was a lot of work to be done in the North just like in the South. At one point he urged her to befriend one of her non-white fellow students, but when she tried to reach out, she only provoked a torrent of verbal abuse. Rebecca became increasingly withdrawn.

Shortly after Daddy's victory against the hospitals, she entered high school. She had seen posters about the debate team and, hesitantly, attended the first informational session. They soon held tryouts, and to her astonishment, she was a first pick for the squad. She had been paired with Max, one of the more popular boys in the school. He dressed like the others—cardigan sweater, khakis, loafers—but stood out anyway. He was tall, six feet, with a Roman nose, high cheek bones, and clear, light blue eyes that seemed to be taking in everything around him at once. He also had a gentle, reassuring smile and a hearty laugh that endeared him to his contemporaries. Rebecca had been shy with him at first, letting Max lead their arguments during debate preparations.

But her strong oral skills soon impressed him, and they developed into a successful unit. They often practiced at Rebecca's house, where he inevitably joined the family for dinner. His own parents avoided talking about politics, religion, or anything else of importance. He had been fascinated by Izzie's tales and work, which percolated through his own thinking throughout high school.

The national debate topic in their sophomore year was: "Resolved: That the federal government should substantially increase its regulation of labor unions." Max had been prepared to take on both sides of the issue; Rebecca was ready to quit. Yet, they toiled on as partners, fortified by their increasingly intense friendship—the two of them became confidants. At one point she admitted to him that she was confused, conflicted, and unsure of herself. Max had listened attentively and was quick to encourage her. He became not only her best friend but a Rock of Gibraltar during her challenging high school years.

♀

Rebecca walks into the condo's large kitchen and looks at the heap of unopened retirement cards on the table. She flips through the envelopes and grimaces, knowing that they will express some variation of "Best Wishes on Your Retirement" in assorted designs and colors. She doesn't intend to open any of them. They were probably glad to get rid of her, she reflects. Rebecca had felt the pressure from the younger organizers. She was not up to par anymore. Too old-fashioned in her ways. Taking up space in the upper ranks that they were anxious to fill.

She runs her fingers through her short, thinning white curls as she considers her situation. She used to have her life in order. Each piece had been painstakingly assembled by the time she was forty. Political activist, union organizer, daughter, and part of a couple. Later, when Susan was stricken with cancer, she had added caregiver. The construction seemed indestructible, as though it would last forever. She had counted on each part to keep her grounded, to make her existence meaningful. It wasn't easy to keep everything in harmony, and she wasn't always successful. But then everything had fallen apart, one by one. Ultimately, only her work recharged her, at least for a while. She had been too busy to nurture friendships, to do the heavy lifting to keep relationships afloat.

Rebecca swallows hard. Now she is alone and lonely. She muses about old age and its victims, those who suffer from chronic illness or dementia, or who pass away—and their grief-stricken loved ones, like her. She has lost her mother, father, and mate, the most important people in her life except for Max and the gang. She wonders how they are faring in their advanced years.

Suddenly, she wants him. She craves all of them. Their friendship had been such an integral part of her youth. She paces the kitchen and then darts back into the bedroom, pulls open the closet door, and rummages around until she finds the frayed cardboard box tucked away in a back corner. The container is bursting with photos of her old comrades—several fading. She bites her lip and reproaches herself for neglecting to put them in albums, certain that most people would have taken the time to preserve them better.

Hands trembling, she inspects a stack of them, lingering on several pictures from the summer of 1965 following their second year at City College. They had volunteered for Project Uplift (PUL), an experimental summer anti-poverty project in Central Harlem. The venture had been sponsored by Harlem Youth Opportunities Unlimited—HARYO—the major social agency in the impoverished neighborhood. After their Freedom Summer in the South, they had decided they would henceforth commit their energies to their own backyard. Certainly, there were sufficient economic and civil rights issues in the North, Malaika had reminded them when they were considering their next endeavor. Rebecca had thought about the segregation in her junior high and her daddy's clear-sighted views about social justice.

PUL was particularly appealing to them because City College was situated smack in the middle of the project's locale. Another strong point had been the self-help aspects of the program, which employed thousands of neighborhood kids aged fourteen to twenty-six as aides, assistants, and associates.

Deanna had been assigned to the remedial reading unit, teaching kids basic language skills, writing, and math; she also assisted in trips to libraries and museums. Malaika was dispatched to one of the several day camps, where she read to the youngsters and helped with educational and recreational activities, dancing, music, and arts and crafts. Russell had participated as an advisor to the enrollees for their eight-page weekly newspaper, *News briefs*, as well as in their preparation of posters, fliers, and leaflets. Max mostly worked with the five booths that provided information about available social, health, housing, and educational services in the city. Keith became part of the Arts Theater group, where he put together a music program that taught the teenagers to express themselves through rhythm and song. Rebecca had ended up with the Community Survey Associates, where she joined block associations and tenant organizations in filing housing complaints and registering adults to vote.

It had been a frustrating but satisfying summer despite the long hours at no pay. They had mingled daily with Harlemites, both young and old, learning of their needs firsthand. At night they slept together on the floor of a community leader's row house. For Rebecca, that had been the highlight of the experience, sharing views about the day's accomplishments with each other. Despite the stifling summer heat, they had stayed up late into the night exploring ideas on social change. Rebecca savored every moment of their discussions.

They talked about the limited possibilities of PUL, that it was confronting poverty with crumbs. They had other reservations about their work. They realized that the driving force was to take Black teenagers off the street, to prevent a repetition of the previous summer's rioting. Max had wanted to talk about their complicity in this and they hashed it out evening after evening.

Deanna had proposed that they instigate block rallies to advocate for welfare rights and demand decent housing and accountability from slumlords. That would have risked them being thrown out of the project by the more timorous participating organizations, and they reluctantly determined to stay the course. They pushed on, playing their small part in assisting individuals in their everyday struggles but questioning the larger political, economic, and social issues that must be addressed. They had been seamlessly intertwined in a sense of camaraderie and purpose, like a colony of honeybees.

Rebecca sifts through more pictures of her friends, warmth radiating throughout her body as she nourishes herself with memories of their shared lives, of her early adulthood. Periodically, she fingers a particular snapshot and holds it close to her chest. An idea is gradually taking shape in her mind as she longs to erase the distance between them.

Yes, she thinks, as she clenches her hands into fists. She eyes the retirement cards again. Why not? Rebecca slips on her navy blue peacoat, wool beanie, and sheepskin-lined winter boots and wraps herself in the cashmere scarf that Susan had knitted for her birthday ten years ago. She walks purposefully to a CVS two blocks away, grateful that the stores have shoveled their sidewalks following the recent snowstorm. Once inside, she heads straight to the greeting card racks and scans them, homing in on what she came for: a pack of purple invitations with matching envelopes. For emphasis, she purchases two bags of lavender glitter. Her heart is pounding, and she closes her eyes for a moment. They will come, she assures herself.

PART II
A Small Circle of Friends: City College of New York, 1963 to 1967

7
Deanna

THE FOLIAGE was near peak grandeur along the lengthy route from the subway exit to the college's entrance on South Campus. Yellow, flaming orange, gold, and rust-brown mingled with splashes of red and purple. The leaves were swaying gently in the light wind and a few were falling to the ground, as if in a slow dance. The azure sky above Deanna was so clear it almost looked artificial, like a crayon drawing by a child. She felt insulted that the smog-filled city had picked today of all days to show off its unadulterated beauty.

The crush of students who had burst forth from the train at the 135th Street train station fed into an endless stream of people heading to classes, some leisurely, others racing against the clock. Deanna threaded her way among them, her head down; she was not in the mood for friendly waves or idle conversation with random classmates she barely knew. She was panicky, on a mission.

She first checked out the well-trodden stretch of lawn around Finley Hall, with its patches of sandy-colored earth and fragrance of sweet dandelions. Despite herself, she inhaled the sounds and beats of instruments and songs. Day-Glo frisbees in assorted colors were flying in every direction. Russell wasn't there.

Deanna sighed and hurried to the cafeteria. She spotted the gang, but he wasn't with them either. Without sitting down, she asked, "Where's Russ?" She then collapsed onto a chair and with a bitter smile said, "He's hard to find these days."

"He may have gone to the library," Max said. "He told me he was working on a paper for his political theory class." He averted his eyes, and Deanna gave him a cold stare.

"I need to find him," she said. "It's urgent." She regarded each of her friends in turn. "If any of you see Russell, tell him to meet me after my three o'clock class. Outside Wagner Hall." Her eyes were watering. She picked up her books and turned to go. "Please don't chase me down," she said. "I want to be alone for now."

Alone? she thought. Among ten thousand students? She walked aimlessly around the campus, clutching her books. Every time she made progress toward her philosophy seminar, she hesitated and shifted direction. Normally, she would be drawn to today's discussion on epistemology. The justification of beliefs. The nature of knowledge. Truth. Opinions. Concepts that fermented in her brain like the production of fine wine. She bottled them in the corner of her mind to sip every so often. To share with her comrades. But on this particular day, she was absorbed in other matters. Deanna slipped her hands under the loosely draped peasant blouse and lightly rubbed her lower abdomen.

She dithered for so long that it was too late to attend class so she sat down near Wagner Hall to wait for Russell, trusting he would show up. The buzzing and jostling of students had died down as they poured into lecture halls and seminar rooms.

A few straggling co-eds scurried past her in hope of reaching their classroom before they were locked out. Several nodded in her direction.

Deanna kicked a small pile of leaves while a squirrel cozied up to her, entreating for a morsel. She searched her pockets. "Nothing today," she said. She rose to stretch, paced around the building, and sat down again. She checked her watch. The hour was stretching interminably.

She finally spotted him in the distance. He was a few minutes early.

"Let's get out of here," she told him, as he sauntered up to her. "I don't want my professor to see me. I blew off class today." He smelled warm and spicy, as if he had just stepped out of a shower. She nudged him along, her expression betraying the angst permeating through her body.

"What's up?" he asked, turning to face her. "I was told there was a pressing matter. You needed to talk to me."

Deanna flinched when he touched her shoulders. She was trembling with resentment. Over the last several weeks, he had been conspicuously absent, on and off, for days at a time. Max and Keith kept making excuses for him, but Deanna suspected they knew exactly what was going on. When she called Russell's house, his mother would say, in an undisguised tone of smug satisfaction, "Sorry, Deanna, he's out." And with an exaggerated sigh add, "And who knows where he's at."

Russell's inexplicable vanishing act baffled and enraged her. But she had her pride and refrained from pushing him about it. Now she had a more urgent matter at hand. "I'm pregnant," she blurted out.

At first Russell was uncharacteristically speechless. "Are you sure?" was all he could manage to say.

"My test results came back this morning." Deanna had seen her gynecologist almost two weeks ago, immediately after she missed her period. She had never been late before. "It must have been that one time I didn't use the diaphragm."

She had been on the pill for nearly a year, but the drug made her feel waterlogged, and she gained not a few pounds. "The diaphragm is sufficient and safer," her gynecologist had said, reinforcing her decision to discontinue the oral contraceptives. Russell had agreed although he had his qualms.

After a moment's hesitation, he edged closer and wrapped his arms around her waist. In the gathering twilight, he kissed her softly on the eyes. "I'll take care of it."

This was Deanna's favorite time of night, when all that remained of the sun was an ethereal glow of rose-tinted lights. Puffs of clouds, purple, white, and gray, arranged themselves prettily in the sky, the trees and college buildings silhouetted against them. The day was fading but it was not quite evening, not completely light or dark. An in-between time that usually allowed her to pause and let her thoughts settle, a short period of calm that defied daily stresses and concerns. And, she should have been relieved; he said he would take care of the situation.

Yet as she stood there in his gentle embrace, the words reverberated in her head, unsettling her.

"I'll take care of it," he said again, in a stronger voice.

Without any input from her, or even discussion, he was ready to get rid of her baby, their baby. Just like that. Poof!

As the sky darkened, the lingering silence chastened her. She was being unreasonable, Deanna decided. She had long considered herself pro-choice, a rational individual who couldn't possibly think of a six-week-old embryo as a baby. Really just a cluster of dividing cells. Russell knew that about her. If she told him what she was feeling, he most likely would have mocked her. *You can take the girl out of the church but not the church out of the girl.* Perhaps it was true. Was her Catholic upbringing embedded in her soul?

"The priests really did a job on me," she murmured, her face pressed into Russell's chest. "Let's go." She grabbed his arm. "It's time to collect the names of docs."

Deanna envisioned the challenging road ahead. Abortion. She allowed the word to make its way from her gut into her thoughts. Banned in every state. New York allowed therapeutic exceptions, mostly to save the life of the woman. Not economic or psychological justifications.

Deanna and Russell sought out their friends to deliberate together, as always. They took the D train downtown to the West End Bar, on Broadway and 114th Street, where the gang met every Friday evening to share a few beers. They liked the atmosphere of the place and its smell of history. Beat Generation writers had hung out there in the 1940s—Allen Ginsberg, Jack Kerouac, Lucien Carr. Nowadays, the pub was home to Columbia University students of all political stripes.

They walked into the dimly lit dining room and, through a thick haze of bluish white smoke, caught sight of their pals.

"Where have you guys been?" Max asked. "We were beginning to worry about you."

A half-empty pitcher of beer sat in the center of the table, and Russell poured himself and Deanna each a glass. She sipped it for a while, nibbling at a bowl of peanuts. From the corner of the room, there were whiffs of marijuana. Deanna felt agitated, like a shaken can of coke ready to explode.

"I'm pregnant," she burst out, hanging her head. "We need help." She let the words hang in the air.

The next days were a blur of activity that she no longer controlled. Deanna gratefully succumbed to her friends' instructions as if she were a lump of clay. A short list of physicians who were willing to perform illegal abortions materialized. An office visit, examination, date for the procedure. Money collected. Each of her comrades raided their piggy bank for the six-hundred-dollar fee, payable in advance.

She soon found herself flat on her back, legs spread, metallic objects moving inside her. Alone with the doctor. Nobody allowed inside. No assistant, no anesthesia. Efficient. In forty-five minutes, the unnerving procedure was over. No niceties. "You'll feel some discomfort over the next few days," was all the doctor had said as he opened the office door and surrendered her to Russell.

She spent the next week at Rebecca's house, waited on by her and Malaika. Rebecca's mother, who had been welcoming, dispensed Tylenol to ease the agonizing pain that seared through her. So much for "discomfort." The abortion had been a harrowing experience, more invasive than she had been told. And she supposedly had been to an actual physician although the office reminded her of a shabby hotel room. The cramped operating area had no pictures on its slightly peeling gray walls. The furniture was sparce, comprising only an examination table and utility cart that held tools and supplies. The place looked as though it could be erased at a moment's notice.

Woozy and shaken during her recovery, Deanna mused about abortion mills, their unsafe, unhygienic conditions, and unlicensed hucksters out to make a quick buck. How many of these procedures were botched, leaving permanent injuries, sterility, and even death in their wake? Countless less privileged women were forced into even more dangerous self-induced abortions.

Or they were obliged to have unwanted babies they couldn't take care of. Often babies having babies. Deanna was like an animal sniffing out its territory. She vowed to join the fight to make abortions legal. No questions asked.

Before long she was back home. Her mother no doubt brimmed with questions about her disappearance but, strangely, had muzzled herself. Deanna guessed that she just didn't want to know. That she was wearing out her rosary beads.

8
Keith

LIKE OTHER boys at the time, Keith had registered with the Selective Service just after he turned eighteen. The year was 1963, a heady time for him and his new circle of friends, and he had not given his enrollment much thought. Vietnam was still a faraway country, a place where President Kennedy had sent a few "advisors." In any case, as a college student, he had received an automatic 2-S draft deferment that made even a stepped-up war still seem remote from his life. Keith's focus was on social justice at home, working with SDS on domestic issues.

But by fall 1965, he and his friends had been sucked into the Anti-War Movement, and it became their top priority. The US had dropped napalm firebombs to clear out bunkers, fox holes, trenches, and, at times, whole villages. The burning gel hit the North Vietnamese Army, the Viet Cong, and civilians alike in horrifying numbers, leaving melted flesh and death in its wake. Making matters worse, the military sprayed Agent Orange to defoliate trees, bushes, and other dense tropical vegetation that had provided cover for the North Vietnamese Army and Viet Cong. The chemical poisoned ever-increasing chunks of forests and arable land—including hamlets—that leaked into bodies, food, and ground water.

National SDS leaders decided that the Johnson Administration must be stopped. And the more the president and his allies lied and concealed the facts of the war, the more they had to be exposed. The City College SDS Organization, now led by Max, agreed to hold a series of teach-ins. He and the other organizers coordinated forums for revealing facts, not Johnson's fictional world. At these gatherings, faculty provided context for the war and let students question the validity of the US presence there and discuss its moral implications, especially the horrific slaughter of innocent people. The all-day workshops were a political education exceeding anything the undergraduates could have picked up in their history, political science, sociology, or economics classes. Keith and his comrades counted on the teach-ins not only to inform but to build momentum for concrete action on a grander scale: rallies, picketing, sit-ins, burning of draft cards—whatever it took. That had been the goal, and they succeeded.

Keith first became known at City College during these teach-ins and later at the campus-wide anti-war demonstrations when large crowds would gather around him. He was normally clad in his signature tight jeans and denim work shirt. His scruffy, short beard was slightly darker than the light brown, long, wavy hair flowing under his black Dutch Boy cap. Strumming on his Gibson J-50, hung over his shoulder by a multi-colored Ace strap, he sang his favorite Phil Ochs songs, "What Are You Fighting For," "Draft Dodger Rag," "I Ain't Marching Anymore," as well as a growing number of his own compositions. He accompanied himself with an ever-present harmonica, held in a brace around his neck. Russell, Deanna, Max, Rebecca, and Malaika were fixtures at his side.

The music not only helped galvanize City College students against the war but became a magnet for co-eds fixated on Keith. He had been remote when Max first brought him into the group, quiet and deep-thinking. Prior to that time, he didn't feel like he fully belonged anywhere. At M&A he had been a loner by choice, content to be on the fringe of diverse crowds. He had been well-liked and good-natured but reserved. There had been acquaintances, guys he hung out with, but none he could call a real friend. Girls had appreciated his good looks and sensitive nature. Yet, he seemed immune to their not-so-subtle advances.

Even though he spoke openly with his new college chums, he was still generally sparing with words, seemingly saving them for his songwriting. He was too preoccupied with politics and his music to date anyone. Once, when Deanna teased him about his lack of girlfriends, he just grinned. "So, you guys are not enough for me?" He looked at Deanna, and in his endearing style continued, "These songs don't write themselves. No time for relationships, at least for now."

♀

In May 1965, Keith became concerned about the government's modification of student deferments. In its ferocious hunger for fighters, the Selective Service had begun to draw from college boys, however unwilling. Keith had been incensed about the selection process, based on class rank and scores on a special standardized aptitude test. He was even angrier that City College administrators were providing class standing status to draft boards.

He enlisted Max, and together they organized a local rally in coordination with a national SDS event. "We can't allow poor

American kids to die because they don't have privileged advantages for taking an aptitude test," he told his comrades. And we can't let our college abet such a reprehensible recruiting process. His eyes flared with contempt. Shortly, their entire clan became involved.

The day of the rally was warm, a relief from the long winter's biting cold. Although the sky was heavy with dark clouds, ready to burst, an assortment of cooing and chirping birds primed Keith for his performance. The hues and fragrances of late spring flowers, bushes, and trees surrounding South Campus invigorated him as well—lilacs, azaleas, peonies, sweet-smelling crab apples.

The six companions were in good spirits, buoyed by the enormous number of students who showed up and flooded the South Lawn. Everyone held clever, colorful signs, the perfect backdrop to Keith's latest pieces that lambasted the Johnson Administration for snatching unwitting kids to feed its avaricious war, like wolves devouring their kill. The songs embodied the dry humor Keith had become known for.

A mysterious girl who had been hanging around Keith for weeks finally caught his attention. Now at the demonstration, she stood near his guitar case, apart from the swarm of people surrounding him. She appeared lost in his music, her closely set dark brown eyes, like chocolate, staring vacantly in a haze of oblivion. She wore a navy-blue jumper over a tie-dyed shirt, two strings of brightly colored handmade love beads around her neck, large silver hoop earrings, and expensive Fred Braun brown leather sandals on her feet. She had a small, yellow daisy tattoo on her ankle.

After patiently awaiting an opportunity, she approached him. "Hey, Keith, come to a party with me. It'll be a blast."

He looked at the unfamiliar co-ed with long, straight, black hair hanging to her shoulders, parted in the middle, hollow cheeks. The girl's prominent nose, pierced with a diamond stud, somehow only enhanced her allure. He turned sheepishly to his friends who were waiting for him. It was Friday night, West End Bar time.

The newcomer pushed back her shoulders and, with a determined look, waved them toward her. "Y'all come along too," she said. "If the chicks sit on the boys' laps, there will be room in my wagon for everyone. The bash is down in the East Village, an easy-breezy drive." She tossed back her head and gave a seductive smile to Keith, who felt pulled in opposite directions, between loyalty and desire.

His pals hesitated, not sure if they should ride with this strange hippie to some godforsaken place. Deanna reacted first, anxious to relieve Keith of the competing pressures. She pulled Russell by the sleeve of his denim shirt. "I'm game for an adventure," she said. The others followed suit.

The seemingly interminable ride was bumpy and uncomfortable, and Rebecca complained the entire way. She kept shifting her weight, inducing Max to softly moan in pain. The girl kept reassuring them: "We're almost there. We're almost there." Sitting on Russell's lap, her elbow poking into Malaika, Deanna wondered what she had gotten them into.

They finally arrived at a tall building that looked more like an industrial workplace. After climbing three flights of stairs, they stepped into a huge loft and were greeted by whiffs of marijuana coming from all directions among the droves of people packed into the place. The partygoers were stretched out on rugs, pillows, beanbags, and the bare wooden floor or huddled together on mattresses and two sagging couches.

Several attendees were standing by a huge window that faced other buildings, other windows, a few darkened by curtains. The immense room was so dim that individuals appeared as mere shadows moving in slow motion, giving everything a surreal quality, like a dream. Makeshift cinder block bookshelves lined the walls, teeming with assorted books, knickknacks, and framed photos that suggested that someone actually lived there.

The mysterious girl whisked Keith away to a dark corner, leaving his friends on their own. She rolled a thin yellow joint, twisting the ends, and lit it up. For the first time ever, Keith sucked in the harsh smoke, which burned his throat and, much to his embarrassment, caused him to wheeze and cough. She stroked his face, brushed back his hair. "First time, huh? That's cool."

She inhaled the weed and passed it to him again. She fed him brownies laced with hashish. He began to feel relaxed, euphoric. Time and place eluded him as his senses became more acute. Hunger washed over them, and they headed out into the clear night. Holding hands, they wandered around the Village, mesmerized by the star-studded sky. Eventually, they found an all-night cafeteria where they wolfed down countless snacks, satiating themselves. Keith felt in love.

"Our Keith is in lust," is how Rebecca sneeringly put it the next day. The girl now had a name, Serena, and she dropped by their cafeteria table regularly over the next few months, typically stoned. She sat there with glazed eyes, pouting at their political talk, pawing at Keith like a dog begging for attention. Every so often she interrupted their discussion, intent on pushing them to join her in a night of what she called "doing drugs." She told them she dropped mescaline, popped pills, snorted powder, tripped on acid. They were welcome to whatever she had. "Can't get Keith to use anything," she said, curling her lips in mock disgust. "At least without y'all."

When Serena wasn't around, they talked about the night of the party, when everyone had become high. Deanna and Malaika had sat giggling in a corner, feeling chilled out, telling wacky stories, both attempting to outdo the other. They kept each other in stitches.

Max had turned quiet, more introspective. "Certain events in my life whirled in my head, replaying themselves in curious ways," he told them. "I wouldn't mind exploring drugs some more."

Russell was less sanguine. "I obsessed about life after college," he confided, "and the prospects made me anxious and depressed." He pushed back a few curls falling over his eyes. "But I'm ready to experiment again too, but only with marijuana or hashish." Everyone agreed not to sample anything stronger, certainly not more serious psychedelics.

Rebecca kept quiet about the evening, and nobody pushed her.

Serena disappeared within a few months. Keith had grown tired of her relentless goading to get high and her apathy about the political events heating up around them. "She doesn't even know who he is," he grumbled to his pals as they were discussing the June shooting of James Meredith by a sniper. "And she couldn't care less about the war or the draft dragging our boys away."

He had to admit to himself that he would miss Serena's uninhibited sexuality and the carnal pleasures he had shared with her. She had been a veritable sensual playground for him. After she was gone, he brought a few other girls to their cafeteria table, but none of them lasted very long either.

9
Rebecca

THAT NIGHT in the East Village loft was a defining one for Rebecca. Unlike her friends, she avoided the weed and instead sipped cheap red wine circulating in gallon bottles. She leaned against a wall, at the far end of the room, observing. She was taken aback by such open use of illicit drugs, joints, and pills passed around like M&Ms. Her attention was soon captured by a woman with big brown eyes whose lids were painted with thick, jet-black lines, heavily coated mascaraed lashes, and copious aquamarine shadow. She had a wide mouth, smeared with plum lipstick, that heightened her dramatic look.

Rebecca stared at her for a while, bathed in feelings of intense attraction, until she glanced back. Rebecca was embarrassed, but the woman's expression was welcoming so Rebecca smiled in return. They kept eyeing each other. Finally, the woman wandered over, touched her arm, and purred, "You're hot." She led Rebecca to an empty nook in the corner of the room and, without warning, kissed her deeply and erotically. For an instant, their tongues intertwined, ravishing each other. Then the woman pulled away, slipped Rebecca a small piece of paper with her phone number, and disappeared into the smoky loft.

The kiss was magical. Those thirty seconds would last forever in her mind, and she replayed the scene over and over. She had never felt anything like it before, certainly not with Max. She had known at a young age that Kitty appealed to her over Matt Dillon, Dale Evans more than Roy Rogers. In second grade, she had developed a crush on the dimpled girl with swinging blonde braids, and, in third, the adorable brunette who sat in front of her. She had pushed such stirrings down, instinctively choosing denial. It was less complicated to veil her eyes than to sort out socially unacceptable feelings. In any case, Rebecca had told herself that she would get over it, develop more natural attractions. She was young, still a work in progress.

But the striking woman with the pixie hairdo, clothed in flaming orange bell bottoms and an embroidered white linen shirt, had shaken her to the core, as if she were falling off a cliff. Her touch exposed buried erotic fantasies: the genie was out of the bottle and could not be squeezed back in. She had been stunned into reality at a visceral level and over the next few days became ever more agitated as the implications sunk in. Her life would be upended. She would never be the same. Her first impulse was to run from the danger like a horse whose blinders are suddenly ripped off.

Rebecca couldn't sleep, tossing and turning into the wee hours of the morning. She binged on sweets—caramels, Snickers, jellybeans—until her stomach rebelled. And she avoided her comrades, claiming that she was overwhelmed with schoolwork; nobody believed her. When she was confronted by Max, she told him to leave her alone.

As time went on, she found herself steadily accepting, even embracing, her sexual orientation despite the future upheaval. Rebecca came to realize that she couldn't hide from herself any longer, that the disconnect between who she is and who she had been pretending to be was just too enormous. Despite her social activism she was living an inauthentic personal life.

Max would be the hardest to confront, the one most affected. Rebecca closed her eyes and took a calming breath. He had tried, really tried, she reflected. He even read through whatever limited books and magazines were available on lovemaking, including the *Kama Sutra*. He experimented, touched her in various places, gauging her response. She had tried, really tried, pleasuring him without being particularly aroused herself. Their sexual relations had love without lust, caring without passion, and he sensed it. They both coveted more.

Rebecca did not want to lead a secret existence any longer, to conceal herself from family and friends. Her eyelids felt heavy. No matter what happened, it was time to come out to them. Yet she waited to tell anybody, struggling to muster the courage. And waited some more. Summer slipped by in a flurry of political activities. It appeared as though everyone and everything demanded Max's attention. The time never seemed right and, despite their closeness, she became increasingly apprehensive about facing him. . .and the others.

She didn't know anybody at the college who was openly gay, who dared to come out of the closet. Being "that way" was taboo, viewed as deviant. Even the American Psychological Association classified homosexuality as a psychiatric disorder. Would Max still love her even though they would have to move on to other romantic partners? Would her pals, notwithstanding their political radicalism, accept her? Rebecca was in new, uncharted territory, and she wrestled again with telling them. Could she bear to lose Max or anyone else in their crowd? They had been her anchor for three years, Max for longer.

That fall she decided to bite the bullet. Max would be told first, and then the others, each separately. It had been an unusually warm September day, and she met Max, as planned, at his classroom door. Rebecca usually threw on whatever clothes she grabbed from her closet, but today she chose her outfit carefully. She had picked out a colorful floral embroidered blouse to top her bell-bottom jeans, a matching headband, and long, clipped earrings. She wasn't sure why, but she had sought to impart a touch of femininity. She even toyed around with putting on some makeup but quickly dismissed that as going overboard.

"You look great," Max said when he saw her. "What's the occasion?"

A bustle of students poured out of classes into the hall. "Let's take a walk," she snapped, avoiding his eyes. Noting his crestfallen look, she added in a gentler tone, "I need to tell you something."

They strolled off campus into the heart of Harlem, passing candy stores, beauty salons, noisy bars advertising billiards, pawn shops, churches, bakeries, and liquor outlets. Women were carrying groceries or pushing baby carriages. Old men sat on boxes playing cards, younger ones on stoops idly passing the day. Inadequate garbage collection was evidenced by overflowing cans and scattered litter along the streets and in the gutters. The area was lively with noise, honking cars, police sirens, rumbling trucks, groaning buses, blaring music. The young white couple, in intense conversation, seemed incongruous with the various shades of dark-skinned faces populating the neighborhood. A few people stared curiously at the two misplaced students.

They found a small playground, mostly concrete, and sat down on a half-broken bench. They remained there for a long while, an unnatural silence stretched out between them. They could hear the shouts of a nearby basketball game, rattling hoops, bouncing balls, thumping sneakers. Rebecca inhaled and exhaled deeply, and with a pained, quivering voice divulged her secret. As she unburdened herself, she began sobbing, releasing months of suppressed emotions.

Max stayed tight-lipped, a pensive expression on his face. Eventually, he took her cold, clammy hands in his. "I'm concerned about you," he said. "It won't be easy to navigate our homophobic world. But I'll always be there, Becca, I promise." He stroked her fingers.

He struggled to find his next words. "But I'm also relieved," he said. "Now I know for sure the sexual problem wasn't me. I had begun questioning myself, my masculinity." They embraced, holding each other tight, a touch of melancholy in the air.

Rebecca approached Malaika a few days later, pulling her away from the cafeteria table. They parked themselves against a nearby tree on the South Lawn, alone but surrounded by swarms of chattering students. Rebecca stumbled over her words as her companion leaned in, raising her eyebrows. After a short interlude, Malaika peppered her with questions in rapid succession. "How long have you known?" "Are you sure?" "What are the signs?" Malaika was also concerned that Rebecca's parents would misunderstand their relationship. "Please reassure your mother and father about us," she pleaded.

Malaika flicked an ant from her skirt and watched its brisk escape. Would it head to the safety of its colony? The insect called to mind the years of warm friendship with Rebecca and how her mother had permitted Malaika to take refuge in their home. "It must have been hard keeping that piece of yourself secret," she said. "You should have known that it wouldn't change anything for me. That our bond is indestructible."

Rebecca shot her a look of appreciation.

Deanna was next. She kept nodding, lips set tightly together, as Rebecca yet again went through her revelatory narrative. "I'm not surprised," had been her first response, quickly followed by, "What about Max?"

"He's good," she said, with a sigh. "And it's not like my charming Max won't find other women. There are probably swarming multitudes already."

Deanna put a comforting arm around her friend's shoulder. "Are you okay?" she said.

Rebecca turned and looked directly into Deanna's eyes. "I'm calmer, more peaceful," she replied. "I think both Max and I feel like a weight has been lifted from our relationship."

The two girls linked arms and walked toward the cafeteria to join the others.

Keith was next. He responded with an enigmatic, "Hmm, thanks for letting me know."

Rebecca's stomach knotted up, uncertain about his terse reaction. Yet at their graduation, he presented her with a song he had composed, entitled "It Is More Than Okay," about a friend who bravely came out of the closet. The recording eventually surfaced on his first and only album a few years later.

Russell was the last one, but by then he already knew. Rebecca was sure that he and Deanna had already picked apart every aspect of her situation. But he indulged Rebecca and listened patiently to her account.

"I'm with you," he said, flashing his warmest smile. "You're our buddy. Nothing can change that."

Her so-called radical mother was the greatest surprise—and disappointment. "I'll never have grandchildren," she wailed. "You and Max would have made such beautiful babies." Then, quick as a blazing fire, she continued, "We'll find the finest psychiatrist for you. Spare no expense. This can be fixed, I'm sure."

Daddy had been more supportive, though she observed a trace of sorrow in his eyes. "Now Nora," he said to his wife, "Rebecca is an adult and makes her own choices. We must trust her." The issue lingered in the air, like a dull, chronic ache for years, though they never spoke of it again. Rebecca felt as though she had let them both down.

10
Max

MAX'S LEADERSHIP of City's SDS chapter gratified his mounting passion to stand up to the military industrial-complex. In his junior year, he attended several national SDS council meetings and conventions held in various cities across the nation. The conferences were a nourishing infusion of ideas. Through workshops, speakers, and casual conversations, he participated in heated debates over strategies for ending the war and developing draft resistance programs on campuses. As the Vietnam Conflict ramped up, along with the volume of draftees, a few SDS organizers insisted on an escalation of their own militancy. For Max, these journeys fueled his political commitment and imparted a shared camaraderie that thus far he had experienced only with his college pals.

Under Max's guidance, City's chapter intensified its demonstrations, both in magnitude and strength. He became so immersed in SDS that he began skipping classes. He and his comrades were particularly irked by the increasing presence of Army recruiters on campus. The government's appetite for soldiers had become insatiable, and City College presented fertile ground for enlistments. The military had set up a large table covered with paraphernalia glorifying the war in front of Shepard Hall. The exhibit was surrounded by huge display boards with colorful patriotic posters: "Follow Me! Your Country Needs You"; "Are You Army Strong"; "Be All You Can Be"; and "I Want You for the US Army," with Uncle Sam pointing his finger to encourage men to join the war effort. These materials were supplemented by American flags of varying sizes waving in the breeze and boxes of smaller ones for students to take with them. Two men, in starched olive uniforms and matching peaked caps, braved their assignment with frozen smiles.

SDS planned a day of protest that involved Max's whole gang. Deanna and Russell designed and photocopied hundreds of provocative fliers pressing for more student power at the college. Each one had a picture of wounded Vietnamese children, underscored with anti-war slogans. They spent weeks handing them out on the pathway between North and South campus.

Rebecca and Malaika set up a countervailing SDS table at Shepard Hall that had its own literature and posters: "War Is Not Healthy for Children and Other Living Things"; "Peace Is Patriotic"; "Make Love Not War"; "Burn Cards, Not People"; and "I Want You to Work for Peace," with Uncle Sam also pointing his finger but this time to elicit anti-war activism. They had several boxes of matching pins to hand out. Other SDS members erected an adjoining stand offering draft evasion counseling, both legal and illegal.

♀

On the day of the sit-in, more than a thousand students showed up. They were a ragtag bunch. Some guys wore beads, earrings, long manes, tie-dyed shirts, beards, and mustaches. Others were clean-shaven with cropped hair and slide rules peeking out of the back pocket of their chinos. There were girls sporting bright, funky outfits and those in more modest shift dresses, mostly in subdued tones. Despite the solemnity of the occasion, everyone appeared in a festive mood.

Students were everywhere, sprawled out on blankets, sitting on steps, leaning against statutes and buildings. Keith, their homegrown Phil Ochs, was there with his guitar and harmonica, leading everyone in anti-war ballads both old and new. He had the usual entourage of co-eds at his side, but he was too intent on rousing the crowd to notice or care. He pushed the crowd to shout "Bring them home, bring them home" at the chorus in his rendition of Pete Seeger's latest song. When he played "Eve of Destruction," they sang along on their own, "You're old enough to kill, but not for voting."

Max was equally intense. He led the gathering in chants: "Hey, hey, LBJ. How many kids did you kill today?" "Peace now! Peace now!" "No more, stop the war." He whipped the students into a frenzy like a Southern Baptist preacher. He stood there sweating, despite the chill in the air, as he moved from one anti-war cry to another.

Then he spearheaded a contingent of several hundred students to encircle the recruitment booth, forming a human blockade. He demanded that the recruiters justify US war crimes and the toxic weapons maiming and killing the Vietnamese people. The crowd began screaming, "Tell us, tell us about the war crimes," and "Hell, no, we won't go" as the two army men sat stone faced. The police eventually appeared and began pushing and pulling students surrounding the stand; a few fought back. One cop with a megaphone was barking, "Everyone clear out now.

The party is over." The crowd refused to disperse, shouting out their First Amendment rights to nobody in particular.

Max attempted to reason with the officers, and he was hit with a baton. That provoked even more outrage and pushback. The day ended with everyone exhausted and some individuals slightly injured. But there was a scent of resolve in the air.

In its relentless attempt to garner support for the war, the State Department had launched a speaker's program aimed at colleges and universities. Emboldened by the previous massive turnout and determination among the student body, Max proposed that City's chapter picket the spokesman, a Mr. Jacob Bartlett, who was to give a talk in the Great Hall. Again, the SDS membership, organized by Max and his crew, mounted a full-court press to promote an even larger rally than before.

This time, over two thousand students appeared, filling the large room and spilling over into the vestibule. The boisterous crowd, waving anti-war signs, did not let the government representative speak. Each time he began his remarks, he was greeted with jeers, hoots, and catcalls. The official had almost been booed off the stage when Max, a tall and imposing figure, stood up. He pressed his index finger against his pursed lips to hush the students. The hall suddenly became eerily quiet.

Max looked up at the man, crossed his arms, and stared directly at him. Despite his racing heart and rapid breathing, he felt in full command of the situation. In a firm voice he said, "We'll let you speak only if you agree to debate with one of us."

The nonplussed Bartlett—hair worn in a crew cut and clad in a pinstriped suit, starched white button-down shirt, rep tie, and shiny wing-tip shoes—stood at the podium, glaring back at Max. He quickly regained his composure and looked around at the young, insolent audience. He must have supposed that this scruffy collection of kids couldn't possibly be his equal because he flashed a cold smile. "Sure. I'll take someone on."

The scraping sound of a chair on the wood floor broke the silence as a student stood up. Everyone turned to Jay Zimmerman, dressed in jeans, a black turtleneck, and a corduroy sports coat, as he walked up to the platform, armed with a small wooden box of note cards. He was short with curly dark hair and a small gold hoop in his right earlobe. The college senior, an SDS affiliate, had been chosen by Max for this likely turn of events. Zimmerman had been a member of his high school debate team and, for the past four years, City's star debater.

The official was too caught up in his jingoistic propaganda to have a chance against the razor-sharp, well-prepared Zimmerman. Every time the speaker spewed out deceptive party lines like a partisan volcano, he was met with point-by-point evidence to the contrary. Bartlett parroted LBJ's statistics on the number of ground troops, extent of air strikes, and imminence of US victory. When Zimmerman challenged him with actual data, the students broke out in loud applause, accompanied by stomping and whooping.

Bartlett was asked to defend clandestine acts of violence, such as the secret bombings over North Vietnam and airstrikes on Viet Cong—controlled villages that engendered huge civilian casualties. He spit out more half-truths, although now he appeared somewhat defensive.

The student debater questioned him about the free-fire zones, which had been cleared of the peasants who worked the land. "Is it true," Zimmerman asked, "that any farmer who refused to leave could be shot like deer in open season?" The Great Hall seemed electrified as one by one Bartlett failed to effectively defend his smoke-and-mirrors arguments. Max's gang was sitting together, nodding their approval.

Afterwards, the undergraduates surrounded Max and Jay, congratulating them on the unqualified success of the event. Max broke away and found his chums, who embraced him. He gave them a satisfied grin and said, "We did it again!" He executed a high five with each of them, and said, "Let's go to the West End. I need a beer." Jay and a few other SDS members tagged along.

♀

Max continued to visit Rebecca's family as often as he could, although these days the situation clearly was more complicated. Izzie and Nora had become his surrogate parents over the last several years as they had for Malaika. Max valued Izzie's input on political tactics as they sat around the dinner table in animated conversation. He had been the one to suggest a student speaker to counter the State Department official; Max had initially intended to organize only a boycott of the talk.

Nora, the gracious hostess, spent much of her time in the kitchen, though at times she too provided thoughtful advice. She was a first-rate cook, and the table was always overflowing with tasty dishes. Nora still treated him like a son, but Max could sense that she was crestfallen about his altered relationship with her daughter.

He still worked hand in hand with Rebecca, as always, as though nothing had changed. But it had. Max felt a longing for her even when they were together. Yes, their friendship remained strong. Yet they were no longer a couple and, for reasons he couldn't quite pinpoint, that made a difference to him. They had been together for such a long time, and now there was a void that his political activism could not entirely fill. She was constantly at the back of his mind, like an unbidden guest, though he accepted their revised relationship as settled.

Max resolved to keep that part of himself under wraps. None of his friends would have guessed that he was heartbroken, and that was the way he wanted it. He would get over this rough patch in his life alone. He plowed on, sinking deeper and deeper into his activism with renewed gusto and single-minded dedication. He became so driven, neglecting everything and everyone around him, that Keith became concerned and warned him to slow down. The entire crew lectured him to no avail. He was a man on a mission.

11
Malaika

GROWING UP, Malaika had felt conscious of her skin color to such a degree that it became a defining aspect of her personality. She had viewed light-skinned African Americans as more attractive, privileged, and socially advantaged than her. Shade mattered, even in a neighborhood of financially struggling families, unemployment, dilapidated housing, and crime. Malaika studied exceptionally hard in part because she believed that to succeed, she had to compensate for her dark complexion.

She had stood out even more at City College, where nearly everyone was white, including the faculty. She didn't face much overt racism, but discrimination was forever there, simmering below the surface like a gently bubbling stew. Malaika sensed it in the look on her college advisor's face when she told him about her intention to attend law school. He had narrowed his eyes and gave her a condescending frown. "Hmm," he said, "perhaps you should have a backup plan."

The college was a white fortress on a hill above Black Harlem—minorities made up less than six percent of the student body. Malaika was often the lone dark face in her courses and in lecture halls, the library, the cafeteria, the South Lawn, student lounges, parties, even at SDS meetings. She was self-conscious when she asked questions in class; it seemed that every eye turned in her direction. She perceived impossible-to-meet demands on her. She felt as though she were on trial and, as usual, had to work harder than everyone else, had to prove that a woman of color could achieve scholastic success. She attained nearly an A average every semester. She tirelessly attempted to conform to white middle-class comportment, behavior, speech, and style. The exertions were exhausting.

Rebecca's parents proved of great consequence to her well-being. They provided Malaika with a bedroom of her own, unlike the shared space at her mother's tiny apartment. Nora purchased a large desk and comfortable chair that facilitated Malaika's studies, as did the unaccustomed quiet in the home. Her high school had not prepared Malaika for the required calculus course, and when she couldn't make up for the deficiency—no matter how much she plowed on—Izzie brought in a private tutor. She participated in the political discussions at the dinner table, often with Max in attendance, benefiting from Izzie's know-how and Nora's wholesome meals. Everyone treated her like family.

She was somewhat protected, too, by her close-knit coterie of friends, who sheltered her from social isolation. They provided Malaika with emotional and intellectual sustenance. She truly cared for them and appreciated their warm companionship. College was a dizzying time for her, and she clung to them for life support. Nonetheless, she craved a romantic relationship, and the dearth of Black undergraduates had proven problematic for meeting anyone.

She first encountered Tommy at an SDS meeting at the beginning of her junior year. He had medium-length, soft, curly, light brown hair, twinkling amber eyes, and a strong, somewhat bulbous, nose. He looked smart in his navy-blue turtleneck sweater, matching beret, leather vest, jeans, and chukka boots. They kept glancing at each other.

Afterwards, he strolled over to her and Deanna and began chatting with them. He was engaging, regaling them with a delicious mélange of anecdotes. She giggled throughout their conversation, partly out of amusement but also out of sheer nervousness. Malaika kept patting her recently straightened hair, self-conscious about her appearance. She wished she had worn something chic. She and Tommy discovered that they were raised in similar low-income Brooklyn neighborhoods, only his—East Flatbush—was mostly white. Race didn't seem to matter to him. They just clicked.

As they shared mutual interests, the budding relationship flourished. He came around to their cafeteria table regularly, and the crew welcomed him. Deanna and Rebecca were delighted that Malaika had met someone as kind and witty as Tommy, especially because he made her—and the rest of them—crack up, at times having them in stitches. He joined them on their Sunday outings to Washington Square Park, Friday nights at the West End Bar, and political meetings.

Four months into their passionate romance, Tommy brought Malaika to meet his parents. She immediately realized that he had not prepared them. When he introduced her, his mother wore a dazed expression and her face turned pale. They were polite but stiff throughout the evening. The tension was unmistakable. She caught his mom periodically eyeballing her, shaking her head—almost imperceptibly—in disbelief.

The next day Tommy greeted her in the cafeteria and, turning his back on the group, asked her to go for a walk. He was visibly shaken as he clenched and unclenched his fists.

"What's wrong?" Malaika asked as soon as they were outside.

He turned to face her, struggling for a gentle approach. He finally gave up, shrugged, and blurted out, "I can't see you anymore."

Malaika stood there, stunned, unable to breathe or think.

"Mom said they would throw me out of the house otherwise," Tommy continued, avoiding Malaika's eyes. Then he pulled her to him. "I care deeply about you, but I have no money and nowhere else to go." The words tumbled out, like he had lost his footing on the edge of a cliff. "Dad also threatened to renege on his promise to put me through law school. From the small inheritance his aunt had left him." He lifted her face and gave a pained look. "I thought long and hard about this, but I have no choice."

Tommy hugged her and walked away, leaving Malaika gazing after him, tears welling but stubbornly refusing to trickle down.

She was shattered, and her friends commiserated, soothing and nurturing her like a pack of wolves caring for its pups. Nora baked her brownies. Even Izzie, who tended to be restrained, weighed in. "You are an exceptional person," he assured Malaika. "You're beautiful, smart, and have a loving heart. You'll find a guy worthy of you, I'm certain." She gave him a weak, appreciative smile.

One evening the girls sat on Malaika's bed, cross-legged, as her emotions poured out in a torrent of tears. They talked and talked, laughing, joking, and sobbing, sometimes all at once. They chewed over the challenges of love, picking up on each other's complaints without missing a beat. Rebecca and Malaika consoled Deanna, who finally admitted her pain over Russell's disappearances. They unpacked details of her relationship with him, giving her fresh insights. The three of them shared longings that they never had revealed before. And they wondered together about what was in store for them in the coming years.

♀

Malaika plunged even deeper into her studies. Juggling work and school left her little time to mope, though she continued to ache for her lost love. Izzie had found her a flexible, part-time job at Local 1199, which paid for her extra expenses. She sometimes worked side by side with Rebecca in the office, absorbing the bustling energy and frustrations of the union's latest organizing campaign. After Tommy left her, she picked up more hours at the union, determined to save what she could for law school. Malaika was fully aware that she could never accumulate enough money for even a semester, but at least she could see a rising balance in her savings account offering the promise that her ambition was more than a pipe dream.

She continued to visit her mother and siblings twice a month, forcing herself to take the dreaded trip. It was not just the time-consuming, tedious trek that Malaika begrudged but also their attitude. Aiysha, who had been forced to take over Malaika's former responsibilities, resented her and made it crystal clear. Her beautiful, flamboyant sister aspired to hang out with her friends and flirt with the guys not babysit Frederick, cook, and shop. At thirteen, she already had a boyfriend of sorts. Julene and Maya showed little inclination to do homework or much of anything else and already manifested signs of delinquency. The pair were impertinent to her and Mom, who couldn't— or wouldn't— control them. They threw out four-letter words with relish, both out of habit and, Malaika suspected, to annoy their serious-minded elder sister. She was concerned about their prospects.

Her mother insisted on straightening Malaika's hair, permitted by her boss after salon hours. She used the opportunity to upbraid her, letting loose with the same refrains, ad nauseam. "If you had stayed here, your siblings would not have turned out so ill-mannered and lazy." She often adopted a defiant tone that at times turned pleading, "Come home. The girls and Freddy need you." Yanking on Malaika's tightly coiled, stubborn locks, she would add, "And ditch your highfalutin' attitude. You're egging your sisters on."

These entreaties tugged at Malaika's heart, but there was no turning back. "Mom," she would answer, "when I return, it will be with the skills to fight for our community, along with the power of a law degree." Was she deluding herself?

♀

At college, she sought out the token Black faculty, eager to take their classes. Fortuitously, two of them, Allen Ballard and John Davis, were both in the political science department, her major. When she entered their classrooms, she felt that she was no longer in a foreign country. Those classes were the first ones in which she could identify with the professor, individuals who looked like her. Nevertheless, rather than coddle Malaika, they pushed and challenged her to such a degree that she developed an even more powerful work ethic and went into overdrive to please them. Neither Ballard nor Davis ever actually mentored her, though; faculty at City College—including the few minorities—lived in an ivory tower, far removed from students outside the classroom setting.

By her senior year, Malaika had begun experiencing unfamiliar stirrings that gave her both greater strength and self-esteem, apart from her comrades. She sniffed a whiff of Black pride that percolated gradually into her consciousness. Black Power, with its call for liberation from white standards, rang true to her, and she began to reject the unhealthy struggles to conform that she had been engaged in over the last several years. She repeated "Black Is Beautiful" so many times that she began to feel more comfortable in her own skin.

The Black Power Movement also raised questions about her allegiances, and Malaika felt conflicted. She heard that CORE recently had voted to become an all-Black organization though the group agreed to work with ad hoc coalitions that included other races. Its rationale made sense to her—people of color must organize themselves to build independence and self-determination. White affiliates had too much power in CORE, undermining the confidence of Black members in themselves and their ability to shape their communities. Malaika agreed that the activities of White allies should focus on their own neighborhoods, where the source of racism resided in the first place.

Where did she fit in? She had spent nearly her entire college years with SDS, advocating for civil rights and an end to the war in Vietnam. But Caucasians were clearly in charge at all levels of the organization. And unlike her, despite their well-meaning intentions, they ultimately enjoyed White privilege. Much of their concern had been the drafting of college boys, who were mostly White. Is that where her allegiance should be?

Malaika decided that she must claim her Black identity. For starters, she would let her straightened hair grow out. She began wearing colorful bandanas to hide the unsightly, uneven growth. In due time, she went to a beauty parlor, avoiding her mother's shop, and had it trimmed. She looked in the mirror with awe at her newly acquired afro and felt liberated. "Black is beautiful," she murmured to herself.

12
Russell

As GRADUATION approached, Russell was frazzled from the emotional tornado of his senior year. In the fall, Deanna had asked him repeatedly about his whereabouts, but he kept delaying a confrontation. Finally, she put her foot down, and he stood up to her. "We're in the midst of a sexual revolution," he growled. "Monogamy is passé." His words hung in the air.

"So, you've been fucking around!" she spat out, a mix of fury, indignation, and hurt contorting her face into an unsightly expression. "How could you do this to me?"

Russell looked down at the floor, arms crossed over his chest. "This is not about you, Deanna. I owe it to myself. . .to experiment. To liberate myself from social conventions." He became even more adamant. "We must shed our sexual hang-ups. It's part and parcel of our radical political mission."

"You've always been good at self-justification," she replied, this time more calmly. She gave him a fixed stare. "What do you suppose is going to happen with us?"

After a brief interval, his heart thumping, he said, "I was hoping you would give me some space. Still be my chick."

"Not likely," she snorted and stomped away.

Deanna didn't speak to him for a month. She gave him the cold shoulder whenever they were together. The air was thick with bitterness.

Russell was rattled by the abrupt breakup and Deanna's silent treatment but didn't question his actions. He blamed the rift entirely on her, the inability to understand how men are wired. They need to play around before settling down, he assured himself, to sample a variety of women. He had met Deanna at too young an age and had been exclusively with her since. He was entitled to more sexual experiences, and she was being selfish. Why couldn't she let him play around without their splitting up? He decided that, despite her radical political views, her moral code for intimate relationships was too conventional for him.

Russell thought about his first one-night stand the spring of his junior year. She had a "make love not war" button pinned to a pale yellow, translucent shirt. Her skirt was short enough to expose her shapely long legs and give a hint of lacy underwear. She had been hanging around with several students who were listening to Keith play his guitar. She had looked up at him with a sensuous smile.

"Make love not war," he had said lamely, immediately feeling foolish.

She giggled, seemingly not put off. They chatted for a while, the unmistakable sexual tension mounting between them. The sun was disappearing, lighting up the sky in a dusty pink glow. Keith had already packed up his guitar, and like everyone else had gone home. Russell listened to the sounds of their silence a while before awkwardly putting his arm around her, unsure of what would happen next. But she took charge. "Let's go. My friend has a place on the Upper West Side, not too far from here." She gave him a playful punch, amused at his apparent hesitation. "No strings attached."

That had been the beginning of a succession of co-eds. Russell became acutely aware of the countless "hot" girls strutting around campus in suggestive attire. He felt as though he were at a smorgasbord, tasting various delicacies. His libido was fired up, like a pot boiling over. And best of all, unlike with Deanna, he could enjoy the sexual pleasures without having to placate their emotional neediness. There was no constant "Do you love me?" or "Where have you been?" from any of these liaisons. He was clear with each one: No attachments. Only two of them even asked when they would see him again, and he had stammered, "I'll call you." He had no intention of entering another relationship, at least for now.

Russell was hugely relieved when he and Deanna eventually settled into an amiable friendship, similar to Rebecca and Max. Like him, Deanna did not want to lose their surrogate family. They were a tight-knit crew, nearly every one of them from demoralizing traditional homes, who had created their own nurturing community. They relied on each other. However, he had to promise Deanna that he would be discreet and never bring any of his casual flings to meet their crowd.

♀

All of them were edgy as graduation loomed ahead. Only Russell had anything resembling a plan, and even his was tentative as he waited for acceptance letters from grad schools. He had spent untold time preparing for the GREs in the fall, including an expensive prep course that his parents paid for. They also financed the costly applications, ten in all, that he had laboriously filled out. He agonized over the required essays, particularly those about why he was pursuing a Ph.D. in sociology. Russell, at this point, was uncertain as to why he was even applying to graduate school, much less a particular field of study. He plodded on, revising the compositions endlessly as his friends critiqued them.

"Why *are* you going to graduate school?" Rebecca asked him, after reading one of them.

Russell squirmed and looked over at the others for backup. But they were studying him, curious to hear his explanation, not the pretenses he had contrived for his applications. "What are the alternatives?" he answered, in a flat, monotonous voice. "I can't make a career out of political activism."

"I intend to," Max said. He looked around the table at his friends with a mischievous gleam in his eyes.

Russell began second-guessing his decision and motives. Was it okay to pursue graduate school only because he couldn't figure out anything else to do? He viewed himself as strong-minded—purposeful—not someone who would drift into the next chapter of his life. He sifted through options for the umpteenth time, attempting to discover something more meaningful. What could he embark on that would allow him to advocate for social justice but also offer him a respectable profession? Instead of derailing his current course of action, he winded up assuaging his guilt by convincing himself that academia was, indeed, an appropriate means for championing causes. He was ready to go full speed ahead.

Russell's parents were ecstatic. Their son was finally coming around to their goals for him. His mother greeted the postman every afternoon before he even dropped the mail into their box. "Nothing yet," his mother said as soon as Russell opened the front door. Her anxious hovering was unnerving.

She also kept poking him about Deanna. "Where's that cock-eyed girlfriend of yours?" she inquired one evening. At another time she said, "Your shiksa hasn't called for a long while. Have you finally ditched her?" As had become his way of dealing with his mother, Russell simply dismissed her spiteful barbs with a shrug. Nevertheless, her words left a sour taste in his mouth.

♀

In mid-April, he and his cronies joined the anti-war demonstration in New York City, one of the largest thus far. Over two hundred thousand people gathered in Central Park and marched to the Dag Hammarskjold Plaza at the United Nations. There had been the usual signs, chants, music, and speakers. The attendees listened rapt as Martin Luther King, Jr. decried the war as a perpetuation of white colonialism and its untenability both morally and politically. The six friends were moved by his eloquent connection between the escalation of the war and the losses suffered by the American poor as the War on Poverty programs increasingly became one of its casualties. Then the rally heated up, like exploding firecrackers, as nearly one hundred and fifty guys rose and simultaneously burned their draft cards in a Maxwell House coffee can. Russell fingered his own card as he watched them with reverential awe.

Max moved closer to Russell, his jaw clenched. "I'm on the verge of joining them," he said.

His friend nodded. "I know. I've seen that coming for a while."

Max squeezed his eyes shut. "But there's too much damn organizing work to do for me to risk jail yet."

Russell looked at him with admiration. "Unlike you, I'm too cowardly to jeopardize my future." He hung his head, mortified by his own words.

Without hesitation, Max brushed aside his comrade's chagrin. "I'm no martyr, nor do I want to be," he insisted. "For me, the escalated bombing and destruction by our forces overseas was a deal breaker. I feel as though I have no choice but to continue the struggle, put a stop to the needless fighting and deaths."

There was a silence as Max gathered his thoughts. "Each of us must make our own way," he continued. "If we keep our goals clear and uncorrupted, one occupation is no better than another." He gave Russell a thoughtful look. "You'll become a professor, a public intellectual. Write consequential pieces. Deliver lectures. Enlighten the next generation on our societal needs and how to redress the inequalities. I won't think less of you, whatever path you take."

Max turned to watch the smoldering coffee cans. "Me, I'll lead the anti-war struggle, eventually burn my draft card, and then most likely leave the country. We'll be going our separate ways, hopefully on synergistic journeys."

They smiled at each other and traded fist bumps.

♀

Russell became more apprehensive about getting into graduate school as the weeks rolled by. However, shortly after the march, the letters started rolling in. His mother could barely contain herself from ripping them open. "What's it say? What's it say?" she would repeat, leaning over him. He knew that she was banking on an Ivy League school, but he was concerned only with finances. His GRE scores, while high, had disappointed him. He hungered for a full scholarship so he could be independent of his parents.

He had been admitted to several places, with packages of aid mostly consisting of low-interest student loans. He would have to go into serious debt, which he had hoped to avoid. A thick packet eventually arrived from Columbia University, and his mother became wild with anticipation. "Open it!" she demanded after thrusting it into his hand.

Ignoring her, he walked into his room and locked the door. Only then did he unseal the envelope. As he read the acceptance letter, he experienced a jumble of emotions. Relief, certainly. The sociology department had offered him a teaching assistantship, which included free tuition and a hefty stipend for five years. But there was also a tightness in his chest. Russell looked toward the door, as if expecting his comrades to walk in. He gave a long, low sigh. This portended the end of his chosen family as a unit. He would be setting off on his own.

PART III
Finding Their Way: Summer 1967 to Spring 1971

13
Deanna

AFTER GRADUATING college, the three women opted to live together for a few years while they decided on their future goals. Deanna's mother had become insufferable, and she was itching to leave her parents' apartment. Dad wasn't much of a presence, mostly because he toiled tirelessly at his job. Starting out as a utilities worker for New York City, he had first operated heavy equipment and then repaired and maintained municipal property and power supplies. Eventually, Patrick O'Connor climbed his way to public works supervisor, where he was on call around the clock. On weekends he was glued to the TV, drinking beer and snacking, mostly immersed in sports. "Maryann!" he would bellow, holding up his can. "More brew." Patrick's favorite game was baseball; he was an avid Yankee fan, and since they lived so close to the stadium, he bought season tickets for himself and his son, Steven. He never considered that Deanna would like to join them, nor had she pushed the issue.

Her mother, on the other hand, was hypercritical and domineering. Now that Steven had started college, she was a stay-at-home mom with nothing to do but clean, shop, and cook.

Maryann was a fastidious housekeeper, harping at Deanna for her messiness. Mom also escalated the tirades about Deanna's atheism. "I brought you up as a nice Catholic girl, and look how you turned out," she would hiss. On Sundays, when Deanna set off to the Village with her friends, she nagged her about skipping church although it had been at least eight years since Deanna had attended. "Church is the place to meet a proper husband," Maryann said. "Not like the ragamuffins you hang out with." Deanna stomped into her room and slammed the door.

The most intolerable aspect of her home life was the derogatory language toward anyone who wasn't Irish or anyone who wasn't like the O'Connors. Maryann thought nothing of throwing out slurs to describe certain people who lived outside their homogenous, working-class neighborhood. She had an arsenal of pejorative terms that she discharged with rancor. Deanna didn't want to think about what her mother would call Rebecca.

Mom would disparage Deanna and her political activities by calling struggling Black single mothers "lazy welfare queens" and "half breeds." "They should just pull themselves up by their bootstraps, like we did," Maryann said, parroting the anti-welfare refrain of the time. "Instead, they breed babies, watch TV all day, drive fancy cars, indulge in expensive delicacies, and rely on us taxpayers to support their lifestyle."

Deanna's eyes flashed with indignation. Sometimes when feeling particularly feisty, she would fire back, "Why don't you get a job instead of freeloading off Dad?" That barb stopped Maryann in her tracks. But most of the time, Deanna released the built-up resentment by jogging or ranting and raving to her friends. By spring of 1967, conditions had become so oppressive that she couldn't bear to be at home and spent more and more of her last semester with Rebecca's family.

♀

Immediately after graduation, the women looked for an affordable apartment and ended up with a fifth-floor walkup on Bank Street in the West Village, not far from Rebecca's family. The place was compact, with only two bedrooms. They flipped a coin and Rebecca won; Deanna and Malaika would room together, at least for the time being.

Deanna was eager to jog in her new neighborhood. She braided her hair, put on a T-shirt, shorts, and running shoes, and mapped out the least complicated route. Although New York City, with its straightforward rectangular grid, was relatively easy to navigate, the West Village streets were convoluted.

It was a hot summer day with cloud cover that provided some relief from the searing heat. She ran hard, a rush of endorphins surging through her brain. An initial stiffness progressed to euphoria, as if she was hyped on drugs. When she got into the rhythm of the run, her worries subsided and tension steadily melted from her body. Deanna felt energy, strength, and power as she headed westward, impervious to the sounds and smells of the city. She picked up speed as she circled Bleecker Playground, then ran north on West Street, east on Jane, south on Greenwich Avenue, and back to her apartment. She found the physical exertion exhilarating after the brief, harried jogging hiatus of the past few weeks.

Deanna plunked down in a chair and pushed a few strands of hair out of her eyes. She surveyed the homey-looking living room with satisfaction, though she grimaced at the green, orange, and gold couch that her mother had donated from their Bronx apartment. At least the ugly piece opened as a bed to accommodate guests. Enclosed in protective plastic for twenty years, it had been in pristine condition when she, Malaika, and Rebecca ceremoniously stripped off the wrapping. Over the sofa hung political prints, some from events they had attended.

The women built a long bookcase across the opposite wall out of cinder blocks and plywood that they painted black. They complemented the books with framed photographs, colorful knickknacks, candles of various sizes, plants, and vases. Deanna stepped back to admire the collage she had fashioned of the six friends that they hung over a worn, comfy recliner. They had ransacked the local thrift stores for the mismatched chairs, beds, dressers, lamps, small appliances, dishes, pots and pans, and sundry other items. They high fived each other when they found an inexpensive, bright yellow dinette set that fit perfectly into their minuscule kitchen.

The guys had assisted them in the move using a rented van. And they helped paint the apartment, though the women were adamant about picking out the colors on their own. Russell wrinkled his nose at the magenta can of paint they selected for one of the bedrooms, muttering "I don't think so." The roommates exchanged knowing glances, and Deanna handed him a paintbrush. He also gave them a condescending smile as they covered the walls of the other bedroom in crimson and the living room in burnt orange. "It's certainly colorful," he said dryly when they were through. The women loved the place.

Afterwards, Max would drop in when he was in town, unfailingly at dinnertime. They cheerfully fed him. For Max, the meals were a welcome reprieve from the peanut butter sandwiches he had been consuming on the road. He usually stayed for a few days on their lumpy sofa. The women eagerly listened to his daring acts in organizing college campuses along the East Coast for the SDS.

Keith came by with his guitar, testing his latest musical compositions on them. He was putting together his first album. Russell, too, popped in periodically, though he was caught up in teaching and grad classes. Occasionally, he and Deanna went out for drinks at a neighborhood bar. He flirted with her, insinuating that he would not be averse to reinstating their more intimate relationship. "You're just jealous that I'm screwing other men," she said with a saucy look. Russell threw her a mock pained look, but Deanna knew that she had stung him.

♀

Deanna had to earn a living, that much was clear. She soon found decent paying employment as a caseworker with New York City's Department of Social Services. She quickly discovered, to her dismay, that in the eyes of the poor and their advocates, she had become "the man." She received phone calls from assorted community organizations accusing her of withholding aid from needy families or harassing them. When she tried to explain that she was on their side, they snickered. To them, she was the enemy.

Her working days were divided between the office and fieldwork. She sat at a tiny, lackluster cubicle in a huge room, surrounded by at least thirty other people in similar compartments. The piles of files on their desks were supposed to be updated monthly. She also had to certify single mothers who desperately required public assistance but had to wait months for official approval by layers of supervisors. Though Deanna tried her best to expedite the process, she was at the bottom of the bureaucratic ladder and had little control once the applications left her desk.

The agency was a drab place, with dull florescent lighting and a lack of spirit. The walls were painted in what she characterized as vomit green like mental institutions. The other welfare workers seemed to be competent, well-disposed people overall, although they were mostly demoralized, sapped of enthusiasm by the predicaments and catch-22s of their disadvantaged clients. The staff had college degrees but few majored in social work and none, including her, had received any training in solving the problems their clientele faced. They were just cogs in the wheel of a mass production line established to manage the poor.

At least twice a week, she visited her caseload on a rotating basis. The purpose of these in-home calls was to investigate whether the beneficiaries were abiding by the rules. She had been warned by her boss to check for any evidence of men living in the apartments, which would disqualify the claimants. Instead, she attempted to take the opportunity to chat with the women, learn about their lives, and offer whatever information she could about the availability of benefits. However, unlike her earlier civil rights activism, where low-income women of color would take in White supporters with warm-heartedness, they were aloof in these encounters, often hostile, grudgingly forcing themselves to converse with her. They relied on the checks. Deanna couldn't wait to move on, to do something more meaningful with her life.

♀

She looked forward to Thursday nights, when she attended a consciousness raising group with Malaika and Rebecca. Deanna found it liberating to integrate her feelings, desires, and experiences as a woman with the overall political agenda she had been immersed in over the last many years. In the past, she had intellectualized matters that affected her; now she was forcing herself to do the emotional work.

At every meeting, they picked a topic and took turns expressing their gut reactions—reproductive concerns, dating, education, sexual harassment. For her, the most anguished and valuable exchange was abortion. For the first time, Deanna found herself verbalizing how profoundly her own abortion had touched her and how hurt she had been by Russell's response. Two other women in the twelve-person group had similar stories. With their support, Rebecca probed the causes of her self-reproach and guilt, which eventually permitted her to let go of the relentless ache she had been experiencing since the procedure.

The weekly meetings continued until the summer of 1971. They covered subjects of importance to them at work and in their individual relationships as well as overall oppression in the patriarchal, male-dominated society. Being in their company had been comforting to Deanna. And sharing the get-togethers with Malaika and Rebecca was particularly rewarding.

♀

One evening at the West End Bar, where the six friends still occasionally gathered on Friday nights, the women decided that it way past time to start a genuine dialogue with the men about their male chauvinism and its effects on them. Deanna, Malaika and Rebecca had recently read Casey Hayden and Mary King's 1965 "Sex and Caste" memo about the subordination of women in SDS and SNCC. At the time, after much amusement by male activists, the prescient piece had failed to ignite any serious discussion, like a bomb failing to detonate on impact.

Deanna folded her hands on the table and looked directly at the men, one by one. "We've never really addressed how our second-class treatment in the movement hurt us," she said. Deanna took a sip of wine and continued. "We would like to share our personal reactions with you tonight. It's important to us."

"I don't see it," Russell objected, narrowing his eyes. "We treat you chicks quite well, in my opinion."

Max agreed. "We've been comrades for years, and I haven't heard any of you grousing before."

Keith leaned back in his chair. "Okay. Let us have it."

Deanna cast a meaningful look at Malaika and Rebecca and said, "Who cleaned up after events? Who held leadership positions in our SDS chapter? Who did the typing and mimeographing for newsletters? Who wrote the first drafts of our weekly articles in *The Campus* while Russell received the credit? Weren't we the worker bees while the guys supervised?" She was on a roll. "Some of the domination was subtle, but we experienced the discrimination, nonetheless. We intend to incorporate women's rights into our political activism. But we also must clean up our personal affiliations, including with the three of you."

Over the next few years, the women handed the men lists of books to read. Shulamith Firestone, Alix Kates Shulman, Jo Freeman, Robin Morgan, Kate Millett. And they soon included volumes on Black and lesbian women that were engaging them as well: Mary Ann Weathers, Frances Beal, Wilda Chase, Ti-Grace Atkinson, Rita Mae Brown.

Keith and Max eventually "got it," like learning a new language. When they met, Keith would lean in, and in an uncertain tone ask if a particular term was acceptable. He spoke in such measured words that at one point Rebecca warned him to knock it off. Max was less self-conscious, though he, too, seemed to have reassessed his attitude. Only Russell was resistant, winking at them with a wily smile when he taunted them with chauvinistic remarks. Deanna would glare at him.

"The feminist movement needs to get a sense of humor," he advised her.

"And you," she would say, "must learn to get with the program."

♀

August 26, 1970, marked a watershed for the six friends. The women were preparing for the Women's Strike for Equality March in the city. They were just finishing breakfast when there was a knock at their door. There stood their buddies, each holding a sign. Russell, with a self-deprecating smile, held up his: "Former Male Chauvinist," written in thick black letters on a crimson poster board.

Deanna gave him a teasing look. "So, you intend to horn in on our rally." She turned to Max and nodded approvingly at his banner: "Men of Quality Don't Fear Equality."

"You guys are really something," she said as Keith, with a touch of pride, showed them his placard: "Men Unite for Equal Rights."

"Let's go," Deanna said. They linked arms as they marched down Fifth Avenue together, the three men conspicuous among the over fifty thousand women.

14
Malaika

MALAIKA HAD not given up on law school but needed to build up her savings from the paltry amount she had managed to accumulate in college. Symbolic dollars didn't count anymore; by her senior year, Malaika had to face the reality that she just couldn't afford to go even if she took on piles of loans. And then there was her advisor's intimation that she probably wouldn't get in. That had sidelined her confidence, at least for the moment, despite the coaxing of her pals.

Early that fall, in their new apartment, she sat for three months at the kitchen table and diligently studied for her LSATs with practice tests she borrowed from the public library. Malaika recognized that she was at a considerable disadvantage; she couldn't afford the expensive prep courses that other applicants enrolled in. She would stare off into space, contemplating the odds against her. Perhaps her advisor had been right; she should have back-up plans. At this point she understood what he had been implying: there were quota systems. Nationwide, law school enrollment comprised of only one percent Black students and less than five percent women of any color. What hubris, she laughed to herself, thinking she could get in. Despite Malaika's unremitting misgivings, Rebecca and Deanna constantly reassured her.

It was a slightly chilly day in October when she finally took the LSATs. Feeling apprehensive, Malaika woke up in the wee hours of the morning to squeeze in another drill. She then threw on comfortable pants, an oversized cotton top, and a lightweight sweater, hopped on the train, walked several blocks to the building, and entered a large classroom filled with anxious, prospective law students. They sat there with rolled-up sleeves, sharpened number two pencils in their hands, and spares on the table, waiting for the exam to begin. Malaika could already sense the cutthroat tension in the room. As usual, nearly everyone was White and male, with a sprinkling of female test takers. Nausea swept over her, and she was ready to flee. As she eyed the door, the proctor said, "Please sit down," and Malaika dutifully took a seat. The clock ticked fast, but she managed to complete the questions.

Deanna and Rebecca toasted her achievement when the scores rolled in. Much to Malaika's surprise given the lack of professional assistance, they were stellar. Her friends urged her to apply to at least one "safe" and a few "stretch" schools. Malaika had to remind them that their advice was sound for White males, but she had to be realistic in the face of the severely limited prospects for women of color. Law school applications were expensive, and she narrowed her choices to five places.

She had become emotionally worn out from the constant push to prove herself at lily-white institutions. She relished the challenges of law school without having to battle racial barriers or perform twice as well as her classmates. Let someone else be the poster child for Black female law students, she told herself. As she filled out the Howard Law School application form, she felt the heaviness in her body slowly melt. To placate Deanna and Rebecca, she sought admittance to the law schools at NYU, Brooklyn, Fordham, and Columbia University as well. But she was intent on Howard.

♀

Money remained an issue that was gnawing at her, and she was at odds with herself over what path to pursue for the year. It was tempting to follow Deanna into social work, where she could get a steady paycheck. She spent a week attempting to talk herself into it. After all, the job would only be temporary until law school started. But she was pulled more powerfully toward less lucrative community work, and she happily succumbed.

Her work at the Community Action Agency (CAA) in Harlem was low-paid and demanding. She was hired to help design the Neighborhood Service Center programs, which were at an incipient stage. The assignment was exasperating because funds were insufficient to develop meaningful services. The best they could offer was referrals to other agencies, where needy families faced bureaucratic hurdles, condescending staff, and often rationed benefits. There were only two of them operating the Center, and they attempted to intervene for their charges, but their efforts were largely futile. She became one of those pesky advocates who badgered caseworkers like Deanna with their grievances against the establishment. The two friends managed to joke about the situation, but Malaika could sense Deanna's defensiveness.

By early spring, the CAA director gave the go-ahead for Malaika to lead a community organizing drive. Part of the legislative mandate for local CAAs had been to empower the poor not just deliver more services to them. Malaika pursued this opportunity with gusto, working with area groups to rally otherwise dispirited single mothers, jobless men, the working poor, and young adults. After jointly compiling a list of their top demands, they agreed to focus first on dilapidated housing. Crowded together at the center, the locals listened to each other's gripes, each one echoing the last. An infestation of roaches and rats. Loud cries of "Amen!" arose from the group. Dangerous, leaking ceilings. More amens. Broken plumbing. "Amen!" Electrical problems. "Amen!" Garbage piling up. "Amen!" Broken windows. "Amen!" After only a month, they were so riled up, they were primed for action.

Malaika next embarked on political education sessions in which she outlined various approaches for them to pursue. She warned that progress would be slow, with no guarantees of success. They would also encounter scare tactics that could get ugly.

"We're ready to go, girl," an old woman shouted from the back of the room. She had a forceful smile, intense dark brown eyes, and only a trace of eyebrows. In addition to deeply wrinkled ebony skin, her face possessed a strong jaw line that gave her a dignified look. She wore a colorful scarf tied around her head like a turban, with a tuft of white hair sticking out on both sides. She stood up and placed her hands on her hips. "Intimidation ain't nothing new for us."

In a front seat, knitting, another senior called out, "Let's go get us some wicked landlords!" Her wide grin displayed three missing front teeth. A roar of approval, like a mountain lion poised to ambush its prey, resounded throughout the room, along with a vociferous series of "amens." Much to Malaika's delight, their passion was equal to hers as they launched what she named Operation Slumlord.

♀

In mid-April Malaika received the first notification from Columbia University, quickly followed by Brooklyn Law. She had been turned down by both places, not even put on a waiting list. Fordham, too, rejected her outright. Rebecca and Deanna angrily blathered on about her stellar college GPA and LSAT scores, as though they had expected her to be admitted despite her gender and race. They stormed around the apartment fuming about racism, wasted energy in Malaika's estimation. "Your temper tantrums won't change the decisions," she scoffed. To calm them, she added, "I'm fine. I was banking on Howard in any case."

As soon as the words slipped out of her mouth, Malaika realized that maybe she had been lying to herself. She became despondent, and tears welled up. A sense of failure and shame floated through her as she lay in bed at night unable to sleep. What made her think she was good enough for law school anyway?

Two weeks later, she slit open the communication from NYU with a detached demeanor as Deanna looked on.

"So? So?" Deanna said, watching the bemused expression that spread over Malaika's face as she read. "Do tell."

Malaika collapsed onto the couch next to Deanna, seemingly lost in reverie. She put the letter against her chest without saying a word. The two of them sat there in companionable silence as she scrambled to absorb the magnitude of the news. She touched her chum's arm and stammered, "I've been accepted." She paused. "And with full tuition. A Root-Tilden-Kern scholarship to train public leaders." She felt her heartbeat racing as the details spilled out in an incoherent frenzy. "Three years tuition—free. Books, fees—free. Loans for other stuff—low interest." The two friends burst into euphoric fits of laughter.

The notice from Howard soon followed. It was a thin envelope, not a promising sign. You can't turn me down, you can't turn me down, she said over and over to the envelope, as if she could will its contents to comply. Her hands trembled as she finally opened the letter. She got in but with no aid package at all. She would be on her own financially.

Malaika sat in the chair for a while, a jumble of sensations churning in her stomach. She had craved an escape from the pressures of being the lone Black face in the classroom, library, cafeteria, everywhere on campus. She closed her eyes and let out a deep sigh. Anonymity, she thought. Not to stick out. Howard Law School called to her like a song sparrow wooing a mate. Could she justify relinquishing the NYU scholarship only to take on loans? Should she renounce the opportunity to attend one of the best law schools in the country?

She conferred with Deanna and Rebecca. Next with Max. Then with Keith and Russell. Unanimous for NYU. Still, she hesitated. She wasn't even sure she was ready for law school. She was devoted to the people in Harlem who were making serious inroads in forcing absentee property owners to maintain their run-down rental units. She felt a strong sense of fulfillment as the community advocates began to rankle managers, landlords, welfare officials, the district councilman, and the mayor, in equal measure. They had so much more to carry out over the next year, and she yearned to remain part of it.

Malaika kept putting off the decision, but the indecisiveness weighed her down. Her insomnia worsened, she couldn't focus, and the stress became unbearable. Even Deanna and Rebecca became tired of the obsessive recounting of options.

During another tedious dinner of listening to Malaika debate with herself, Rebecca finally took a stand. "Decide," she demanded. "You're making yourself and us crazy." She softened her tone.

"Both of your alternatives are advantageous."

Deanna touched her arm affectionately. "Yes, this is a win-win situation. You can't mess up either way."

Her roommates' optimistic assurances settled her down. That night, in bed, a decision snuck up on her. She would accept NYU but request a deferment for twelve months. During this period, she could continue her work with the Harlem residents, perhaps push them to combat additional issues along with their decaying housing. She mulled over possible avenues for them to pursue and fell into a deep, blissful sleep.

15
Rebecca

REBECCA WASN'T sure whether to take the full-time job offered to her at Local 1199 despite her deep-seated admiration for the union's commitment to social justice. During her childhood, she had been regaled with anecdotes of its laborious campaigns and triumphs, and she had experienced a few of them herself during her part-time work in college. Yet she hesitated. Her father had pulled strings to obtain a desirable position for her. As an adult attempting to make her own way, should she be so entangled with him? Was she overly dependent on him, like a child unwilling to shed training wheels on her bike? Ultimately, she decided to accept the post, at least for the short haul.

It was a rewarding, whirlwind venture. The union first assigned her to a team that was negotiating for hospital personnel across New York. She met with frontline workers, nurse's aides, orderlies, and housekeeping staff in an attempt to appreciate their priorities. Rebecca was sobered by the conditions engendered by their poverty-level wages. She heard stories from single mothers who had to choose between their own medical care and nutritious food for their family despite steady, grinding labor. There were others who persevered in the face of back injuries and lack of medical insurance. She learned that employees toiled for decades without the prospect of a retirement benefit, like Sisyphus forever rolling a boulder up the hill. But many of them were fearful of being fired if they pushed too hard even though they were somewhat protected by the union.

From the beginning, Rebecca's colleagues were aware that negotiations were her forte, and she became increasingly confident in her skills. She and her team would sit face-to-face with the employers and their lawyers across a huge oval mahogany conference table. The adversaries were intimidating, but she learned to focus and exude calm.

Her debating days taught her that success depended on gathering copious information and carefully studying it, so she was always well-prepared. She would lean back in the chair, hands folded behind her head, and ask pointed questions, always sure of the answers in advance. The hospitals threw obstacle after obstacle at the union representatives. "Budgets are tight." "You're going to force us to shut down." "We're doing the best that we can." Rebecca invariably had a ready response. These fast-paced back and forth exchanges fired her up like an opening act before the headliner. Then she would move in for the kill before the rest of the 1199 delegation could rally behind a weak contract.

She savored the victories. An increase in minimum pay. Better wages. Retirement pensions. Health insurance. The union even secured a large training fund, one of the demands of the nursing assistants. There were setbacks, to be sure, that the indefatigable Rebecca faced with a frustrated shrug before she moved on. The negotiations were hard work, and she was usually spent in the evenings.

♀

The three roommates agreed to rotate household tasks on a weekly basis. They put up a whiteboard denoting the various duties and who was responsible for them. Dirty dishes piled up for days when it was Rebecca's turn. Deanna and Malaika objected, but Rebecca grumbled, "The apartment should have a dishwasher." The plants desperately screamed for attention on her watch, and the other two were forced to water them to keep them from dying.

Rebecca seemed allergic to mops, brooms, and vacuum cleaners. Her own room was dusty and filled with clutter that occasionally overflowed into the living room. Files, books, paperwork, clips, receipts, magazines, and newspapers were spread everywhere. Deanna once called her out on the mess then winced, fearing she was turning into Maryann. She and Malaika were relieved that Rebecca had her own room and were content to keep it that way.

They tolerated Rebecca's slovenliness mostly because she made up for it with loyalty, compassion, and generosity. Now and then, Deanna would have a date sleep over, and Rebecca unfailingly relinquished her room to the couple without question. She was unstinting in her praise for her comrades' triumphs and would drop everything if one of them needed her, even for the slightest reason. Besides, she was an extraordinary cook who tutored them on culinary dishes from her mother's seemingly endless recipes. She could always be relied on for preparing meals and soon became the main household chef. They cleaned up after her.

The women led busy lives, and Rebecca often came home late after long, tedious meetings with either the union leadership or disgruntled members. While certain complaints were consequential, most involved squabbles between employees and their supervisors; Rebecca was obliged to mediate.

In nursing homes, a nurse's aide might be forced into a double shift when they were short-handed. "I can't do it," she would say. "I'm exhausted and don't have a babysitter." In one instance, an attendant protested that they were adding three more patients, two with dementia, to her already heavy caseload. "I'm treating incapacitated residents as if they were on an assembly line," she had told the RN in charge. The head nurse simply shrugged, insisting that there was nothing she could do; the facility was understaffed. These types of incidents occurred frequently, day and night, often on weekends. Rebecca attempted to support the caregivers as best she could while muttering under her breath, "If they paid adequate wages and benefits, the place would be overflowing with applicants."

On the occasions when she, Malaika, and Rebecca were home together, they confided in each other, engaged in back-and-forth banter about their day, and dissected the ongoing escalation of fighting in Vietnam and its brutal carnage. They remained actively engaged in the anti-war movement along with their Thursday night consciousness-raising group.

Every so often they played board games—Monopoly, Clue, checkers, Scrabble—and cards, mainly gin rummy and pinochle. As with everything else, Rebecca was a cutthroat competitor who both nettled and amused her roommates. She just liked to win.

Rebecca had what she called her not-so-secret vice. Certain evenings when she came home too dog-tired for conversation or diversions that required brain power, she would park herself in front of the TV to binge on miniseries, made-for-TV movies, sitcoms, and variety shows. Her favorites were *All in the Family*, *The Mary Tyler Moore Show*, and *The Carol Burnett Show*.

The television, which Rebecca's father had purchased for them, was hidden in her room because Deanna refused to let them put the set anyplace else. She viewed watching TV as a bourgeois pastime for people who had nothing better to do and found it embarrassing to even possess what she called an "idiot box." She was haunted by disconcerting images of her mother riveted by daytime soap operas, an empty look in her eyes.

Nevertheless, Rebecca sometimes managed to entice Deanna and Malaika into watching a show or two. She would put out bowls of popcorn and chips for them but mostly polished off the snacks by herself. The women sobbed, chortled, and laughed uproariously during these programs. The boob tube became their collective guilty pleasure.

♀

Rebecca's success at work was not matched by her romantic life. She developed a clandestine crush on one of her coworkers but was terrified of taking the infatuation any further despite hints of reciprocation. She had not come out to any of her colleagues in Local 1199, fearful that they would shun her. Even the most rabid organizers among them were suspicious of gays and lesbians. It was conceivable that she could be fired given the public's view of homosexuality as "abnormal" and the laws supporting its criminality. Cure, convert, and suppress—not accept or respect—were still the standard attitudes toward same-sex intimacies. She was also anxious about the possibility that she was under FBI surveillance for her political activities; her sexual orientation could make her even more of a target.

Every so often she would slip into a lesbian bar in an attempt to meet someone. However, Rebecca found the scene humiliating and antithetical to her temperament; she disliked dancing and preferred conversation, not loud music. She sensed that the assorted women frequenting these places tended toward one-night stands, and she was seeking a genuine relationship. She envisioned a person of substance, one with similar values and life goals as herself.

One evening, after two pitiful hours at a bar, she admitted to herself, with consternation, that she was in quest of a female version of Max. She toyed around with joining the periodic picketing and sit-ins for gay rights erupting in the City, where she might meet someone. That would be going overboard, she decided. Her plate was already overflowing with organizing, anti-war activism, women's marches, and the consciousness-raising group. She was also determined to keep up with the burgeoning feminist and gay literature. She drew sustenance from the developing feminist philosophies and fertile evening exchanges about them with Deanna and Malaika.

♀

She was spending more time at home with her parents, increasingly concerned about her father's health. She would catch Izzie bending over in pain even though he never acknowledged the agony. His skin had acquired a yellowish tinge, like the fingers of long-term smokers. She and her mother had been prodding him to see a doctor, but he resisted. He'd always had a hearty appetite, so when he started picking at his food and his pants became baggy, they forced the issue.

Rebecca went with him, anxious to hear the details. Despite Izzie's forceful opposition, the doctor sent him to the hospital for a workup. She took time off from work to stay by his side for three long days of countless tests and examinations. Assorted specialists walked in and out of his room, like a parade of ghosts. Rebecca attempted to waylay them, determined to get a professional opinion, but they were forever in a hurry. "We'll get back to you." "We must wait until all of the results are in." "We're reviewing the reports." She paced the halls, yearning for a hopeful prognosis while her distraught mother sat at his bedside, motionless. She had retreated inwardly and wanted to be left alone.

The diagnosis, when it finally materialized, was devastating. His primary care doctor came into the room with a grave expression, sat down, and looked directly at Izzie. They waited for the physician to speak amid the cacophony of sounds: beeping monitors, whirring machines, droning IV pumps, clanking carts, and dinging call buttons. He did not equivocate. "You have pancreatic cancer." The doctor hesitated. "And the disease is at an advanced stage. It has metastasized to nearby organs."

The end came quickly. He was at home, in hospice care, when he died. Rebecca stayed with him every weekend for six months, tending to his needs as best as she could. Max came by, cheering up Izzie with tales of his latest organizing feats. And Dad, in turn, reciprocated with his own stories. Malaika, too, came around often, mostly tending to Nora, who was having trouble taking in the situation. She remained numb and unresponsive, preparing dish after dish for visitors who stopped by the house. Only Malaika could penetrate Nora's protective emotional shell. With a mix of empathy, sensitivity, and steadiness, Malaika charmed her into sharing her thoughts, at least to some degree. Rebecca was both grateful and a tad jealous.

The funeral was a blur of decisions. Picking out a coffin was the most unnerving part. Rebecca and her mother stood in a room full of caskets while the mortician detailed the pros and cons of each one like a snake oil salesman. Her dad once confided that he preferred to be cremated; Izzie was not one for fanfare, especially in death. Nora would have none of that. Finally, Rebecca chose a basic wooden box that she thought her father would approve of and that suited Nora's financial situation. She knew Mom would have a limited income and didn't intend to deplete her assets on already expensive burial rituals.

The funeral director looked at Rebecca with a condescending sneer. "You intend to bury your father in that?" Rebecca found herself bullied into a more costly casket.

Then there were the handshakes, hurried embraces, and perfunctory exchanges with countless individuals who lined up to convey condolences to the family. The hall was bursting with friends, relatives, acquaintances, colleagues, neighbors, and even strangers, at least to her. Izzie had been a beloved leader in the Labor Movement, and the mourners' stirring testimonials moved her to tears. At Rebecca's firm directive, there was no religious service; such a ceremony would have been abhorrent to her free-thinking father. Instead, those in attendance were encouraged to say a few words about their connection to Izzie and how he had affected their lives. Max and Malaika's poignant tributes touched Rebecca deeply.

During the next several weeks, as she attempted to sort out finances for Mom, Rebecca stayed with her. The house had an unnatural stillness without Izzie and their feisty debates. She found herself whimpering in anger to no one in particular, "No! no! How could you leave me!" She had been fiercely attached to her father and felt abandoned. For the first time ever, she started smoking.

Her friends were her lifeline. Their presence was calming; with them she could release some of the anxiety lodged in the pit of her stomach. They shared hilarious memories of Izzie, sometimes parodying him, each attempting to one-up the other. They laughed until they cried. One evening, she and Max had a heart-to-heart talk that lasted way into the night and it boosted her spirits enough to propel her back to work.

At her request, the labor union moved her to the newly formed National Organizing Committee, dubbed Union Power, Soul Power. Rebecca was delighted that Coretta Scott King agreed to be honorary chair of the ambitious endeavor. Rebecca met with her once, and they had a long conversation about the limited role of women in the Civil Rights Movement. In truth, Rebecca was so awestruck that she was uncharacteristically silent and mostly just listened, hanging onto her every word. As 1199 fanned out to marshal healthcare workers into a national union, Rebecca became a leading force. She only wished Dad could have shared her achievements.

16
Russell

As a graduation present, Russell's parents gave him money for a month-long excursion to Europe, a journey he had coveted for a while. He had never been outside the US and wanted to expand his horizons before enrolling in graduate school. On the day the gang finished painting the Bank Street apartment, he took Deanna aside and asked her to come along; if they were frugal, he had sufficient money for two. She was tempted—it would be the trip of a lifetime—but at this point, she was intent on disentangling herself from Russell.

He packed his knapsack and headed off to Europe alone. After a three-day stay in England, he caught a train to France. As in every country he visited that summer, there were students of every nationality touring around like a swarm of locusts, mostly staying in hostels or cheap hotels. He easily linked up with others, especially women traveling in twosomes or by themselves. While exploring the history, culture, and sights of unfamiliar places, many of the women were open to flings, and Russell took full advantage. He was rarely companionless.

For two weeks, he visited a few popular attractions in Paris and was impressed—Versailles, the Louvre, the Eiffel Tower—

but preferred roaming the streets, sitting in cafés watching Parisians promenade by, and wandering around places like the bustling, mouthwatering Bastille Market. He devoted days to strolling the maze of narrow, winding cobblestone-paved streets and alleyways of the Latin Quarter on the Left Bank, relishing the bohemian atmosphere, impromptu performances, and eclectic open-air bookshops, boutiques, bistros, galleries, and theaters. He contentedly lived on wine, cheese, bread, and pastries. At night, he would stop by one of the bars or jazz clubs peppering the district, generally with a newly befriended female or an ad hoc assemblage of young travelers.

He moved on for a week-long stretch in Rome and instantly fell in love with the city. Russell was awed by the historical sites—the Pantheon, the Colosseum, and the Sistine Chapel—that he had studied in various courses. His favorite spot was the Piazza di Spagna; he sat on the steps sipping wine and devouring gourmet cheeses and crusty ciabatta bread. The Trevi Fountain and its majestic baroque statues more than met his expectations. He threw the requisite coin over his shoulder, half-believing in the guarantee of a return visit.

Next on his itinerary was Venice, where he explored the small workshops producing jewelry, ceramics, Venetian masks, mosaics, and perfume in the quiet back streets. He splurged on a gondola ride that took him on smaller canals as well as the Grand Canal; the loop provided a different perspective of the enchanting city. Later, he hopped on a public water taxi to Murano, where he watched, fascinated, as glassblowers created delicate pieces of art; he purchased three unique necklaces for Rebecca, Deanna, and Malaika. The rest of the time in Venice, he nursed a cappuccino at St. Mark's Square while people-watching. As in Rome, he gorged on the usual Italian five-course dinners: antipasto, pasta, main dish, fresh vegetable, and dessert. Of course, wine flowed, served in a carafe which, without preservatives, tasted like freshly crushed grapes.

He spent his final few days in Munich, beginning with an inspection of the remains of Dachau. His interest in concentration camps had first been piqued by a history course on the Holocaust, which included a heated political discourse on *The Rise and Fall of the Third Reich.*

There were a handful of intact buildings, a library, and special exhibits that he studied for hours. He was sickened by the depiction of conditions in the overcrowded Dachau forced-labor camp—thousands had died of disease, malnutrition, physical exhaustion, beatings, and execution. Torturous medical experiments had been conducted there as well. Toward the end of the war, survivors were sent to various death camps elsewhere. What stood out for Russell from the literature and displays in the camp was the multiplicity of victims: not just Jews but artists, intellectuals, communists, homosexuals, gypsies, and the handicapped. What kept cropping up in his head was that it could have been him. Or his circle of friends.

Intrigued by Dachau and the role of the German people, he set out to learn about their current outlook on the genocide. Most of his life, he had heard his parents disparaging Germany for the atrocities against the Jews. They had relatives who lived in Warsaw during the 1940s, and a few of them died in the ghetto or later in concentration camps. "They are evil people," his mother had said. "Murderers, every single one of them." She would chastise anyone who drove a Volkswagen: "How could you support such a vicious country?" She had kept a careful list of German products and imposed a personal boycott on them, pressing her ban on anyone who would listen. Russell had not been one of them. In defiance, he even took German as his language requirement in college.

For the remaining time in Munich, he frequented taverns to speak with working-class people, speaking and listening as best as he could with his rudimentary German. He moved from place to place, unaccompanied, drinking beer with the locals. He also meandered in and out of shops, striking up conversations with employees and proprietors alike. He sat on park benches, engaged adults watching over their kids in playgrounds, and walked around college campuses talking to students, most of whom spoke English.

In the end, he concluded that post—World War II generations abhorred Germany's previous barbarism, genuinely repented, but wanted to move on. "No use dwelling on the past," was the common refrain, followed by, "We must make sure that such crimes against humanity never happen again." Russell held his tongue as he thought of recent massacres perpetrated by dictators around the world and the conspicuous lack of action by other nations, including Germany.

♀

Upon his return to New York, he was enthusiastic about starting graduate school. However, the first year left him disillusioned with the intellectual vitality of university life. Instead of a lively exchange of ideas with his fellow students, which he had been accustomed to among his clique, Russell now found himself in the midst of mean-spirited conversations about departmental politics. He managed to ferret out a few graduate students who would engage in more fruitful dialogues, but even they tended to be intellectually cautious and preoccupied with careerism.

Classes proved equally mind-numbing as professor after professor droned on about irrelevant social theories and debates about research methods. Russell was concerned with social justice, inequality of power and income, and a war that was killing innocent Vietnamese children. Not old white guys with outdated ideas like Talcott Parsons, Vilfred Paretto, Robert K. Merton.

The saving grace was that he had been assigned as a teaching assistant to Frances Fox Piven, a radical sociology professor and political activist with interests akin to his own. Thirteen years older than Russell, she took him under her wing, inviting him for drinks and thought-provoking chats at the nearby West End Bar. Much to his gratification, she introduced him to Daniel Bell, Amitai Etzioni, and Immanuel Wallerstein, three other esteemed leftist professors in the department. He intended to attend as many lectures as he could with the four of them, riveted by their powerful intellects, and partake in the cutting edge of their still developing philosophies.

His parents had been mollified; in their view, their prodigal son had finally come home. This is what they had dreamed about, their only child attaining a Ph.D. at Columbia University even though they were a bit confused about his area of study. "What exactly is sociology?" his mother inquired with a hint of disdain. She clearly would have preferred a field such as medicine or law. But she shrugged off her qualms. "You were throwing your life away. At least now you're back on track."

Russell was less sure. After six months, he questioned his decision to give up a life of political organizing. He was still an idealist, someone who sought to be part of the action. He yearned to confront and change the system not just study it. He felt isolated in the ivory tower, like a goldfish in a glass bowl gazing out at the world. In the past he had felt connected. With his comrades. With a cause. They lived in the moment. In the academy, he was expected to surrender a meaningful daily life for tomorrow's promise of personal achievement.

As he was second-guessing his chosen profession, Columbia University exploded in a student revolt. Tensions had been brewing since the spring of 1967. Like City College, the university's SDS chapter had been at odds with the administration over its backing of military recruitment on campus. Petitions, peaceful protests, debates, and educational leaflets had proved sorely ineffective. Mark Rudd, its leader, and his supporters were now, a year later, pressing for more militant action. The national office, too, was leaning in that direction after years of eschewing violent campaigns. On April 23, Russell listened to Rudd deliver a galvanizing speech before a gathering of four hundred undergraduates, calling for disruptive, confrontational encounters including civil disobedience.

The SDS had two major demands, which Russell enthusiastically endorsed. Columbia had become a major military research contractor, profiting from extensive secret agreements to develop lethal weapons. The local group sought to force the University to cease its complicity in the bombing of the Vietnamese people and the destruction of their land. Second, SDS called for putting a stop to Columbia's construction of a new gymnasium in an adjacent community recreation area, Morningside Park, enjoyed by Harlem residents.

It was a heady experience for Russell as he was swept into the momentum of the crowd storming the gym construction grounds, knocking over its fence. He was in the thick of the action again, reveling in the moment. After skirmishes with police, the demonstrators moved on to take over the Columbia administration building, Hamilton Hall, holding the dean hostage in his office. Over the next several days, nearly a thousand students occupied four more buildings as the administrators refused to give in to their demands, which by now included amnesty for the protestors.

Russell decided that he could not just walk away despite the risk to his assistantship and perhaps his future in academia. He joined the two hundred graduate students who took possession of Fayweather Hall. The experience was exhilarating as they bonded through six days of singing, chanting, and barricading the doors. Several of them, including Russell, entered into deep discussions about the Vietnam War, the ethical obligations of a university, and the duty of graduate students to uphold such concerns. They questioned the effectiveness of peaceful strategies as opposed to more hard-hitting ones, especially the use of violence. It was the first time Russell felt a kinship with his classmates and a sense that they were part of something larger than simply seeking a degree. A few were even transformed by their involvement in the sit-in and deliberations.

After attempted negotiations with administrators, who refused to budge on any of their ultimatums, Columbia's president summoned the police. As instructed, the students did not resist but sat down limply, waiting for their arrest. Nevertheless, they were kicked, punched, and beaten with clubs along with bystanders and reporters waiting outside. The peaceful demonstration had turned into a bloodbath as over seven hundred students, shrieking in pain, were dragged away—including Russell. This was the first time he was badly assaulted in a protest, but he didn't regret his participation.

Max had come back to New York to help with the Columbia protest by assisting in feeding the buildings' occupants and providing them with sleeping bags, books, magazines, newspapers, and other paraphernalia. Along with other members of the SDS, he raised bond money for them, with Russell first on his list. As the bloody students gradually wandered out of the detention center the next morning, mostly dazed, Max waited outside. When he spotted Russell, the two embraced. He was hurt badly. That afternoon Rebecca, Deanna, and Malaika came to his apartment to nurse his wounds.

Since the university remained unwilling to relent even though a group of faculty members was struggling to broker a deal, Rudd and his student committee declared a university-wide strike, and undergraduates began picketing classroom buildings. Columbia was effectively shut down for the remainder of the semester. Instead of regular classes, various faculty held "liberation seminars," mostly on university grounds, that were well-attended. Mostly mended, Russell opted to teach two of them, which his old pals attended to support him. Keith joined a gathering of amateur musicians, surrounded by throngs of students, performing protest songs. Russell felt well taken care of by his community of friends.

♀

His mother, on the other hand, was hysterical when she read about what the newspapers called a "riot" at Columbia University. She tried calling Russell numerous times, but he refused to answer or return them; he was not in the mood to hear any tongue-lashing from her. A week later, he heard a persistent knock at his door. Not expecting anyone, he opened it warily, and there stood his mother with a stern look. "I haven't heard from you. Dad and I were worried about the insurrection at school." Her tone was the usual blend of concern, blame, and bitterness. Russell's mood darkened as she slumped down onto a chair at the kitchen table, still wearing her jacket. "I couldn't wait for your father to come home, so I took the subway." She paused. "All the way from Brooklyn." As if he didn't know where she lived.

She regarded his bruised arms and black eye. "Ha!" she said. "I knew you were involved." She looked around the efficiency apartment, noting the huge posters of Che Guevara, Malcolm X, and Stokely Carmichael hanging on fading white walls. The place was mostly bare except for a sagging king-size mattress on the floor, two large round black pillows for seating, and the rickety kitchen table surrounded by four weather-beaten chairs. She started whimpering. "Why are you doing this to us? Where did we go wrong? We didn't raise you this way."

Russell kept his temper in check. "Mom," he replied, "this is not about you. It's about me. I know you want me to get a Ph.D. from Columbia, and afterwards a professorship at another elite university. You would like me to marry a strait-laced woman, live in a ticky-tacky house with a white picket fence, and have 2.3 kids. However, I have my own desires and dreams and can't live yours. You and Dad must let go. I need to find my own way."

He handed his mother a tissue. Wiping away her tears, she stood up, walked over to the refrigerator, and looked inside. The shelves were bare except for a six-pack of beer. She stared at him. "No wonder you're so skinny," she said. "Let's go to the supermarket. I'll buy you some groceries."

His mother looked old and tired. He didn't regret his actions but was sorry he had caused such pain. To mollify her, he said, "I'm still on track for the Ph.D. And I didn't lose my scholarship." Max had secured him a volunteer lawyer, and the charges of disorderly conduct and trespassing had been dismissed.

17
Max

EVEN AS a child, Max had appreciated the design of certain buildings and their imposing and decorative facades. When the family had driven across the George Washington Bridge, his eyes were fixed on the magnificent skyline of soaring structures along the Hudson River. The silhouette mesmerized him, especially at night when the buildings were lit up. In his college architecture courses, he had explored innovative materials, styles, and shapes. He toured New York City often with Rebecca, pointing out the most impressive edifices in the urban landscape. He pursued a major in architecture at City College and intended a career in that field.

After graduation, however, he was less certain. As President Johnson stepped up the bombing of innocent Vietnamese civilians and more American soldiers were killed, his commitment to end the war strengthened. He debated with himself and sought advice from Rebecca.

She looked him straight in the eye and said, "If anti-war activism is where your heart leads you, go for it."

That fall, he joined SDS full-time, serving as a regional field representative. The goal was to build a national movement. He traveled in his beat-up blue VW Bug from campus to campus throughout the Northeast visiting existing chapters and assisting in organizing new ones. He immersed himself in the work, taking pleasure in galvanizing undergraduates to fight the Washington establishment. Twice he brought Keith with him, using his music as a magnet for recruits. As they clustered around him, singing, Max handed out leaflets and addressed their questions. It was an intoxicating time as students streamed into the newly established local chapters.

His paltry wages necessitated that he scraped by as best as he could. When he was on the road, he found students willing to share their dorms, where he slept on the floor in his shabby sleeping bag. He mostly ate peanut butter sandwiches unless he could mooch a decent meal somewhere. In New York City he could count on his comrades. Rebecca invariably greeted him with a wide smile.

"Just in time for dinner," she would say. "There's plenty for you."

He'd give her a grin in return. "Good, I'm hungry." She had become as proficient a cook as her mother.

He stopped arriving unexpectedly at Russell's apartment. He had tried twice, and both times his buddy answered the door with a sheepish look. On each occasion he had caught a glimpse of a different half-dressed woman on his mattress. Instead, he and Russell took to meeting occasionally at the West End Bar for beers. Russell encouraged him to order food and invariably paid the bill.

In addition to recruiting students, Max was involved in the national umbrella committee—MOBE—that organized a huge anti-war rally. His five friends had driven down to meet him. Nearly three hundred thousand people gathered at the Lincoln

Memorial, listening to speeches by Norman Mailer, poet Robert Lowell, and Dr. Benjamin Spock. Max leaned over to Keith and said, "Our parents should be here. They raised us on Spock."

The October day was sunny and glorious, with colorful foliage in its full autumn splendor. There was a strong sense of solidarity among the crowd. Pithy signs and banners, deafening chants, and evocative music made it feel like something momentous was about to happen. As he looked around, Max drank in the moment; he felt as though there was nowhere else he would rather be. At 3 pm, as planned, he bid his friends goodbye and rushed toward the throng of demonstrators marching to The Pentagon. Despite their peaceful intentions, the action eventually degenerated into bedlam. Max was arrested for disorderly conduct along with nearly seven hundred other protesters; they were bailed out by a squad of volunteer lawyers at the ready.

Because of his effective work with MOBE, Max was elected to one of three SDS officer positions, interorganizational secretary, and moved to the national office in Chicago. There, he shared an apartment with the rest of the fifteen-member team. His role was to coordinate with various other activist groups that had been proliferating like wildflowers throughout the country. He was determined to strengthen SDS's fraying ties with the Black Panthers and initiate connections with women's organizations. Since he was paid only fifteen dollars a week, Max still had to get by on a subsistence budget.

Shortly thereafter, he met Kathy, the newest and youngest of the office personnel. She had auburn hair cascading to her shoulders, radiant brown eyes flecked with green, and long, dark lashes that made her eyes even more luminous. Her arched eyebrows gave her a look of perpetual surprise that was somewhat softened by full, pouty lips. They were attracted to each other immediately and became involved after only a few days. From the start, she viewed them as a couple...Max, not so much.

Kathy had dropped out of Berkeley after two years, where she had been politicized, and departed to join the SDS staff in Chicago, her hometown. She seemed like a "flower child" to Max, garbed in tie-dye shirts, granny dresses, wraparound Indian skirts, fringed shawls, love beads, assorted headbands, oversized dangling earrings, and leather boots. Her conversations were punctuated with "cool," "groovy," "outta sight," and "bummed out." Unlike her, Max chose his words carefully. She indulged in psychedelic drugs. He only occasionally smoked pot. He was not interested in a long-term commitment, and she badgered him about their future together even though he was clear about his intentions. Max felt fenced in by her; she fended off any woman who came near him. Still, she fired him up in bed, and they had an intense sexual relationship for six months on and off.

Though based in Chicago, Max and his VW bug were still constantly on the road. He gave speeches on campuses everywhere and reported his observations in *New Left Notes*, the national SDS newsletter, which was distributed to local chapters. Kathy often pleaded to come with him, but Max preferred being alone. His long trips gave him uninterrupted spells to reflect on political issues, organize his thoughts, and flesh out arguments for his talks.

The year 1968 was traumatizing for the nation, and Max routinely woke to catastrophic news. Not long after Johnson withdrew from the presidential race, Martin Luther King, Jr. was killed. Max was paralyzed for hours as though he'd been hit by the bullet himself. There were uprisings in over a hundred US cities including Chicago, leading to civil disorder across the country. From SDS headquarters in Chicago, he observed the looting, rioting, and fires set by angry mobs, the billowing smoke partially obscuring the view. He watched as National Guard troops and the regular army, in full combat gear, violently assaulted residents in the streets, nearly all people of color. A few troopers, holding batons up in the air, raided their SDS office, confiscating documents. Max and his team protested, demanding their constitutional rights, but backed down when threatened with a beating. Even so, as the officers were departing, one of them wacked Max on the leg, leaving a deep gash.

In August, he half-heartedly assisted in organizing protests at the Democratic National Convention to pressure delegates to vote for Eugene McCarthy. At that point, it was evident that Hubert Humphrey, the establishment candidate, would win the nomination. Nonetheless, as an SDS officer, Max felt obligated to align his group with other organizations bent on disturbing the process and, as usual, he drove himself hard.

The rally in Grant Park was supposed to be peaceful, but Mayor Daly refused to grant a permit to the organizing committee. Regardless, thousands of demonstrators arrived, finding themselves confronted by the city's police force along with national guardsmen and army troops. Mayhem broke out as protesters as well as spectators and journalists were clubbed, beaten, kicked, dragged, and sprayed with tear gas. Rocks and bottles flew helter-skelter through the air amid screams and poisonous fumes. Max, who remained on the sidelines, witnessed the unprovoked violence firsthand; nearly one hundred people ended up in the hospital. His role was to orchestrate the posting of bail for the SDS members among the seven hundred individuals arrested.

"We are truly a police state," he reported to his female friends when he arrived the following week at their New York apartment. "It was just as bad as the attacks on civil rights workers in the South."

By 1969, Max was increasingly hopeful that the American populace would finally recognize the futility of the Vietnam War and its disastrous consequences. Every night on TV, they were accosted by shocking images. Civilians rounded up. Children burned. Deafening detonations over fields, lighting up the sky like fireworks. GIs coming home in body bags, assembly-line style. The Tet Offensive in early 1968 jettisoned any illusion that the US was winning: communist forces had initiated simultaneous surprise attacks in over 140 towns and cities, catching US leaders and troops unprepared. The Viet Cong were far from defeated, and the conflict wouldn't end soon despite President Nixon's assurances to the contrary. Tet helped turn the tide of American opinion against the president and the war.

Max left SDS after his year-long stint as national secretary, frustrated with the internal feuding. The organization had become increasingly polarized among various factions—Progressive Labor (PL), Revolutionary Youth Movement (RYM), Worker-Student Alliance. He was tired of wasting his time on such nonsense. There were also serious debates about SDS escalating its level of militancy, something Max understood but didn't care to be a part of.

He drifted for months, traveling in his VW bug around the country, not sure what he would do next. On October 15 he landed in the US capital for the Vietnam Moratorium. Over two million people assembled in cities across the United States, including 250,000 in Washington, DC. As he surveyed the diversity of groups holding up signs, he felt relieved that the American public was wising up to the immorality of the war: Teachers Against the War; Social Workers Against the War; Teamsters Against the War; Vietnam Veterans Against the War. There were middle-class mothers with kids, elderly people walking with canes, high school and college students, union representatives, women's groups, and a healthy mix of races, religions, and ethnicities.

His mood of optimism was punctured the next day when Nixon, in a televised broadcast, dismissed the marchers as a bunch of hooligans and declared that under no circumstances would he be affected by them or their unruly demonstrations. The president appealed to a so-called "silent majority" to support him in winning "peace with honor," not American humiliation. Max itched to throw a rock at the TV but instead left the room.

He returned to DC to attend the Second Anti-War Moratorium, held on November 14. Two days prior, the press had shocked the nation with details of the Mỹ Lai massacre. Apparently, US troops had tortured and slaughtered hundreds of unarmed Vietnamese civilians, mainly women, children, and the elderly. The sheer brutality and immorality of the atrocity put another significant dent in the public's approval of the war. Nixon ignored this rally as well, and business as usual continued at the White House.

By now Max was thoroughly dispirited. Despite widespread hostility toward the senseless killing of US troops and Vietnamese civilians, nothing had succeeded in stopping it. Not petitions, not peaceful marches, not even elections. Indeed, the bombing over North Vietnam had been worsening as the protest movement swelled. Though Max avoided electoral politics, he supported activists who had backed Robert Kennedy, believing that he would have ended the war and broadened civil rights. Kennedy's murder had been a further blow to Max's spirits and his faith in the system.

Now he drove to New York, knocked on the door, and collapsed on his friends' couch, anguished and discombobulated.

"You look like you just came home from combat in Vietnam," Malaika said. "What's wrong?"

Max began slowly, as though he were thinking out loud. "I've quit SDS. Too much sectarianism. Most of the activists I worked with have since left, are in jail, or are out on bail for one or more bogus charges. Only the Weathermen remain, and as much as I like many of them personally, their tactics are too violent for my taste. They've become terrorists." He rubbed the back of his neck. "The Days of Rage at the Chicago Eight trial were just too much for me," he continued. "Did you know they went out in the streets for three days, shattering shop windows and smashing cars? It's the end of SDS. . ." He stopped short, heartbroken about the turn of events.

"Go on," Rebecca whispered.

"I'm burned out," he said. "I've had FBI agents trailing me for two years. Informants infiltrated the national office staff, so I never knew who I could trust. Even the phones were tapped." He looked grimly at each of the women, in turn. "Nixon and his Washington establishment don't give a damn about what Americans think or want. This war isn't going to end anytime soon. I've wasted my time."

He gave a scornful laugh. "As you know, I've drawn a low number in the draft lottery. I can't go to Vietnam. Slaughter may be in my brothers' DNA, but it sure ain't in mine. And I've already publicly burned my draft card, in any case."

Max felt a flame in his chest, making it hard for him to breathe. He finally blurted out, "I'm heading for Canada."

Rebecca stared at him, deep in thought. She grabbed both of his hands and held them tight.

18
Keith

KEITH DEPARTED his apartment building on Cornelia Street, a quaint solitary block in Greenwich Village, and greeted two old men sitting outside, playing chess. The sublet was surprisingly affordable, in part because he had agreed to care for the couple's cats and water the plants that were sprawling everywhere in the spacious residence. The two felines were a study in contrasts: the Persian, soft blue eyes and pure white, was quiet and reserved; the Burmese, intense green eyes and pitch-black, cried all day demanding attention. Their toys were scattered over the hardwood floors, like a child's playroom. Keith lavished them with affection, as if they were his own.

He had always wanted a pet, preferably a Labrador Retriever, but would have been content with a cat or even a gerbil. His parents had dismissed the idea out of hand. "I don't have the time or energy for any critter," his mother had said. When he had pleaded that he would take care of it, she raised other objections: "They're dirty." "We'll have hairs all over the place." "It will chew our furniture and smell up the apartment." "Our musical instruments will be at risk." Neither parent would relent despite his constant pestering.

He envied other children who had the companionship that Keith was certain only a dog could provide. He watched with longing as kids cuddled their dogs, ran with them in parks, threw balls for them to chase. At one point he hid a turtle under his bed, but his siblings squealed on him. For now, the two cats filled a hole in his heart.

Keith walked to work, sauntered really, soaking in the aromas wafting from restaurants and cafes lining the Greenwich Village streets. He passed one of the many head shops sprouting up in the area and paused to examine the hodgepodge display of paraphernalia—posters, candles, pipes, rolling paper, earrings, T-shirts. He soon reached the Folklore Center on MacDougal Street. Izzy Young's book and record shop, the walls lined with instruments, had become the gathering place for folk musicians. It was where Keith first encountered Bonnie, whose uncle owned Kettle of Fish. The bar, which was situated above the Gaslight Café, had become like a second home for aspiring and established performers alike along with writers, poets, and locals. Tourists, too, frequented the Kettle, careful not to gawk at the better-known patrons.

Keith and Bonnie paired up in the summer of 1967. She was a talented guitarist with a hauntingly lyrical voice. They would often harmonize, and she added a fresh quality to his musical compositions. Bonnie was reasonably good looking—short wavy hair, sparkling coffee-colored eyes, cherub face, and quick, easy smile. Keith was drawn to her sense of humor and uncommon wit. She introduced him to her Uncle Steve, who was seeking a trustworthy bartender for Kettle of Fish. Keith was hired, and while concocting drinks, he spent many an evening sharing ideas, gossip, and songs with the likes of Phil Ochs—his idol—Dave Van Ronk, Joni Mitchell, and, at times, Bob Dylan, who tended to be standoffish.

The dimly lit Kettle was perpetually crowded, humming with chatter, music, and laughter. A haze of tobacco and marijuana smoke permeated one's senses, psyche, and every inch of clothing. The long, ornate bar, made of dark, polished wood, was well worn but charming. From his station, Keith witnessed the not-so-inconspicuous exchange of drugs, snorting of cocaine, boozy intake of alcohol. The place was a veritable candy store of illegal substances. Keith kept his distance, sticking to an occasional beer.

Downstairs in the basement, at the Village Gaslight, a mélange of folk musicians took turns performing, passing the hat for tips. Bonnie knew the owner and somehow wrangled a short gig for Keith that showcased two of his original songs. His act was well-received, and soon he joined jam sessions and Tuesday night open mic hootenannies at the Bitter End, a club up the block. A few times, his five buddies came to watch him, their deafening applause outstripping that for any of the other impromptu players. They embraced Bonnie, often imploring Keith to bring her along to their get-togethers. The women were disappointed when the relationship ended a year later. Keith never revealed why. "We just drifted apart," was all he would say.

♀

In February 1969, Keith and his friends attended a Joni Mitchell concert at Carnegie Hall. He was impressed with the building's grandeur, magnificent acoustics, and subtle but splendid lighting. "This place is awe inspiring," he said to Max when they first arrived. "It's not the Village Gate, or Café Au Go Go, that's for sure." He wondered whether his parents would appreciate him playing on stage here with his guitar and harmonica, at least fulfilling their dream to some small measure. He didn't even know if they viewed folk songs as an authentic form of music. They had been baffled when he gave up the violin, telling him how much he had disappointed them. The acoustic instrument had not made up for it.

Perhaps he should seriously pursue a musical career, he thought. After all, Joni's debut album, *Song to a Seagull*, had come out only eleven months ago, and it had not taken her long to reach Carnegie Hall. Bob Dylan, Patsy Cline, and Johnny Cash played there as well. Why not him? Over the years, everyone had applauded his musical talent, proficiency on the guitar, and original songs. After the concert, over drinks at a nearby bar, Deanna and Rebecca spurred him on.

At the Kettle, he talked to Phil Ochs about his ambitions. Ochs, in turn, introduced Keith to Fred Weintraub, owner of the Bitter End, who had heard him play a few times. In a short while, Keith worked his way around scores of clubs in the Village's musical circuit, an exhausting but intoxicating whirlwind of performances. His music was lauded by his contemporaries in the folk scene, and eventually he was offered a slot opening for Arlo Guthrie at Gerdes Folk City.

Six months later, Steve Lamoure, a record producer and music critic, came to see him at Kettle of Fish. Apparently, he had heard him years earlier at one of the civil rights demonstrations. "I loved your compositions when you were just a college kid," Lamoure said. "Your music has matured since then. I just heard you over at Gerdes and would like you to audition for me."

Shortly thereafter, he signed Keith to Capital Records, which recorded his first and only album. Flabbergasted, he had quickly seized the opportunity, yet at the start had second thoughts. Keith had to fight to keep "It Is More Than Okay" on the album. The piece had been his way of supporting Rebecca, and he refused to cave in.

"You will turn off too many people with a song about homosexuals," Lamoure argued. "Let's stick to anti-war themes for now, while they're still hot." Keith prevailed, but Lamoure's associates tinkered around with the arrangements, tempos, and timbre of every song on the album, jarring him.

As part of his contract with Lamoure and Capital, Keith had to promote the LP. That meant performances in small venues across the country, pushing radical protest songs on apolitical disc jockeys, and doing interviews with a parade of local reporters. He toured in a peach-colored Volkswagen Westfalia Camper equipped with a bed, sink, refrigerator, and stove. Dressed in a turtleneck, tweed jacket, jeans, and his signature cap, Keith traveled from town to town, barely filling clubs, now and again facing half-empty establishments. In some places, he played his heart out to people engaged in loud conversations, barely listening. And his album sold poorly. His spirits were dampened by the demoralizing, lonely undertaking.

Lamoure told him that it was tough to promote a first album, that he shouldn't be discouraged. He would need time to build up a fan base. The producer suggested a second album with a longer, more intensive tour, but he was reluctant to go on the road again.

Keith took on a pensive expression and considered the options. In the last few years, he had been drawn into the nascent environmental movement and had written songs about ecological issues that he was eager to share. He quickly learned that environmental action would not simply happen; people had to become sensitive to the issues. What better way for him to contribute than an album and cross-country promotional trip?

He reflected on his first involvement with the Environmental Movement during a summer weekend in 1968. He had been invited to perform at the Clearwater Festival, an annual benefit concert founded by Pete Seeger to clean up the Hudson River. There, Keith had been introduced to all manner of sustainability and social responsibility issues. A year later, Seeger built and launched the Sloop Clearwater, a wooden sailing vessel, to draw attention to the Hudson's hazardous conditions. Keith was further motivated by Tom Winslow, a folk singer who wrote a song about the event, "Hey Looka Yonder, It's the Clearwater."

In 1969, a fire erupted on the Cuyahoga River, the first of many over the years that stemmed from the waterway's oil slicks. They simmered in an unremitting toxic soup, ready to ignite at the slightest spark. Lifeless rats floated by; dead fish periodically dotted the shoreline. This latest flare-up finally captured public attention and inspired Keith's first song on environmental activism, "The Cuyahoga Ablaze."

The river fed into Lake Erie, which itself had become a dumping site for industrial waste and chemicals. Fertilizers and pesticides from surrounding farms added to the noxious mix. Keith sang about the devastation of the lake in his next composition. After that, he gave tribute to David Brower's fight to save the Grand Canyon from destructive dams. He warned about the dangers of the thousands of acres newly opened for oil exploration on Alaska's North Slope. He wrote about the Union Oil platform, an offshore rig that poured three million gallons of crude oil into the ocean, leaving thirty-five miles of slime along the coast of Santa Barbara. He advocated against the testing of nuclear bombs, with their huge mushroom clouds and radioactive byproducts. His lyrics spoke to manmade environmental disasters past and present and called for greater ecological awareness and integrity.

♀

Keith looked around the cramped, windowless producer's office, and sighed. It was a tough choice, but he would make another album, this time on environmental issues, and go on the road again to promote it. With renewed confidence, he tells Lamoure what he has decided.

Steve Lamoure was having none of it. "Nobody cares about the environment," he said, barely concealing his irritation. "We need you to sing protest songs about trendy issues. We are in the business of selling albums. Think sell, sell, sell." He leaned back in his chair. "And we must adjust some of your rhythms and work on your overall message—it's too gloomy."

Keith was like a wild animal caught unawares in a trap, struggling to escape. Nobody was going to micromanage his music again. He paced the room, a sheen of sweat forming on his forehead. Music was his way of galvanizing activism for causes he deeply believed in. He was not a commercial product, a money-making machine. He hadn't signed up for that kind of life. He yearned to be part of the emergent Green Movement, strumming his guitar. He hungered to draw attention to contaminated rivers and oceans, forests stripped bare, the polluted air that we breathe. To debunk the notion that the wreckage is part and parcel of so-called progress.

Keith glanced at the producer, who was checking his watch, his lips pressed in a scowl. Keith shrugged and walked out.

PART IV
Should I Go?: June 2025

19
Rebecca

THE DAY before the reunion, sitting on the porch at The Mountain House, Rebecca becomes apprehensive. She scowls, chiding herself. She should have included an RSVP in the invitation. Why did she assume that they would come? She hadn't heard a word from any of them since she sent the invitation nearly six months ago. She'd assumed that they didn't bother letting her know because it was a given that they would attend. Now she's not so sure. She had been anxiously awaiting this day, the emptiness in her very being filled with anticipation as she painstakingly planned every detail of the three-day weekend. Today she is second-guessing everything. Even if they do show up, is she setting herself up for disappointment? Can they really pick up where they had left off? It's been decades since they have been together, and she's not even sure they will like the old dyke she has become. "Rebecca, Rebecca, Rebecca," she says aloud to the silhouette of mountains in the distance. "Why couldn't you just be content with the magical memories?"

Oddly enough, she has reservations about the clothing she haphazardly packed for the trip. Never concerned with fashion, Rebecca is accustomed to throwing on the first garments she touches in the morning, even if they are mismatched. She loathes shopping, especially picking through clothing racks spilling over in assorted colors, styles, materials, and sizes; she rarely buys anything. Jeans, generally elastic at the waist, and oversized solid or striped cotton shirts are her everyday attire.

Her co-workers had persuaded Rebecca that she should take on a more professional look, and she grudgingly purchased three pantsuits that she alternated for work. In her view, the outfits had made her appear more stodgy than usual, like Hillary Clinton. As soon as she arrived home from work, she would tear off the outfit and slip on sweats with a sigh of relief.

She particularly resented having to wear a bra, the tight undergarment pressing uncomfortably on her chest. She recalls the protest at the 1968 Miss America Pageant where a small group of women threw bras and girdles—along with other "instruments of female torture"—into a large "freedom" garbage can, and her enthusiastic endorsement of the brazen act. "Go girls, go," she had shouted at the television screen. Too bad they weren't allowed to burn their bras, she thinks, even though the press consistently asserted that they had done so. Since retirement, she walks around unbound whenever possible. It feels liberating.

Nonetheless, she is uneasy about what she has brought to the reunion—raggedy old things that are decidedly frumpy. Although she never had given much thought to how she presented herself to the gang, she is suddenly self-conscious and agonizes over her present wardrobe. She begins to fixate on her image. Deanna will show up looking chic. Malaika, too, will come across as classy, putting her to shame. The more she obsesses, the more she realizes the madness of her concerns. They are getting together to take pleasure in each other's company, not to pass judgment on each other. At length, she tells herself that if her comrades want the authentic Rebecca, the companion they had respected decades ago, they should be okay with however she looks. This does not entirely assuage her, but at least it sets her mind temporarily at ease.

She wanders around the secluded property, taking in the beauty of the place. Rebecca wonders whether any of them can walk great distances anymore, take full advantage of the five-acre estate and its several hiking trails. She pictures Deanna, long blonde braid flying every which way down her back, jogging around their former neighborhood as she prepared for yet another marathon. "Come join me," Deanna had once said, only half-seriously.

"I can barely walk to the subway station," Rebecca replied with a self-conscious laugh.

Susan, too, had tried with mixed success to get her out for treks in the woods. She even bought Rebecca hiking boots. Her partner had been somewhat of a gym rat, working out every day. Rebecca called it boot camp.

"I'd rather get a root canal than go to the gym," she had said.

"You're out of shape and overweight," Susan retorted. "Physical conditioning protects your heart and improves your body and mood."

"My dour personality suits me quite well," Rebecca said. "And I'm perfectly comfortable with my body as-is. It's Rubenesque." She had struck a pose, as though modeling for a magazine cover. "Besides, I don't like to sweat."

Susan persisted, attempting to cajole her into some type of fitness program, but Rebecca was adamant. "I log ample miles at work. I'm always on the move, running from place to place." She sighed. "At home, I prefer a sedentary existence. To read or watch TV. I'm an incurable couch potato."

One evening, Susan had tried to talk her into yoga, but Rebecca snapped, "I would feel silly in leggings and a tight tank top." She grimaced and said, "Face it, my love, I'm just not the athletic type."

Old age has not made Rebecca any heartier, though she brought the barely worn hiking boots with her to the reunion, just in case.

♀

Rebecca saunters into the cabin and surveys the great room with satisfaction. It has a huge stone chimney, perfect for a cozy fire; a cathedral ceiling; sizeable windows in every direction, some with views of the pool; dark, knotted wooden floors partly covered with a lovely Persian rug; two posh wrap-around couches facing each other; and a leather chair. The room is attached to a large dining area, fashionably furnished with a huge round, glass table that seats ten, a wine rack, a serving cart, a designer display cabinet, and two accent armchairs.

She walks into the kitchen. The brightly lit area is equipped with every conceivable small appliance including a specialized coffee machine and cappuccino maker. The counters are white marble with flecks of light and dark brown. An abundant supply of copper pots and pans is hanging on an overhead rack and side wall. Not that they will be cooking. To allow maximum time for them to reacquaint themselves, she has hired two chefs to shop and prepare their meals. A knowing smirk plays on her lips: it is certainly an upgrade from their makeshift New York apartment.

Rebecca has come a day early to inspect the place, make sure that everything is in order. But the extra hours give her too much time to worry. Details swirl in her head in a whirlwind of random and anxious thoughts. What if they have special diets, like she does? What if they don't enjoy the food? Is there enough firewood for three nights? What if there isn't sufficient propane for the barbeque? Will they be able to find the house? Rebecca wanders out to the deck and sits on the swing to calm herself. She gently sways for a while, but that doesn't work. Her stomach is churning, and she's feeling dizzy. For the hundredth time, she questions whether they will come.

She's becoming a nervous wreck, double-checking everything about the arrangements. It is her modus operandi—no detail is too small to merit scrutiny. Such attentiveness had served her well as a labor organizer, especially when confronted with resistant employers or even employees. She likes to have the facts at her fingertips to challenge any misinformation or untruths.

Fastidiousness is an integral piece of Rebecca's overall type-A personality that she highly values in herself. She may be a worrywart, but she is capable of multitasking, focusing on goals, accomplishing. And she is decisive, taking quick action and then moving on to the next problem. The downside, as her laid-back partner had been quick to point out, was chronic stress; she was incapable of "stopping to smell the roses." Anxiety propelled her, but it also undermined rewarding aspects of her personal life, especially in her relationship with Susan.

But she had fit in seamlessly with her college friends, who tended to share her driven, workaholic tendencies. They meshed, each with their own identity, like sections of an orchestra. Rebecca once viewed herself as their woodwind, a supportive role that added color and sustenance to the group. Now she is their conductor, leading and coordinating a weekend with unforeseeable outcomes. She's sure that Max and the others would call her loving leadership "bossy."

The nervousness has triggered her appetite, and she checks the refrigerator. To her delight, the shelves are already fully stocked. No worry about tonight's dinner. She brings in the wine from the car and inserts each bottle into the elaborate dining room rack. There are several cases of beer as well, but they are too heavy for her. She'll let the guys load them into the fridge. Rebecca arranges cheese, crackers, and grapes on a plate, pops open a bottle of red wine, and watches the striated pink and blue sunset from the swing. She isn't looking forward to the lonely, sleepless night ahead.

20
Max

MAX'S SEVEN-AND-A-HALF-HOUR flight from Vancouver to New York has been delayed twice, a problem with the plane, it is rumored. At the airport, his daughter wants to stay with him until the very last minute, afraid that he will get lost, but he waves her off. She is forever concerned about his safety and has no inkling as to why this reunion is so important to him. He eventually told her and Noah more about his young life in the States but had held back most of the details, including his relationship with Rebecca and the rest of the gang.

Given their strong distaste for the US, his children had not exactly encouraged him to talk about his earlier life. Nevertheless, since adolescence, Noah and Johanna followed current events south of the border, and the more they learned about the US, the greater their aversion. Over the years they had regularly cross-examined him about what seemed anathemas to them. "Pop," they would ask, "why are Americans so anti-immigrant?" "Why do they hold such harsh views on abortion and LGBT rights?" "Why is the country stingy with vacation time and maternity leave?" "Is it true that they value work at the expense of family life?" Noah and Johanna were horrified at the nation's deficient healthcare system compared to their own. "How can a country leave millions uninsured and with devastating bills?" they had asked. They also ranted about the low US Coronavirus vaccination rate and the climbing number of infections and deaths.

Max had not tried to defend his native country from their attacks, which made him squirm. "Obviously, these are some of the reasons I left in the first place," he told them. But Noah and Johanna kept pointing out the harsh realities in the States, taking obvious pleasure in nettling him. Their condemnations escalated during the Trump Administration, which had left Max at a loss for words.

As much as Max tried to fit in over the decades, he still stands out as an American. "You can't entirely erase your past," he informed his thoroughly Canadian children when questioned on certain habits. They badgered their father about his failure to say "thank you" or to apologize in situations that seemed nonsensical to him. Max drives his points home in a stronger, louder voice than his Canadian counterparts, much to their chagrin. And his pronunciation of certain words, despite their constant corrections, had not fundamentally altered. But he developed a love of ice hockey, a pastime he enjoys with them and the grandchildren.

♀

Despite the early hour, YVR is bustling with people. It is a beautiful airport, adorned with First Nation artwork, including sixteen-feet tall intricately carved figures, arms raised to welcome arriving passengers. Visitors are also greeted by a massive, nearly thirty-three-foot totem pole, that Max admired when they first entered the place.

"I can navigate the airport on my own," he says to Johanna. "In any case, I have to change planes in Toronto, and after I arrive in New York find my way to New Paltz, and to the cabin by myself." He knows the winding multi-leg journey will be challenging, but he dislikes his kids treating him like a child, and he constantly reminds them that he is a grown man.

Before she departs, his daughter hands him a book of brain teasers to keep him occupied. Max frowns and dumps the book into a bin as soon as she is out of sight. He intends to devote the long hours on the plane to sorting out his feelings about the reunion. He often had his friends in mind but seldom communicated with them.

He reflects on their correspondence over the years, mostly through mindless holiday and birthday cards. He had called Rebecca frequently in the months after Susan died and had intermittent phone contact with Deanna, Malaika, Keith, and Russell, although less frequently in recent decades. Just as he hadn't shared particulars about his American youth with his kids, he kept his Canadian existence separate from the crew. He had become a closed book to them despite wheedling from Rebecca. And that was the way he had decided it should be.

He had carried out the most sustained contact with Keith and Russell in 1977, when Jimmy Carter issued an executive order pardoning the hundred thousand or so men who had evaded the draft, most relocating to Canada. Like Max, the other American emigres were embraced by their new country, where they flourished; only half eventually returned. For some people, however, the pardon gave them a new lease on life.

His friends had hoped that Max would come home, and the two men took turns attempting to lure him back. "This country needs you to keep up the good fight against oppression." "You could accomplish so much more in the US." "You're a natural-born leader." "Maybe you should run for political office like Tom Hayden and Julian Bond."

None of their arguments had won him over. By then, Max was totally alienated from American society. He didn't want to reside in what he considered an amoral nation, a place with persistent racism, stark income inequality, and a history of hatred and persecution. He was done with that and had settled into a new life, taking pride in his newly acquired Canadian citizenship. It was unfortunate, he reflects, that his buddies were collateral damage.

Max is not sure why he decided to meet up with the gang now. What does he want from them? What do they expect from him? Since receiving the invitation, he purposefully put his emotions aside, but he can no longer do so. The time has come to address them head-on.

♀

He has learned how to deal with his incipient dementia as best as he can. So far, there is only mild cognitive impairment, mostly periodic memory lapses. He jots everything down to avoid forgetting things or getting lost. He has detailed instructions on his cell phone for this trip and feels relatively confident as he finds his way. He is grateful that Rebecca found a venue that is easily accessible. He arrives in New York at 5 pm, takes a cab to Port Authority to catch a Trailways bus, and steps off in New Paltz an hour and thirty-five minutes later. He grabs a taxi to take him to the bed and breakfast that he reserved for the night but impulsively directs the driver to the reunion cabin instead, a half hour away.

Max dismisses the cabbie, even though the house is dark inside. He walks cautiously to the entrance, luggage in hand, with only two dim porch lights guiding the way. He turns the knob, but the door is locked. What has he done? he asks himself. He knocks loudly and presses the doorbell.

Rebecca has fallen asleep on the couch. She wakes with a jolt and looks at her watch. Eleven o'clock. Frightened, she parts the blinds and sees a tall figure hovering at the entryway. She gives an incredulous stare, trying to take it in. He stands there, his finger still on the buzzer. Rebecca is dazed, frozen. She finally stirs and, as though sleepwalking, opens the door.

"Becca?" he says, his voice trembling. "Becca?"

She stands there, barefoot, in saggy jeans and an oversized plaid shirt. She is an older version of his first love, with wrinkles and white hair. His mouth turns into an impish grin, still recognizable after so many decades.

"Aren't you going to let me in?" He puts out his arms, hugs her close to him, and presses his lips on her forehead. "It's been too long," he says. "Far too long." He doesn't let go of her.

Rebecca closes her eyes and drinks in his familiar smell, woody and spicy, like the scent of patchouli oil in an old-time head shop. She takes a step back, and with an upturned face, touches his cheeks. A slow smile spreads across her face. This extra time with Max before the others arrive is more than she could have hoped for.

"You're here," she finally says.

Rebecca pours the remainder of the wine into two glasses while he raids the fridge. They settle on the couch, and stories from their shared past spill out in surges of uninhibited emotions like a tsunami rushing the shore. They talk to each other, talk over one another, howling in delight.

"Do you remember the day when the mimeograph. . ." Max begins.

"Purple stains on everyone's hands and clothing," Rebecca squeals, without missing a beat.

"The look in Deanna's eyes when Russell goaded her with chauvinist barbs," Max says. More bursts of laughter.

"Do you remember? Do you remember?" they say, followed by half stories, finished by the other.

Despite the late hour and his long, arduous trip, Max is rejuvenated. They open another bottle of wine. By 3 am, they are both so exhausted that their eyelids are drooping. Wordlessly, Rebecca leads Max up the stairs, holding firmly onto the handrail, to one of the bedrooms. He stumbles into bed, fully clothed, and promptly falls asleep. She pulls the cover over him and watches his rhythmic breathing for a short while. She feels calm, an unaccustomed lightness in her chest. For the first time in years, she senses that everything will be okay.

21
Malaika

Two months prior to the reunion, Malaika decides not to attend. She is reluctant to leave Darryl, who is starting to require more help. Despite his objections, the family finally insisted on hormone therapy. Between prostate cancer and the drugs, he has been experiencing painful urination, swelling legs, increasing fatigue, and, more recently, trouble concentrating and memory lapses. He, however, is most disturbed by the impotence. Malaika tries in vain to reassure him, but depression has set in.

His characteristically placid demeanor turns angry when she tells him she is staying home. He glares at her, shaking his fists.

"You must go," he says. "I would never forgive you or myself if you give up the reunion for me."

Their children are equally emphatic. "I'll take care of Dad," Kayla says. There is such resolve in their voices that Malaika finally relents.

Despite her husband's debilities, she knows that he is worried about her. Ever since she retired, she's been walking aimlessly around the house. At first, she kept herself busy by emptying her office box by box, which she insisted on doing on her own.

She shooed anyone away who offered to help, grateful to have something to occupy her attention, at least for the time being. It was a slow process as she evaluated each book, journal, memento, file, photograph, and other paraphernalia as to whether they should be discarded or moved to her home office. Malaika discovered an unknown piece of herself: that she had become a pack rat, unwilling to let go of anything.

She attempted to advise the newly hired lawyers in the firm who seemed younger and younger every year. They were polite, feigning interest in her suggestions, but Malaika knew that they would ignore her. The senior personnel who had worked under her guidance for years were less deferential and made clear that they were now in charge. She eventually pulled back entirely from her former law practice, which further sapped her self-esteem. A feeling of hopelessness washed over her, a sense that her future was yesterday.

Darryl's recent neediness gave her a new role, caregiver, but that hasn't been sufficiently fulfilling. Besides, Malaika was told by his doctor that he probably doesn't have more than a year or two to live, and that realization only intensified her uncertainties. Yes, my family is right, she decides. Maybe the trip will be good for her.

♀

She spends a week in New York City prior to the reunion, staying with her youngest daughter, Shanice, and two grandchildren. She hasn't seen them for six months. Shanice is busy with her law practice, and the grandsons—Lamonte and Booker—are both in college, one at Columbia University and the other at NYU. Now a senior, Booker had taken a sociology course from Russell prior to his retirement but was reluctant to let him know he was Malaika's grandson. "Great teacher," he had told her. "Considered one of the best at the university." She could not sway him to introduce himself to her friend.

After a few days with her daughter, Malaika visits two of her sisters who still live in Brownsville. The neighborhood is more rundown than she remembers, seemingly untouched by government programs and Black Lives Matter. Poverty is everywhere. Deteriorating public housing. Garbage overflowing from containers and dancing down sidewalk gutters as if they were an essential part of the scenery. Men, the generation after her own, still hanging out in doorways. The walk from the subway makes her question whether she and her comrades had any effect on the squalid living conditions at all. Her old neighborhood is still a dangerous place to live for children and teens, for women, for males targeted by cops. Even so, nobody bothers her; she is just another invisible, wrinkled old Black lady shuffling down the street.

The visit is demoralizing. Her sister Julene, who had struggled on and off welfare as a single mother, begrudges Malaika her success. After high school, she had secured a hair stylist license but soon became pregnant. The second child arrived shortly thereafter. She tried to work, to support her family. Momma helped, babysitting the kids, but after suffering from complications of diabetes, she could no longer care for them. Time has not eased Julene's bitterness; at seventy years old, she continues to throw poison darts at her elder sister. "Momma gave you everything," she sneers. "Me, what did I get? Nothing." The expression in her eyes is venomous. "You believe that you're better than us, don't you?"

Her brief stopover with Aiysha is equally troublesome. She had parlayed her beauty into an advantageous marriage to a

Caucasian entrepreneur who traveled for long periods. After fathering their three children, he died of a heart attack at age forty-two. While attempting to make funeral arrangements, Aiysha discovered that he had a first wife, who would inherit everything including her house. She had reached out to Malaika for legal assistance, but there was little she could do. Malaika tried to explain that she wasn't a family lawyer and didn't even have a license to practice in New York. She could only provide advice and take her to the Legal Aid Bureau, where she had interned during law school. Aiysha lost everything, ended up in Momma's apartment, kids in tow, and held Malaika responsible for her dismal situation.

The family had lost track of Maya, who disappeared into the world of prostitution at age seventeen. At Momma's insistence, Malaika had hired a private detective to locate her to no avail. The investigator said that Maya most likely did not want to be found. Momma accused Malaika of not trying hard enough, of stinting on her baby sister.

Malaika had long since cut off her brother Freddy from her life. He joined a gang at age twelve and since then was in and out of prison for increasingly severe crimes. She had tired of his incessant requests for money and finally severed ties when she heard him regaling her son, Cornell, with the romanticism of life as an outlaw. After she chased him away, she discovered a few pieces of expensive jewelry missing.

♀

The long subway ride back to her daughter's house is tiresome, but Malaika is relieved to escape her siblings. Worn out from their chorus of blame, she is even more anxious to reunite with her chosen family of friends. On Thursday morning, Malaika assures Shanice for the nth time that she is perfectly capable of driving by herself. "I'm eighty, not one hundred," she says, forcing a laugh. Her daughter peppers her with warnings in rapid succession. Her eyes are narrowed in such loving concern that Malaika humors her youngest child with assurances before setting out for the Poughkeepsie countryside in a rented Honda.

For the nearly two-hour trip, images of her companions roll through her mind like reels of an old film. Moments that were hilarious. Poignant. Chilling. Challenging. Defining. Darryl and their children are counting on her friends to ignite a spark of enthusiasm that they've been unable to achieve. Malaika views their expectations as magical thinking. She intends to just sit back and revel in a weekend with a bunch of old codgers rattling on about yesteryear.

She pats the colorful head wrap covering her neatly trimmed salt and pepper hair. For decades she had worn it in a voluminous afro, much approved of by the younger associates in the law firm; the bold style had given them license to experiment with their own hairdos. But she was strict about dress codes. "African Americans must always wear professional clothing to gain credibility," she told the staff. "Especially civil rights attorneys." She didn't even allow business casual in the office like so many other law firms. She hasn't quite ditched the habit despite retirement. For this trip, she is garbed in gray linen pants, a textured round-neck purple silk blouse that matches her head wrap, and black leather sandals. She keeps to her full makeup regimen, even for today.

Malaika turns onto a long dusty side road. She is surrounded by acres of forest, not a house, billboard, or traffic sign in sight. There are no cars, and except for chirrups, buzzes, whistles, and rustling leaves, there is an eerie silence. After a long stretch, she sees a clearing ahead and, with relief, catches sight of the large cabin. The trees and bushes are decorated in purple and lavender balloons and streamers, flapping in the wind. She sucks in a quick breath, overwhelmed with both anticipation and misgivings.

22
Russell

Russell waits for the limousine at the front of his building, two small suitcases at his side. He has been frugal his entire life, both out of principle and habit. He scorns people like his parents who are forever trying to keep up with "the Joneses." Their craving for a fancy new car was incomprehensible to him; he has driven the same beat-up Honda for fifteen years. Reliability should be the key, not social status. His mother could never understand why he had turned up his nose at their annually purchased new Cadillac. "You should be proud that we can afford such a car," she would say.

He abhors materialism, always has, as though you could achieve well-being through the purchase of objects. Like his college comrades, he always felt driven to avoid waste and transcend the need for unnecessary "stuff." Clothing was never important to him, although he had tried to keep up a professorial image. And he refused to take on debt for anything. "Interest on purchases only profits banks," he would bark if one of his wives had coveted something they couldn't pay for without borrowing money.

Luckily, he and the university had contributed hefty sums to his retirement fund for decades; his assets now amount to a few million dollars. He had assuaged his guilty conscience about investing in the stock market by picking only socially responsible funds—portfolios of companies concerned with social justice, environmental sustainability, clean energy, and human rights. His earnings hadn't suffered; only his choice of wives put a serious dent in the savings. Two divorces had cost him a hefty share of his wealth.

Ever since his second heart attack, Russell has loosened up a bit financially. At first, he resisted using a chauffeured car to attend the reunion but soon warms up to the idea. Why not, he reasons. At eighty, what is he saving for? Envisioning Deanna's contempt when he arrives, he momentarily thinks the better of it. Ultimately, he makes the booking.

As he waits for the limo, he looks down at his luggage and curls his lips. The large side pocket is filled with medicines along with bottles of vitamins his several specialists have insisted on. In his youth, he and his friends had largely eschewed the drug culture of their times. They had smoked marijuana occasionally but refused to experiment with mescaline, peyote, magic mushrooms, LSD, cocaine, or heroin. They valued mental clarity and an ability to concentrate far more than hallucinatory trips. Now he is swallowing a plethora of pills night and day—for cholesterol, blood pressure, clots, prostate problems, bladder control, general anxiety, nutritional deficiencies. The medicines fatigue him, cloud his mind.

At the moment, he is especially weary, having spent the night in mortal combat with Beth. She has not let up on the reunion for six months, alternating between sullen looks and belligerence. One day she found an old photo of Deanna and shoved the picture in his face. "I bet she hasn't aged well," she said with an ugly laugh. "Do you like her better than me?" she asked at another time. His wife is mostly upset that she wasn't invited to the reunion and that he will be with Deanna without her.

He would love to extricate himself from the everyday fracases which began long before the invitation arrived. The hateful arguments have been ratcheting up for years to a point where he and Beth can't have a civil conversation. Retirement made everything worse; they are around each other for hours at a time. He mostly hides in his study like a crab burrowed in the sand. He fantasizes about divorce, but that would make him a three-time loser. In any case, he blanches when envisioning yet another financial settlement with an ex-wife. He is finally through with child-support payments and college for his four kids. Luckily, NYU paid most of the tuition for them, a sizable benefit for a faculty member as prolific in progeny as he had been.

♀

Russell's mother referred to the grandkids as broods one, two, and three—two kids with the first wife and one each with the second two. She had kvelled when the first infants arrived, insisting on babysitting at least twice a week. "Nothing more rewarding than being a grandma," she had said with a satisfied look. Both of his parents were chagrined at the first divorce but pacified when his new wife bore them another grandchild. By the second split-up and his marriage to Beth, they were far less enamored of daughters-in-law and grandparenthood. At the announcement of Beth's pregnancy, his mother initially pretended that she misheard and walked away without comment. Never at a loss for words, she later called him. "Enough is enough," she said, with more than a trace of rebuke in her voice. Nevertheless, Mom had treated the latest baby as tenderly as the others.

All three unions were problematic at the outset. Lynda was a graduate student when she caught his eye. Their relationship, which had been an open secret, raised eyebrows among the faculty and their spouses. Supposedly, Lynda was on the pill, but one day she informed him, in a hushed, excited voice, about his impending fatherhood. Russell was adamant about her obtaining an abortion, legal by then, but she would have none of that. He reluctantly married her in an elaborate ceremony demanded by Lynda's family. But they tore at each other relentlessly, and their union became a verbal battlefield. The age difference didn't help; they had such different youths and outlooks on life. Before long, he was on the prowl, engaging in one-night stands as well as somewhat lengthier affairs. One of these, with Nicole, led to an acrimonious divorce, limited access to his two children, and a second spouse.

It felt like déjà vu when the shouting matches began shortly after the wedding ceremony. He felt as though Nicole had lured him into matrimony, trapping him in another combat zone. She complained that he spent too much time on his writing, that he attended an inordinate number of conferences, that he neglected her. Nicole accused him of being tightfisted with money while he viewed her as a spendthrift. They were poles apart on most everything of importance to them.

He endeavored to walk out several times, but she dissuaded him by threatening to take their son from him. He finally had enough, once more suffering through another bitter break up. This one had hit him even harder in the wallet. Russell did his best to maintain a connection with his teenage offspring despite unremitting battles with Nicole over visitation rights.

He was forever juggling weekends in his efforts to keep in regular contact with his three children. He wonders if he had tried hard enough; he barely sees any of them these days, including the five grandchildren. At least he has a warm relationship with his youngest child Allison, something he could possibly jeopardize if he divorced Beth.

♀

There is heavy traffic and, when the limousine arrives, the driver is forced to maneuver around it into a tight parking spot. Russell climbs in and leans back in his seat. Would the situation be different if he'd hung onto Deanna? If only she had put up with his healthy, youthful libido, allowed him a chance to experiment. They could have had an open relationship before settling into fidelity. "I need some space," he had told her. He envisions her, hands on hips, cold eyes. "You just can't keep it in your pants, can you?" she had shouted. "Find someone else who will put up with such a self-indulgent libertine."

Their romantic relationship was over just like that. She had been so quick to leash him in then cut him off. They were just college students, for god's sake. Russell's heart is pounding, and he is beginning to sweat. She wouldn't listen to reason. He had tried so hard to explain how men are different from women. How he had to fully explore his erotic fantasies before settling down.

He replays the scene with Deanna again and again, her heartless dismissal of him. Surges of adrenaline rush through his body. If only she had let him exhaust his sexual appetite, perhaps they could have had a lasting relationship. He gets more worked up. Deanna had been his soulmate, could have spared him three failed marriages. His resentment spins out of control. Exhausted, he drifts off to sleep for the rest of the trip.

23
Deanna

It has not been a good morning. Deanna feels the stabbing pain as soon as she awakens in the dreary hotel room. She chides herself for putting off the knee replacement surgery that would have eliminated the constant throbbing. What was she thinking? She is heading out to a country house tomorrow and can barely walk. She imagines the rest of them hiking down the trail while she hobbles behind with a cane. She hears their "Go Deanna, go," but she can't. "I'm hurting," she moans, letting the words hang in the air. She aches everywhere. Even getting out of bed is a chore.

Moving her bowels is an excruciating undertaking as well. Since being forced to give up regular exercise, her body has rebelled. The massive amount of Tylenol she gulps down daily has intensified the problem. At times, her hemorrhoids are so inflamed that she must sit on an inflatable donut cushion to ease the discomfort. Nothing has been effective, not the high-fiber diet or quarts of water. She even stuffs prunes into her mouth, reminding herself of her mother. Dulcolax tablets sometimes help but not today, most likely because she is anxious about the reunion. The eight-hour plane ride from California to JFK yesterday wreaked havoc on every part of her body.

Deanna also gained weight from the inactivity, though she has lost a few pounds through a crash diet. She was determined to get into her size twelve wardrobe for the reunion, but that turned out to be an overreach. She sighs. She is still a little thick around the middle. During the six months leading up to the reunion, she experienced an internal war: she obsessively counted calories while berating herself for dieting. I'm eighty years old, she thinks, and still obsessed with my body image. She covers her face with both hands. How can she face them? She feels like such a mess.

She pictures the six of them together so many years ago. They had been an intrepid crew, ready to face danger to put their values into practice. They had believed that they were invincible, that in partnership with each other they could accomplish anything. How she yearns to be young again, naïve but striving to make a difference in the world no matter the odds.

Deanna reflects on her relationship with Russell, something she hasn't done in quite a while. Sam had swept away any lingering regrets over the end of her romantic ties to Russell, but she still questions how he could have let her go so easily. She thought their bond had been too strong to break for a series of one-night stands. He had been so caring about people in general, willing to sacrifice himself for humankind. Fight for the disenfranchised, the underprivileged. Yet he couldn't give himself fully to one person. To her. She had felt sidelined by a succession of girls who meant nothing to him.

Deanna's mind drifts to the abortion. How could he have been so stoic about getting rid of their baby? He didn't even want to talk about it, however hard she tried. What would her life have been like if she had given birth? She does not second-guess the abortion; she clearly was not ready to raise a child at that point in her life. It's just Russell's cavalier attitude about the situation that still rankles her despite warm feelings of friendship for him.

The abortion was a defining moment in her life, motivating her to pursue a career as a gynecologist. After receiving her medical degree, she spent decades working part-time at clinics making sure that other women had access to affordable, safe abortions. Deanna did not want anyone else to endure the same tragic experience that had left her sterile.

She can't count how many abortions she has performed over the decades for girls and women who were in desperate circumstances. Despite the fact that an abortion was eventually legalized, so many of them still had to face angry, threatening protesters waving nasty signs accusing them of killing their babies. As they walked to the clinic entrance, they had to be protected by volunteers, at times by Deanna herself.

And she had spent decades with grassroots organizations advocating for women's rights, even testifying before Congress several times. Deanna was especially proud of her support for anti-poverty programs and universal childcare. She had refused to be a single-issue activist and fought to advance social and racial justice. However, since the Supreme Court's overturning of Roe v Wade, paving the way for states to ban abortions, she has intensified her pro-choice lobbying as best as she could.

Deanna regains her composure. What she's accomplished should be enough, not what she looks like. She peers into the mirror and grimaces, not totally convinced. Okay, so she would like to have her sexy, fully functioning body back. To turn heads again. There, it is said! Now get over it, she tells the reflection with a quick laugh.

Tomorrow she will head out to New Paltz, but today she has set aside for priming herself by visiting a few old hangouts in the City. She grabs a cab to Washington Square Park, walks through the familiar marble arch, cane in hand, and sits by the gushing fountain. A colorful assortment of characters still roams about, but the social and cultural milieu feels different. Deanna barely escapes being hit by a skateboarder who whizzes by without even acknowledging her existence. Homeless people are scattered throughout the park, some so young she feels as if she is in a Charles Dickens novel. Glassy-eyed drug addicts wander amid the musicians who sound louder than she remembers. She also senses a heightened police presence, which detracts from the vitality and spontaneity of the place. She stays for a while, absorbing the perplexing vicissitudes of time.

Deanna hails a cab to Bank Street and asks the driver to navigate the streets of her prior jogging route. Instead of giving her reassurance, the tour conjures up losses. How she had savored those runs; they nurtured both her body and psyche, kept her fit. She had taken such pride in her athletic prowess. Her spirits are dampened until they stop at the small building where she had lived with Malaika and Rebecca. Deanna would like to knock on the door, ask if she could check out the apartment, but is dissuaded by the five flights of stairs. Instead, she just looks, rummaging through the dustbin of her brain for long-lost memories. Recollections of their friendship kindle feelings of deep affection.

She is on an emotional roller coaster, rushing through tight turns and steep slopes but Deanna refuses to disembark. "City College, next," she tells the cabbie. "138th Street and Amsterdam Avenue." She asks him to wait while she wanders around South

Campus. She takes in the vast changes, first in confusion and then in shock. There is little remaining of her college days. The imposing Romanesque Finley Student Center has been demolished along with the dungeon-like cafeteria and its ghostly whispers of their intellectual dialogues, political intrigues, and camaraderie. Also gone is the South Campus Lawn and its crowds of undergraduates, Day-Glo frisbees, songs, and laughter. In their place is concrete—new dorms, specialized academic facilities. Despite students spilling out of buildings on this glorious June day, the campus appears almost sterile.

Her final stop, the West End Bar, is equally disheartening. "On to 2911 Broadway," she instructs the driver. She intends to have dinner and a glass of wine in their old Friday night haunt. She discovers that the pub is long gone, since 2006. The edifice is empty, bereft of its exalted history as a gathering spot for the 1940s Beat Generation novelists, poets, artists, newsmen, and later for the political activists of the sixties —Mark Rudd and Columbia University's radical cadre. Deanna and her clique had been a part of that story. Her eyes begin to water, and without warning tears course down her cheeks. The vacant structure seems as wistful as she for its heyday.

Back at the hotel, Deanna grieves over the relics of a bygone time; she mourns her youth. The more she rummages through the rubble of her past, the more she feels weighed down by old age. Her journey to their former hangouts has deadened rather than sparked enthusiasm for the reunion. She doesn't relish further disappointments. Did she really think she would find comfort in revisiting the escapades of her younger self? She toys with going straight back to California, backing out, but in the morning Deanna takes the bus to New Paltz.

24
Keith

KEITH IS riding in the passenger seat next to his granddaughter, Jenna, in his Toyota Prius, the Sirius XM radio thundering music from the 50s and 60s. They sing along at the top of their lungs, harmonizing with each other. They have been singing together for years, their voices matching seamlessly. The two of them have been musical pals ever since her sixth birthday when he bought her a Martin Djr-10. She took to the instrument immediately, developed proficiency over the years, and picked up the violin and cello along the way. Keith was gratified that she was gifted with perfect pitch, most likely in the family genes.

In high school, Jenna had been selected to join the recently formed Boston Philharmonic Youth Orchestra, where she studied and played violin under the mentorship of its conductor, Benjamin Zander. The ensemble performed in prestigious venues—Symphony Hall and Carnegie Hall—and traveled abroad for weeks at a time. Eventually, she attended Julliard in New York but returned to Boston, where she earned a seat with the Boston Philharmonic Orchestra. Keith pats her arm. If only his parents could have attended her concerts: Jenna had become the violin virtuoso they had dreamed of.

As with Keith, the guitar was her first love, and they often played together. He taught her techniques that she quickly mastered—strumming styles, finger picking, chord inversions, rhythms, timing. She advanced to a point where she would give him tips. Jenna has become his muse; after the Parkinson's disease slowed him down, she would arrive at his house once a week, pushing him to write songs and play the guitar.

For his seventy-fifth birthday, she had surprised him with a puppy, much to the dismay of his wife. "I'm allergic to dogs," Sara said. But the golden lab soon won her heart. He would lie on his stomach and demand, with a tapping paw, that Sara pet him. The dog was quick to learn and obedient, which also ingratiated him with her.

None of that mattered to Keith—he fell in love instantly. It was a fantasy fulfilled, having been deprived of a pet his entire life, first by his parents and then by Sara. His wife agreed to endure steroid nasal sprays, anti-histamine eye drops, and other remedies that didn't always work. But the spark in Keith's eye when he was with the dog rendered her allergic reaction, which lessened over time, a sacrifice she was willing to make.

He named the lab Che, and the two became inseparable. Che proved to be a one-person pup, loyal to Keith. He would cuddle with him in "the Monster," listen when he strummed the guitar and walk patiently at his master's side, despite the slow pace. Otherwise, the dog was high-spirited and jaunty, lifting Keith's morale when he felt despondent about his declining health. For the reunion, he reluctantly left Che at home, abiding by Rebecca's heavy-handed injunction against pets.

♀

His granddaughter had insisted on driving him to the reunion. "I understand that family is not invited," she said with a chuckle. "I'll stay in New Paltz for the weekend with friends." He protested, but she was firm. "Grandma and I want you to go. We know that you are eager to see them."

And he was. His friends had been his second family during a period when he needed both validation for his musical aspirations and fortification of his budding political outlook. They had been a refuge for him against his parents' onslaughts. The five of them carried him through his ill-fated journey as a would-be folk music star. Because of them, he had become a better version of himself.

Keith and his granddaughter suddenly hear a shrill voice through the deafening sound of "Rock Around the Clock," and he turns the radio down.

"Recalculating. Recalculating," intones the tiresome mechanical voice. "Make a U-turn in five hundred feet."

♀

"Uh-oh," Jenna groans. "I missed the turn." She sighs. "I'm so dependent on that GPS lady."

"Me too," Keith assures her. "It must be in the genes."

They both laugh. Jenna glances over at her grandfather. "Are you anxious about the weekend?"

"A little," he says. "Mostly about my ability to get around. Without you and Grandma." He pauses for a moment, pondering what lies ahead. There is a companionable silence between them. "It's been so long," he finally says. "I just hope they haven't turned into strangers. But I'm mostly looking forward to seeing them."

They drive up to the house, where the gang is seated in a circle on the front lawn, absorbed in animated conversation. They get up to greet Keith, surprised to see a young woman with him. Jenna gets out of the car and without a word attends to her grandfather. She moves his feet into position and wraps her arms under his armpits, bracing him. He leans on her as he steps out of the vehicle. She hands him two canes but leaves the walker in the car. Together, they amble haltingly toward the group, Jenna still propping him up.

Jenna is taken aback as she gazes at his friends. She had heard so many anecdotes about their exploits that she felt as though she would know them. The plucky six who engaged in battles for social justice. Unapologetic badass activists. Grassroots organizers. Undaunted by conventional norms. Now she is facing a bunch of wrinkled, balding, white-haired, slow-going elderly folks. Of course, she chides herself. Like her grandfather.

Keith breaks away from her grip and embraces each friend in turn. He basks for a moment in their warm familiarity, like a lost dog who has found his way home. To him, they are the identical feisty comrades that he consorted with in college. Older but still full of life.

"They haven't changed a bit," he whispers happily to his granddaughter. "They are exactly as I had visualized them."

Jenna glances around again at the group, wondering if she and Poppy are looking at the same people. She would like to ask if he's kidding but realizes that her grandfather is seeing what he wants to see, that he is observing his pals through rose-tinted glasses. And that's okay, she thinks. She takes in her grandfather's chipper mood. Maybe she should buy a pair of those specs for herself.

Deanna and Russell link arms with Keith. He feels safe with them.

"Meet my granddaughter, Jenna," he says, adding firmly, "and she's leaving soon." Keith doesn't want Jenna to get any ideas about staying on to help him.

She shakes her head at her wily grandfather and brings his suitcase, guitar case, and walker from the car.

"You take care of Poppy," she says to his friends.

"Don't worry," he tells her. "My buddies will be here for me. They always have been." Jenna turns to leave. "And take the walker with you."

PART V
The Reunion: June 2025

25
The First Night: Getting Re-Acquainted

"Martini anyone?" Russell says, retrieving the fixings from his room. "I make the best."

"Go easy," Rebecca says. "Tipsy is okay but drunk is not."

Deanna nods in agreement.

"Bossy women," Russell says. He prepares a cocktail for himself and Keith, who rarely imbibes in hard liquor. The rest of them stick to wine and beer. Russell eyes the vodka longingly as they nibble on hors d'oeuvres—spinach dip, baked brie, and an assortment of olives.

For dinner, they are served baked Dijon salmon; a roasted vegetable medley of red peppers, zucchini, baby carrots, and asparagus; and scalloped potatoes. The wine flows freely.

Deanna hesitates about dessert, moving the piece of freshly baked cherry pie around her plate with a fork.

"Go, Deanna, go," Rebecca says.

Deanna scarfs the pastry down, promising herself it will be the last time for sweets this weekend.

"What a feast," Max says to the husband-wife chef team as they are leaving. "Thanks for a terrific meal."

The friends gather in the great room, satiated with food, drink, and camaraderie. Rebecca procures a wicker basket and places it on the coffee table. "For your cell phones," she says. "We're putting them away for the weekend." Her tone is insistent. "And don't forget to turn them off."

"You're as controlling as ever," Russell says. He drops his device into the basket, and everyone else follows suit.

Rebecca sticks the basket in the hall closet. "There, that's done with," she says with satisfaction.

"Don't be surprised if Jenna turns up unannounced," Keith teases, a twinkle in his eyes. "She will be unnerved when she can't get in touch with me."

"You're pretty close to your granddaughter," Malaika says. "Me, too. With the seven of them. And my four children as well."

"Well, bully for both of you," Rebecca says. "We may as well get it over with. Why doesn't everyone take out the pictures of their adorable offspring. Then we can move on."

A hush falls over the room as though the conductor has raised his baton for the concert to end. Malaika sizes up Rebecca, whose arms are crossed. She decides to take the plunge, breaking into the quiet. "So, what's got your goat?" she asks. "You have an aversion to kids?"

"I don't care to talk about it," Rebecca says, not wanting to revisit the pain she had long buried. This weekend, she envisions basking in the warmth of their friendship. Sharing pleasurable times with them. Indulging in carefree jesting and humor. Not opening old wounds. Everyone can hear her heart thumping in the pregnant silence. Still, no one says a word. Rebecca is inundated with sentiments that she hasn't felt for some time. It enfolds and crushes her so forcefully that she blurts out, "We ached for them so badly. Susan and me. They wouldn't let us." Rebecca's lower lip trembles and tears sting her eyes. Without warning, they flow freely like a dam that has been breached.

Max puts his arms around her, holding Rebecca tight. "Tell us about it."

She hesitates. Not even she and Susan had discussed the enduring sorrow in the aftermath of their final, fruitless efforts to adopt. Then again, her friends seem so willing to let her unburden herself like they had in earlier years. Rebecca pulls away from Max and takes a few quick breaths. "We went from agency to agency," she begins. "We were desperate. Until the late 1990s, it had been impossible for lesbians to legally adopt in Maryland. By that time, we were in our mid-fifties, too old to be parents."

"Sorry," was the constant refrain when the agencies discovered they were a gay couple. "We wish we could help." The staff never seemed sorry in the least.

"It's not like we had to have a Gerber baby," Rebecca says. "At the time, there were so many Black and Brown infants without homes who ended up in foster care. Rather than put children with willing and caring families, like us, they ended up getting shuffled from place to place." Rancor flares within her as she thinks about the evidence, since then, that kids thrive just as well with same-sex couples. . .that what they require most is love and stability, which they would have provided.

"Over the years," she continues, "Susan and I assured ourselves that children would have weighed us down. The union became my baby. I nurtured it, devoted my life to the cause. I was enmeshed in a dizzying flurry of activity, day and night. Susan devoted herself to teaching and writing. We moved on. We were happy, just the two of us."

Her friends receive this last assertion with looks of such compassion that Rebecca finds herself pushing toward a truer reckoning. "No," she says. "We weren't okay. We carried on with our daily routines without so much as a ripple. We worried about meetings, paying bills, petty office politics. But neither of us ever actually got over the void in our lives. Even today, the sound of children's laughter brings sadness, reminds me of what we never had. Kids. Grandkids. The whole shebang. And it took a toll on our relationship."

She is stirring up painful memories, like chafing the scab of an old wound, and Rebecca clenches her fists. "I was born too early," she says. "I missed out on the reproductive technologies that freed LGBTQ couples to choose parenthood. I was so envious of young gay couples strolling in the park with baby carriages. It could have been Susan and me."

Rebecca gives Max a doleful smile. "I would have asked you to father our baby," she says. She tries to visualize holding a tiny Max in her arms. "Would you have agreed?" she asks.

"That was many years ago, Becca."

"But would you have?" She looks up expectantly, not willing to let him get away with the evasive response. She doesn't understand why, but it's important for her to have an answer.

He searches Rebecca's eyes. "I'd do anything for you. Let's leave it at that."

Tears are rolling down her cheeks again, and she fails to suppress a sob. Max takes her hand and strokes it. Each of the friends embraces her except for Keith, who blows her a kiss. As she drinks in the moment, a sense of calm rolls over her. She sinks back into the couch. For the first time since Susan died, Rebecca feels that she is not alone.

"I couldn't have kids," Deanna lets slip into the stillness. "I'm sterile." She glances at Russell. "Because of the slipshod abortion."

Russell fidgets in his seat. Does she really have to bring that up? He scowls. What is he doing here? Everyone turns to him, waiting. "What do you want me to say?" he mumbles, after a while.

Deanna had not intended to broach the subject. After all, it was nearly sixty years ago. The strength of her lingering anger at him takes her unawares. As he sits there looking exasperated, her indignation only intensifies.

"You treated me heartlessly," she says, her voice quaking. The wine is loosening any restraints. "Like the pregnancy was just an irritation in your life, a fetus to get rid of. I mourned the loss for decades, especially after I learned I couldn't conceive again."

The air is charged with an intermingling of anticipation and foreboding. The intensity of Deanna's passion has caught everyone off guard, especially Russell. It's been forever since he's turned his thoughts inward, seeking to find answers in himself. Beth has insisted that he go into therapy, but he views that as her way of shifting blame for their failing marriage onto him. This feels different. Deanna is in obvious pain and, for some unfathomable reason, he is willing to take some responsibility. Maybe it's the expressions on his friends' faces. Everyone seems to expect something of him. He's fearful of digging too deeply but doesn't want to disappoint them—or her.

Emboldened but wary, he says, "I was scared." He winces.

"Go on," Malaika urges.

Russell feels a heaviness in his chest, reminiscent of his two heart attacks. "I know this is irrational," he says, "but I had assumed that Deanna's Catholicism would kick in. That she would insist on having the baby. That my life would be ruined." He is reminded of the overwhelming dread that had engulfed him at the time. He had felt as though he were drowning.

"What about Deanna?" Malaika says gently. "She suffered too, and you weren't really there for her."

At first, Russell is confused. Didn't he help set up the abortion? He even went with her, waited throughout the entire procedure.

He turns to Deanna. "Perhaps I was lax during your recovery." He pauses. "I didn't spend enough time with you afterwards."

"I'm not counting hours," Deanna retorts in a sharp tone. "I longed for you to connect with me, to understand that aborting the fetus—our fetus—was traumatic." She stares straight at him. "I was desperate for reassurance. I had felt emotionally abandoned."

Russell grimaces. She is right, of course. He had panicked and wished for Deanna and the situation to just go away. He didn't want to contend with her neediness. He was preoccupied with his own concerns. Humility doesn't come naturally to him, but he forces himself to say the words. "I'm sorry," he mumbles. "Truly sorry."

"Say it louder," Rebecca commands.

He puts his head down. "I'm sorry. Sorry for everything. You had been my soulmate, the love of my life. I never meant to hurt you." He squeezes his eyes shut. "Okay. I was an asshole."

Deanna softens. She is assuaged by his heartfelt apology. As she scrutinizes him, she envisions the Russell of earlier days. Their bond of friendship over the decades, which has endured over time and distance, is far too important for her to hang on to the bitterness. She must leave any remaining animosity behind.

As the others signal approval, Deanna moves across the room and curls up against him. Russell reaches out and caresses her cheek.

"You're still beautiful," he says. "So beautiful."

♀

"It's incredible that such intense feelings from our youth haven't faded with age," Malaika murmurs, almost to herself. "Even at eighty. I for one have hung onto so many childhood fears and insecurities."

Max pours her more wine. "Such as?" he asks.

Malaika feels panicky, as though she's falling off a cliff. She is sorry she spoke up and pulls back. She has not been able to talk about the malaise that has been eating her up over the last year or two—not with Darryl, not with her children. Why should she share her apprehensions with them?

But as she regards her pals, she is struck by how open they've been with each other, with her. Malaika decides to take a chance.

"I was an uncertain kid from Brownsville when I had first met you guys," she begins. "In college, you helped me gain self-confidence. I'm forever grateful. . ." Malaika breaks off in mid-sentence.

Before her friend can have second thoughts, Rebecca spurs her on. "You seem so depressed. Even in your body language. What's troubling you? Spit it out!"

Jolted by Rebecca's forceful voice, Malaika resumes. "I've had a highly successful career, lots of kudos from all walks of life. I've been celebrated as a first-rate lawyer. I drove myself hard, but it was fulfilling." She covers her face with her hands, hesitant to expose herself. Suddenly the words spill out. "But since

I retired, I feel as self-doubting as I did as a teenager. I'm just floating through life. I don't even know who I am anymore."

"I know what you mean," Deanna says. "I stare in the mirror, see an old lady, and wonder who she is. Even when I'm engaged in meaningful activities, the younger women look through me as if I'm invisible. I've become the other."

"But unlike you," Malaika says, "I'm not doing anything worthwhile. I sleep far more than I should. My will has been crippled."

"What about your kids?" Max says. "They must give you some measure of comfort. They do for me."

Malaika sips her wine, uncertain how to respond. "My four adult children have busy careers of their own. The seven grandchildren are grown up. They are still part of my everyday life but not central to who I am." She takes a deep breath. "My world seems to be shrinking every day. Darryl has Stage 4 prostate cancer and will require a full-time aide soon. The only role I'll have left is part-time caregiver. In an emotion-choked voice she adds, "And his prognosis is not very good."

"That must be devastating for you," Deanna says, clasping her hand. "When I lost Sam, it was as though my life support system had been pulled from under me. I floundered for a long time. My daughter and grandchildren weren't enough. They live on the other side of the continent in any case. But my clinic responsibilities had rescued me."

"Me too," says Rebecca. "The union was my lifeline when Susan died."

"Exactly," says Malaika. "And retirement has taken that away from me. It has stolen my very identity."

"But there's more to you than your profession," Max says. "You're awesome. Always have been."

"But that's the point," Malaika says, shaking her head. "Without my law practice, I feel like a nonentity. Darryl keeps suggesting different hobbies. And the kids are keen on sending me on a long cruise."

Everyone lets out a collective snort. "Hollow diversions are for old people," Max sneers. "Not for people like us."

There is a gnawing at Malaika's conscience. "One more thing," she says, the combination of camaraderie and wine erasing any lingering reticence. "My family was never enough for me. I feel as though I were a neglectful mother and grandparent, letting my offspring remain secondary to my clients." The statement punches her in the stomach, like a hit-by-pitch baseball. "I know grandparents whose whole world is their grandchildren. From the day the first one was born, I was never like that." Malaika is mired in self-reproach. "Even when I was at home, my mind tended to be elsewhere, drafting an argument, mulling over a legal question." She is whispering, as though hiding her words from the family. "I was never fully there for my children or grandchildren. Not for Darryl, either."

Malaika wonders why this long-simmering issue is bubbling up now. Nonetheless, it's out. She is finally owning up to her inadequacy as a parent, grandmother, and wife. Her eldest daughter had attempted to broach the subject several times, but Malaika brushed her off. "Nonsense," she told her. "I raised you just fine." Darryl, too, had desired more of her. "It's not just your physical presence," he said. "You always seem far away, even when we're together." She never owned up to her mental absences but forced herself to spend more evenings and weekends with the family.

From the lingering quiet, Max says, "You were a good enough mother, Malaika. Good enough." He gives her hand a squeeze.

A wave of relief permeates her body. She has exposed the most vulnerable pieces of herself, yet her friends are nonjudgmental, accepting her for who she is. Reminiscent of how they used to be.

She scans the room and sees loving, understanding faces. "Maybe I'm brooding about personal failures from my past because I can't move forward," she says. "I need to figure out how to take the next step."

♀

Deanna turns to Max. "Sounds like you're quite the family man. Tell us about them."

"It's just my son, daughter, and five grandkids. No wife. Never married."

"Guess I made up for you," Russell says. "I'm on my third." He ignores Deanna, who is rolling her eyes. "So how did you escape tying the knot?"

"Can we skip the history?" Max demurs.

"No fair," Rebecca argues. "We're filling each other in."

"Okay, I'll try. But first I'd like another beer."

He takes a while at the refrigerator, hoping they'll move on to something else, but when he comes back, they're patiently waiting.

"I'm not sure where to start," he says. "It's been a long journey."

"How about with your kids," Rebecca says. "Who is their mother?"

"It's complicated. When I first escaped to Canada, I had wandered around Ontario for several years, picking up odd jobs. It was hard labor and not very gratifying." He yearns to chug his beer but instead takes a long swallow. "Then I found a commune."

"You lived on a commune?" Russell asks with equal parts awe and incredulity.

"For five years. We heated our cottages with wood and solar energy. I learned to garden. Can food. We grew vegetables and berries. Had fruit trees. Hens. In the winter we tapped our maple trees and sold the syrup to the locals. It had been labor intensive but a simple, rewarding life." Max visualizes the log cabins, kitchen for preparing their common meals, laundry room, and fireplace where they gathered for warmth, music, and dancing. "It suited my needs at the time. I had given up my family and all of you. It had been unsettling to feel totally alone in the world. The people on the commune gave me companionship."

"And your children?" Deanna asks.

"I'm getting to it." Max finishes his beer. Russell gets up to grab him another. "I was in a sexual relationship with one of the women. Nothing more." His voice is clipped, impassive. "One day she told me she wanted a baby. No obligations for me. And I thought, why not? Maggie seemed like a decent person. I could do that for her."

"What a story," Russell says.

Rebecca has a burning sensation in her chest. That could have been my baby, she thinks. Scrunching up her face in sullen resentment, she demands, "So, what happened?"

Staring straight at Rebecca, he says, "She asked me for a second one. A sibling for Johanna. Noah was born two years later." Max's blue eyes are solemn. "And less than a year later, Maggie disappeared. No one knew where she had gone. She left a note telling me to take good care of the kids.

"At first, I wanted to bury my head and wake up when it was over. We stayed on the commune for another year. Everyone helped care for them." Max furrows his brow. "But it soon became clear to me that I had to become more responsible. I was the father of two, living on a collective farm. Penniless and dependent on others. My children would grow up without a formal education. None of the advantages that I had."

He gazes around the room at his friends. "So, we left. I took them west. I cobbled together odd jobs. It was taxing as a single parent." His face is grim. "But then I received an inheritance from my parents and enrolled in a graduate architecture program at the University of British Columbia. The Vancouver Campus. The money had been sufficient to get me through school.

"My brothers begrudged me my share. But the will specifically had stated that the assets be divided equally among the three of us." He shakes his head. "I had to get a lawyer, which prolonged the process."

Max flashes back to his siblings, who had been outraged that he was included in the will. He can only imagine what they said to each other. "Can't believe our parents left any of their assets to that commie deserter." "Didn't even have the guts to come back for their funerals." They did not know that his mother had been surreptitiously sending him money during his early years in Canada. Much to her delight, he had reciprocated with pictures of the grandkids that, in time, she shared with her husband. By the time he reached Vancouver, he was communicating with his father as well.

Max raises his beer to toast them. "That was such a long time ago," he says. "I don't like dwelling on the tough times. It worked out. My children turned out to be dependable and ethical individuals with generous hearts. And they're raising the grandkids that way." He narrows his eyes. "I just wish they would hover over me less. Since the memory lapses, they've been overprotective, sometimes smothering. But I put my foot down when they go too far."

"Oh Max," Rebecca says. "How bad is it?"

"Incipient dementia, at least that's what I've been told. But I'm fine. Getting around the beast. Lots of sticky notes. I got here on my own, didn't I?" He gives them a thumbs up. "Being here with the old gang has been a tonic for the ole brain." Max puts a finger to his lips. "Enough for now."

♀

Deanna smiles at Max. "My daughter was abandoned by her mother too," she confides. "When Angela was an infant. Sam and I had wanted children, and when we found out I couldn't conceive, we decided to adopt. It was a long, frustrating process." She glances at Rebecca. "But for us it turned out well."

Deanna laughs. "I hate to admit this, but when we went to collect Angela from the agency, I brought pink blankets. Pink baby clothes. Pink booties." She blushes. "That day, I put aside my feminist sensibilities for a princess fantasy. Sam had been taken aback, but he indulged me."

"I'll bet that thwarted any future for her as a women's libber," Russell says, winking at Deanna.

She gives him the evil eye, enjoying their former good-natured banter. "Actually, Angela is a dedicated political activist," she says. "Has been since law school. Right now, she is legal counsel for Women of Color Against Violence.

"My daughter is an impressive woman," she goes on. "The teenage years were rocky, but later we developed a strong bond." Deanna remembers the trajectory of their relationship. It was like negotiating a road bike on a path full of potholes.

"In her early twenties, Angela decided to find her biological mother. Sam and I helped, of course. The adoption agency refused to give up her identity, but my daughter was dogged."

"I wonder who she takes after," Russell chuckles.

Deanna nods. "Once Ancestry began DNA testing, she laboriously went through every possible connection and eventually found her. It was bittersweet. Her biological mother turned out to be a spiteful woman whose only interest in Angela was what she could get from her. Mostly money. Her stepsisters and stepbrothers had their hand in the till as well. She was disconcerted but felt more at ease with herself for having found her roots."

Deanna turns pensive. "Our visits are few and far between these days. Angela and the family rarely come west," she says. "And the trip is hard on me. We mostly communicate through Zoom, but that's not the same thing." Deanna realizes how much she misses the in-person discussions with her daughter and warm embraces with the grandkids. She and Sam used to fly to DC regularly and felt part of their lives. Nowadays she is isolated from them. Misgivings are lurking around the edges of her mind. "I should move closer to them." The statement takes her by surprise.

"You're fortunate," Russell says. "At least you have a relationship with your kids. Except for Allison, the youngest, none of my children have any interest in me. Two of them have broken ties completely. The other one only invites me to special occasions, like bar mitzvahs. And that's only for the gift. As if any of them need money." Russell has a sour taste in his mouth as he calls his offspring to mind. "I never missed a child-support payment for any of them. And I paid for their college—at least everything that NYU didn't cover."

"What happened?" Malaika asks, wondering if she could survive a falling-out with her children and grandchildren.

Russell doesn't hesitate. "My first wife had been so angry about the divorce that she poisoned the kids against me," he snaps. "I never had a chance with those two." He recalls the juggling of weekends when they were young. "I saw them as much as Lynda would allow. Every other Sunday, sometimes the whole weekend. I took them camping, to sporting events, played board games with them." His cheeks are burning as he sifts through the endless confrontations over the children. "She had a habit of canceling at the last minute with some lame excuse. She even asked me at one point to give them up, let her second husband adopt them. Told me that he is well-to-do and would provide them with a better lifestyle." He shakes his head in dismay. "I refused, of course. That was a no-brainer. But to get even, she put an even tighter leash on their visits with me."

"Why didn't you take her to court?" Max asks.

"I guess I was too beaten down." Russell avoids eye contact with his friends. "And I was unwilling to take on that kind of fight. Lynda was determined to punish me, and David and Cory were her weapons. In retrospect, I should have. It really hurt to see them raised by their stepfather. I had so little influence over their upbringing." He wags a disapproving finger. "They're both money men. The oldest, David, is an executive at Morgan Stanley, and Cory manages a hedge fund like his stepdad."

Russell stares vacantly into space. "They steadily withdrew from me over the years as our values increasingly clashed. When they were in college, they claimed that every time we were together, all I did was lecture them about their political views."

"Did you?" Deanna goads him.

"Yes, of course," he says, taking the bait. "I couldn't just ignore their fucked-up outlook on life. They turned into Trump Republicans, for heaven's sake." He spits Trump's name out as though it were an obscenity. "And the grandkids have followed in their footsteps." He is worked up. "Ultimately our heated arguments turned into slanging matches and now they want nothing more to do with me." He is feeling a mix of humiliation, indignation, and guilt. "Nor I with them."

"My third son is mostly apolitical," he goes on. "Very conventional. Just like his mother." Russell has a long face as he considers his disappointing children. "Brett is an electrical engineer, lives in a suburban middle-class neighborhood in a gated community, and plays golf on weekends. The Women's Movement passed him by. His wife is a stay-at-home mother even though the kids are long gone. Black Lives Matter eluded him, as did every other social and political movement, right or left."

He throws up his hands in exasperation. "Since childhood, he showed no interest in literature, no matter how many books I gave him. No curiosity about the world around him. He had craved building kits, erector sets, anything having to do with math or science. He turned into a staid, unadventurous man who mostly holds mind-numbing conversations." Russell gives his friends a sheepish look. "The bottom line is that I don't respect him. Or the other two."

He searches his friends' eyes, one by one. "Does that make me a bad person? Regarding my own children with contempt?"

Rebecca leans forward. "Sounds like you've been judgmental of them their entire lives. Perhaps we would have been as well, but only in our minds. You don't have to approve of their politics or lifestyle to love them." She weighs her words carefully.

"You are seeing your kids in black and white. Their beliefs, political or otherwise, are only a part of who they are. That doesn't negate the whole person."

"She's right, Russell," Deanna says. "No, you're not a bad person, but you've been cold-hearted as a father. You gave your kids financial support but dismissed them as people. You are not responsible for how your kids turned out, but you are accountable for the blanket condemnation, the verbal abuse."

"It's not too late," Max says. "No matter how old they are, at some basic level your boys need their father. It's possible to recognize the parts of them that are admirable rather than to dwell on the negatives. You must accept them for who they are, not what you want them to be."

Their comments remind Russell of his own parents, who were always pushing him toward their vision of a good life. They could not accept him as his own person with aspirations of his own. He eventually did carry out their dreams for him, but at what price? He recalls a recent funeral he attended for a professor emeritus at NYU. The memorial tributes concentrated on the man's warm and loving relationships with his wife, children, grandchildren. They were so heartfelt. What will they say about me, he muses, beyond a list of my academic achievements? He has ruptured connections with nearly every one of his offspring. There is only Allison left to acknowledge his tender, affectionate side as a father. Still, he hesitates.

"Could you refrain from commenting if your children and grandchildren held deplorable political and social viewpoints?" he asks the group. "If they were Trumpians?"

Malaika studies him before speaking. "They're your family. Try to find the good in each of them," she says. "And enjoy a relationship based on those qualities."

Russell considers what his friends are telling him. "I know I should let go of the resentment, the condemnation. But I'm not sure I can do it."

"You are eighty years old, my friend," Deanna says. "You don't have much time left to make amends."

Russell shrugs. "I'll try," he stammers. "Okay, I'll try to patch things up." He's not quite convinced it's even possible.

♀

"Keith," Deanna says. "You've been so quiet. How are you doing?"

"Everything is hunky-dory," he says without missing a beat. "My legs are unsteady. I've mostly lost my sense of smell and taste. My guitar fingers wait for 'on' times. Sara will sooner or later have to care for me full-time. And I'm dependent on medicine to function. Besides that, I'm good." He sits back on the couch with a playful dance in his eyes.

Everyone exchanges knowing glances. "Guess we can move on," Russell says.

"Same ole Keith," Deanna adds. "Still keeping to himself."

Keith gives a soft moan. "I'm really not up for a conversation about my health. Right now, my hands are functioning. If you bring me the guitar, I'll sing a song I wrote for you. It's called 'We Knew Each Other at the Start.'"

The friends sit back and listen to the ballad, which captures images of their years together. It's like watching a home movie as the verses evoke memories that spark delight and elicit groans. The lyrics recall the civil rights and anti-war struggles and the camaraderie they had forged together. And the playful times that had brought joy to their lives. He conjures up their days at Woodstock romping barefoot in the mud to the music of Jefferson Airplane, Joan Baez, The Who, Janis Joplin. He pays homage to Washington Square Park, the West End Bar, their cafeteria at City College, and the South Lawn. He sings about Max's celebratory calls to each of them in April 1975 when the Vietnam War was officially over. The gang cheers, almost drowning Keith out. And he ends with an ad hoc tribute to their enduring communitarian spirit.

"Nothing can match that," Deanna says with wistful tears in her eyes.

"Bravo!" Max shouts out.

Rebecca claps her hands and the others join in. After the applause dies down, she says, "Let's hear some of the anti-war songs we shared back in the day."

Keith brightens. "Can do," he says. "At least as long as my fingers hold out."

"Where's the harmonica?" Max asks.

"It surrendered to Mr. Parkinson," Keith quips. "But that's okay. I've learned to accommodate myself to the disease's will."

They settle in as Keith strums several of their old favorites. As soon as he concludes "I-Feel-Like-I'm-Fixin-to-Die Rag," they whoop and holler in appreciation. Together they sing "If I had a Hammer" and "Kumbaya." There is a magical mood in the air as they allow themselves to succumb to nostalgia. The daunting impairments and challenges of old age fade away as they immerse themselves in their youth. It feels as though time has stood still.

After an hour, Keith says, "I'm tired. Can someone help me to my room?"

26
Second Day: Linked Throughout the Decades

RUSSELL STAGGERS into the kitchen, craving a cup of coffee. He's a morning person, always has been, but can't seem to get started without the caffeine surge. He used to drink several cups a day. But recently, after more than one cup, he becomes agitated, shaking like a wet dog. The cooks have already brewed a large pot for them, and he inhales the aroma before pouring himself a mugful. He sips contentedly, relieved to have a second alone.

His long-standing habit of writing for three hours every morning has given way to briefer stretches since retirement. He mostly composes short opinion pieces for online publications rather than scholarly articles. He comments on Facebook and Twitter, now X. Much of the time, he mulls over national and international events for inspiration. Today, however, he contemplates last night's conversation. Does the world need yet another critique from him? Perhaps he should put more energy into his relationship with his family.

Russell lays out eight pills on the table and scowls. Before he can swallow them, he hears the thump of Keith's deliberate footsteps and proceeds to help him into the kitchen. He serves his friend a steaming cup of coffee, black like his.

"I'm supporting the entire pharmaceutical industry," Russell says dryly as Keith eyes the array of medicine. "Doctor's orders. All of them. Since my heart attacks."

"Me, too," Keith says. "Couldn't function without my Sinemet tablets or whatever the generic is called." His hands are shaky. "The drug has worn off. It usually does by morning." He takes out his pill container along with vitamins and places them on the table. "How ironic," he says. "We're now dependent on Big Pharma. In our youth, we would have been battling against their egregious prices."

"At least we're insured by Medicare. It's our kids and grandkids suffering the most from their profiteering. We must fight for them," Russell says, conscience-stricken over his lack of political engagement in recent years.

"Easy for you to say, pal. I'm depleted of energy these days." Keith appears unruffled despite his trembling hands. "It's up to the younger generation to take up the mantle. I battled big business my entire adult life. Done my share."

Russell lightly touches his pal's arm. "It must be hard to navigate through such a debilitating disease. I can only imagine."

"It's not too bad. Just grateful that I can still play the guitar. And compose songs." His dispassionate demeanor turns tense. "It's Sara I worry about. Before long, she'll be saddled with my full-time care. I don't require much help now. Nonetheless, I'm steadily going downhill." He lowers his voice as if taking Russell into his confidence. "Sara and I have been married for forty years. We've fought side by side against ecological exploiters. Even now, she's at the forefront of the movement. I don't want her to give up everything for me. When the time comes, I intend to go into assisted living despite her resistance. I couldn't live with myself otherwise."

"I suspect you'll have to fight your granddaughter on that as well," Russell says with a sly smile. "From what I've seen, she could be an even more formidable force than your wife."

He gives Keith an appreciative once-over. His appearance has not changed much, like a well-preserved old car. He has the same scruffy beard and longish hair spilling out of a Dutch Boy cap, only now it's silvery white. His fine-featured face has few deep wrinkles or discoloration. His attire, too, has been unaffected by time, except that his denim work shirt and jeans are looser.

Russell rubs his own bald head. "Despite everything, you look great," he says. "None the worse for wear."

Russell fetches two glasses of water, and they both down their pills.

♀

Deanna sits on the patio swing lamenting her self-indulgent binging at brunch that morning. The table was laden with a variety of tempting goodies: Belgian waffles with strawberries and whipped cream; quiche Lorraine, freshly baked; assorted bagels and cream cheese; English muffins; a choice of jellies; and a large bowl of sliced fruit. She couldn't resist despite her resolution to restrain herself.

Rebecca comes out of the house and pulls up a chair next to her.

"It's your fault," Deanna says, patting her stomach in disgust. "Forcing such delectable fare on me."

"Don't you think it's time to give up dieting? For an old lady, you look fabulous. Who are you trying to impress anyway? Just enjoy yourself this weekend."

"I know. I shouldn't care about my weight. I'm a dyed-in-the-wool feminist." Deanna stares down at her feet, avoiding Rebecca's gaze. "The truth is that I obsess about my appearance. Aging is supposed to give us freedom from worrying about our looks, but I find myself more concerned than ever." She pauses, embarrassed. "Some people try to hide their age. I make a point of announcing it as a test. I look forward to hearing, 'You don't look that old.' It boosts my morale. Unfortunately, it's not always forthcoming these days." Deanna has a pained expression. "Remember how I used to turn heads?"

"Yup. I was a little in awe of you. You had the whole package."

"And now I'm wrinkled, bent over, and afflicted with arthritis." Deanna sighs. "I miss jogging. It released my anxiety, made me feel free of cares. Nowadays my knees hurt so badly I can barely walk." She stares at her friend. "We had such an indominable will and sense of invincibility when we were young, didn't we?"

Rebecca thinks about her father, who told her that he intended to age gracefully. "Dad had argued that it's too easy to grumble about the inevitable downsides," she says. "He would say, 'Since you can't stop it, embrace it. But make sure you hold onto your core values and purpose in life.' It helped that he had a charming sense of humor—obviously not something I inherited."

"Nope. But you have his wit," Deanna assures her.

"My father had such a positive outlook on life. Then again, he died before he had to cope with chronic illnesses and retirement like us."

Malaika comes out of the house and sits on the steps near the swing. She is dressed more casually today. She has discarded the head wrap, exposing her clipped salt and pepper afro. She is wearing white flared jeans, a blue striped T-shirt, and sneakers. "Such somber faces," she says. "You both seem as though someone has died."

"We are grieving for our youth," Rebecca says. "The Grim Reaper has abducted it."

"Hmm," Malaika says with a weak smile. She softly squeezes Rebecca's shoulder.

The three women sit in companionable silence. The day is hot, but the porch fan cools them off like a gentle sea breeze. They catch faint whiffs of the vibrant display of red and yellow roses along the side of the house. The scent is mingled with that of white and pink peonies on the other side of the porch. The neatly cut lawn is bordered by wildflowers, sundry small and large plants, and sculptured bushes. They can hear the distant sound of the Hudson River as it courses south.

"It feels good being here with you guys," Rebecca says. "I haven't devoted much time to developing friendships over the years. There's lots of acquaintances but no confidants." She taps her fingers on the arms of the wooden chair, musing about relationships. "I didn't miss the closeness with other people when Susan was with me. After she died, I had my work. Retirement made clear how alone I am."

"Did you ever try seeking a new partner?" Deanna asks.

"Actually, I did," Rebecca confides. "It was a disaster. I went out with three women I met online through OkCupid." She snickers. "The first turned out to have multiple chronic illnesses. She was seeking a caregiver not a significant other. I didn't mind tending to Susan, but I'm not willing to take on someone new. The second one was ready to move in after only three dates. Her neediness freaked me out. The third was decent enough, but her politics were to the right of the Koch Brothers." She shrugs. "I'm through with finding another mate. I don't even think I have the patience to break in another relationship. Too much effort at my age."

"Same here," Deanna says. "Sam and I had settled into a satisfying, affectionate marriage, but it took time and inordinate effort to hammer out our differences."

She dredges up the litany of conflicts they had to work through. "He wanted to move to the East Coast, but I preferred the warmth of California. We fought over that for years. Then there was the issue of children. Angela was enough for me, but Sam would have liked more. I just couldn't go through the adoption process again. I don't think he ever got over that. He had insisted on us buying a huge house because, I suspect, he hoped that I would eventually give in."

Deanna cups her chin in her palm as she contemplates the concessions they made to each other over the years. "We even differed as parents. I was strict, and Sam had such a soft touch. In the end, the disagreements had melted away, but I don't want to make compromises again at this point in my life."

"Tell us about Sam," Rebecca says.

Deanna touches her small, antique locket with his picture inside. "He was a fiery redhead, freckles over his entire body. Sam was tall, six feet three, with a gap-toothed grin and ruddy complexion. He reminded me of Howdy Doody. And he had such elongated fingers, piano hands really. They stretched to nine notes. He was quite the musician. When he played, he was as intense as when he performed surgery."

She gives a weak smile, remembering a holiday debacle. "One Thanksgiving, Sam cut two fingers while carving the turkey. We had to rush him to the emergency room. He was so worried about not being able to operate anymore. I, on the other hand, was mostly concerned about the spoiled meal—there were twenty people at the table and blood on everything. Sometimes I had such misplaced priorities."

Deanna hugs herself. "It does get lonely without him." She tilts her face toward Malaika. "Despite everything, at least you still have Darryl."

"Yes," she says. "And he's a very loving man."

"How did you meet him?" Rebecca asks.

"At NYU. He was one of two Black law professors. I took several courses with him. He was my secret crush. I never even told either of you about him. And Darryl was careful to maintain a professional distance from me." Malaika has a glint in her eyes. "But I was smitten. He had a tidy afro, a wide mustache, and thick brows that he often furrowed in disapproval at his students. In the classroom, he had a forbidding demeanor and was demanding. In reality, he turned out to be a teddy bear." She closes her eyes, contemplating her first images of him.

"Years passed," she continues. "Then one day, I was introduced to him at a party. In DC. He had moved to Georgetown Law School. I wasn't even sure he remembered me. We began seeing each other on and off for a long while before we married. He was hesitant, mostly because of our age difference—fifteen years. He turned ninety-five last week.

"Darryl has been good for me. His upbeat and easygoing nature tempers my intensity. We went through a challenging period in our marriage and split up for a while, mostly because of my workaholism. Then we went into therapy, figured some things out, and reconciled. Through everything, his love has been steadfast." She breaks off to regain her composure. "It's hard to accept that he's dying."

Deanna and Rebecca sit down on each side of their friend and wrap their arms around her.

♀

The men are sitting around the swimming pool with rolled-up pants, dipping their toes into the cool water. To relieve himself from the searing heat, Max tucks his long white ponytail into his cap and splashes his face with water. Despite the temperature, he feels relaxed, at home with his companions.

"Have either of you requested your dossier under the Freedom of Information Act?" Max asks. "Mine is fifty pages, most of it redacted. I was considered a subversive."

"Me too," Keith says, with a bit of pride. "The terms *insurgent* and *agitator* are dotted throughout my record."

"You would think that the FBI had better things to do," Max says. "Their COINTELPRO Project had been zealous. Apparently, agents followed us around for years. My file indicates that our activities also were infiltrated by informants."

Russell leans back on his hands and tilts his face upwards. The sun is peaking in and out of the clouds. "The FBI intimidated my parents as well. The agents called them communists. And I discovered that the IRS audited my mother and father for years." He flashes back to his mother's hysterical phone calls during his first year of graduate school. "'I keep getting threatening messages,'" she had screamed at him through the line. "'They're going to take revenge on us if you don't stop your political shenanigans.'" She never actually knew who the harassers were, but she was sure "they" meant business.

Russell scrunches his face. "The Bureau also enlisted Columbia benefactors to demand that the board of trustees revoke my teaching assistantship. Fortunately, the directors refused to cave in."

"What sleazes," Max says. "It took me forever to obtain my records. Once I did, the amount of personal information they had collected on me was chilling. It went on even after I fled to Canada."

"For me," Keith says, "the surveillance continued during my years with Greenpeace. The FBI used the full array of weapons in its toolbox against us greenies. We were harassed, intimidated, threatened, and arrested on dubious charges. Agents released phony leaflets and wrote anonymous letters castigating our actions." His voice is trembling with anger. "And its massive domestic surveillance is ongoing. Not just environmental groups but any protesters seeking social justice. Black Lives Matter. Native Americans. LGBTQ. Trans. Radical feminists. And much of it is legal since 9/11. We are living in a veritable police state."

"We're too old for them to care about us anymore," Russell quips. "We could blow up buildings and still fly under their radar."

Max's face takes on a self-satisfied smirk. "Old age does have its benefits."

Soon the clouds drift eastward, subjecting the men to the relentless strength of the midday sun. After baking in the heat for an hour, Russell says, "Anyone up for the game room? It's air-conditioned."

"Sure," Keith says. "Though I'm not sure what I can do. My coordination is shot."

"Let's give it a try," Max says, as he dries his feet with a towel. "I heard that exercise is good for Parkinson's."

"So the experts say," Keith retorts. "Easier said than done."

As they enter the enormous room, Max is impressed by the

game tables: There's foosball, ping-pong, air hockey, pool, shuffleboard, darts. "Rebecca sure knows how to pick a place. Let's start with rotating ping-pong."

Keith groans. "Too much for me. I'll watch."

Max and Russell compete for twenty minutes then flop onto chairs, sweating. "I'm too old for this," Russell says, only half in jest.

"I used to be quite good," Max says. "Haven't played for a long while. I enjoyed that."

"Let's try our hands at darts," Russell suggests.

Keith is uncertain. "I think I'm too unsteady on my legs, though it is my Parkinson's 'on time.'"

"We'll play seated," Russell says.

The men pull over folding chairs and engage in several matches. They give Keith a handicap to level the score. "Yes!" he shouts when he wins the first round. His friends abruptly rescind his advantage.

"Pool, anyone?" Max says.

"I'll sit this one out," Keith says. "The experts call for exercise, not an endurance contest."

Russell is no match for Max, who gives his buddy a playful grin. "My son and I play regularly. I have a pool table in my rec room."

After two more games, Russell throws his hands up. "I yield to the maestro. Let's call it a day."

"Let's go find the women," Max says. "And grab some beer."

♀

Deanna stands alone at the edge of the pool, barefoot. She is wearing a black one-piece bathing suit concealed by a long, floral shirt. She had to work up the courage to put on the swimsuit, shy about displaying her body. Her once-admired figure is fleshier and, despite herself, she feels self-conscious about the buildup of cellulite on her thighs and the dark veins on her legs. As usual, Deanna is disgusted with herself. She says, under her breath, "Nobody should capitulate to the unrealistic portrayals of women in bikini ads, least of all a person eighty years old." She takes off the cover-up.

Deanna observes the white and blue glitter patterns of the circulating water, reflected by the sun like ice crystals. She is at once dazzled and mesmerized by the swirling movement. The cool, clear liquid calls to her. She surveys the grounds, but there is nobody in sight. She dives in.

She swims effortlessly back and forth, unencumbered by the arthritic pain, fatigue, or inertia that has impeded her in recent years. She glides through the water in freestyle, her mind liberated of concerns. She does the butterfly for a few lengths, and then moves on to the breaststroke, her legs following with frog kicks. She feels as carefree as she had in the past when jogging. After she tires, she floats on her back, eyes closed. Deanna speculates on why she had surrendered to her infirmities without a fight, foregoing any exercise. I'm a physician, she reproaches herself. I should have known better. She vows to swim every day when she returns home. Take a membership in a club.

She is startled by the sound of voices. The men open the gate and park themselves on chaise lounges, beers in hand.

"I'll join you soon," Russell tells her. "As soon as I finish my brew."

Max and Keith salute her with their cans, and she waves back. Deanna is so soothed by the swim that she has left behind any unease about her appearance. The men, who have put on swimming trunks, certainly don't have any reservations about exposing their bodies, she laughs to herself. "Throw me one of the pool floats," she instructs Russell. "The one with the headrest."

Deanna lies back on the raft, listening to their indistinct chatter and hoots of laughter. They are like teenagers again, ribbing each other, cracking jokes, parodying political figures. They haven't changed much, she notes happily.

Malaika wanders out to the pool after her nap. She has put on a bathing suit, covered by a T-shirt that says, "Black Women Are Powerful."

"Great T-shirt," Max says.

"My daughter bought it for me. I thought you guys would get a kick out of it. I don't usually advertise my politics on my chest. Too gauche."

Malaika sits with the men and joins in their convivial exchanges. Their dialogue now sizzles with snappy repartees, challenging her mind and nourishing her spirits. With them she feels alive, retrieving tucked away pieces of herself. She can't remember the last time she abandoned herself to unmitigated joy, and deep, satisfying belly laughs.

Eventually Rebecca saunters out onto the pool deck, fully dressed. Her eyes are heavy from sleep, and she yawns.

"Hey, Sleeping Beauty," Max calls out.

"Aren't you going to swim?" Deanna asks. "The water is delightful."

"Everyone's going in," Keith adds. "And you're going to roast in that attire."

Rebecca has no intention of swimming. She has an aversion to pools, always has. She doesn't like the feel of chlorine on her skin, stinging in her eyes, or water in her ears. But mainly swimming is too taxing for her taste, and she doesn't see the point of just standing in the water.

"The dudes just want me to bare my voluptuous body," she says dryly. "I'm saving it for Prince Charming."

"You are the same ole Becca," Max says. He jumps into the pool, purposely drenching her shoes and pants. Rebecca shoots daggers at him.

One by one, the others follow him into the water. Russell and Max dump Deanna off the raft. She feigns annoyance and then takes part in their games.

They play a rowdy competition of Marco Polo, and Malaika struggles to keep up.

"I'm really out of shape," she says. "And I'm not getting any younger. Can we take a break?"

"Sure," Max says. He moves to the edge of the pool and splashes Rebecca, who is reading a magazine. "Can you get us a beach ball? It's in the storage bin."

She tosses one to him and returns to her reading.

"Ready?" he asks the others. "Let's play volleyball."

"I'm through," Malaika says as she climbs out of the pool.

"Me, too," Keith says. "I'll have to up my Levodopa pills to keep pace with you guys."

Max, Deanna, and Russell whoop it up, hitting the ball back and forth. As it dances through the air, it becomes a blur of rainbow colors. At one point, Max hurls the ball too high, and it lands near Rebecca. She scowls. "Nope. I'm not getting it."

Malaika pitches it back into the water.

"Enough for me," Russell calls out.

"I'm ready to pack it in as well," Max says.

"Guess I'm the grand winner," Deanna shouts, holding her fingers up in a V sign.

♀

"Cocktail hour," Russell announces as everyone gathers on the lawn chairs. He prepares martinis for himself and Keith. Malaika brings out wine and beer for everyone else. Deanna supplies glasses, Max rounds up small outdoor tables, and Rebecca returns with the hors d'oeuvres. The chefs have arranged plates of stuffed mushrooms, bruschetta, fried calamari, cheese and crackers.

"Everything looks yummy," Rebecca says.

"You certainly picked great cooks," Max says.

"I give up," Deanna mutters, digging into the food. "Nobody could resist such a spread."

The sun is setting, and a slight breeze cools the air. The friends watch the orange, yellow, and red blaze spread across the horizon. The rays catch the edges of clouds, shading the sky with gradations of gray, white, and pink. The mood turns mellow as they sip their drinks and snack on appetizers.

Keith beholds the beauty of the place, luxuriating in the greenery, fresh smells of wildflowers and pinecones, and the sounds of rustling leaves, gurgling stream, chirping crickets, and hooting owls. Warmed by the liquor, he says, "I feel so at peace in the countryside." He puts one trembling hand over the other to quell them. "Too bad we're destroying the planet at such a rapid rate. What kind of world are we leaving to our grandkids? I wish I could have done more to protect the splendors of nature, to let future generations take advantage of what Mother Earth has to offer."

"You are only one person, in one organization," Max says. "You did what you could." He sips his beer. "You were an environmental warrior, and I admire you for that."

"Everyone's concerned about climate change these days," says Malaika. "But you were at the cutting edge."

Rebecca leans forward, toward him. "What were some of the highlights of your green campaigns?"

"I'll need another drink for that," Keith says, holding up his glass.

"Two more martinis coming up," Russell says as he stands to make another round.

"Cheers," Keith says, raising his fresh drink shakily in the air. "This should loosen me up a bit." Everyone's eyes are on him. "I held every position imaginable in Greenpeace USA: researcher, campaign director, political strategist, organizer, trainer. But the most satisfying part was participating in direct-action campaigns." He turns to Max. "I learned from you, early on, that organizers must accept danger if they are going to be effective. As we discovered in our youth, you don't get what you don't fight for."

Keith sorts through the mélange of projects, his life work, that are stitched together like patches on a quilt. There is a glint in his eyes as he recounts his crusades against Big Oil. "In 2015," he begins, "Sara and I joined a procession of kayakers intent on blocking a Shell Company drilling rig, Polar Pioneer, from leaving the port in Seattle. The platform was proceeding toward Alaska, ready to plunder the coastline. We formed a physical barrier with a floating line of kayaks. We raised huge banners that said, "Save the Arctic." The skipper steered the rig right through us, almost hitting several of our crafts, but ultimately, he was forced to turn around." Keith's facial muscles are stiff from the Parkinson's, but he manages a satisfied smile.

"Just as dangerous, a month later thirteen climbers suspended themselves on ropes from the St. Johns Bridge in Portland to block a Shell Oil icebreaker, the *Fennica*, from heading to the Arctic to make way for a drilling project. A few of us remained on the walkway above them to assist. Long yellow and red streamers, tied to the dangling protester's harnesses, flapped in the wind. It was a sight to behold. The campaign was a risk everyone had been willing to take to defend one of the only pristine places left on Earth." Keith frowns. "These were only temporary wins. Baby steps. Now the next generation will have to take on the struggle to save the Arctic, indeed the planet itself."

"Tell us more," Malaika says, entranced by his stories.

Keith recalls the early years, before he was affiliated with Greenpeace. He had been moved by the dangers of nuclear power plants and the grassroots forces attempting to stop its spread. To him, the government seemed unconcerned about the dangers of uranium mining, the disposal of radioactive waste, or even a potential accident. "In the late 1970s, I had freelanced," he says. "Against the nuclear power industry. I had helped train several local advocacy groups in civil disobedience tactics."

Rebecca thinks back to the mass anti-nuclear protests she read about in the newspaper. She would have joined the campaigns, but Susan objected. "You're already spread too thin," she had argued. Rebecca relented but cheered them on from the sidelines. "Which ones were you involved with?" she asks.

"Two," he says. "The Clam Shell Alliance in New Hampshire and the Abalone Alliance in California. I coached them in nonviolent, direct-action strategies. For the first one, 1976, we sought to halt construction of the Seabrook Station reactor. Six hundred demonstrators sat down at the proposed construction site. Nine months later, two thousand citizens occupied the spot again. I was arrested, along with hundreds of others. We succeeded in obstructing the construction of the plant for nearly a decade."

"And the other action?" Rebecca says.

"The Diablo Canyon plant eco-event was just as fierce, if not more so. At first, we had fifteen hundred activists with forty-seven arrests. A year later, five thousand individuals rallied against the plant. We also organized pickets against Pacific Gas and Electric offices across California. The plant had been experiencing serious safety concerns. In 1981, nearly thirty thousand activists attempted to close it down. Can you believe they arrested nearly two thousand people? But the ten-day action brought attention to the defects." Keith lets out a soft laugh. "Because of us, the Nuclear Regulatory Commission revoked PG&E's operating license. That cost the company $3 billion in repairs and three years without revenues."

"At least you accomplished something," Max says, "even if you didn't shut down either plant permanently. The confrontations certainly raised public awareness of the hazards of nuclear power. It probably spurred the quest for safer energy sources."

"Unfortunately, we were assisted by the 1979 accident at Three Mile Island," Keith scoffs. "Officials had to remove a hundred tons of damaged uranium fuel from the core. Millions of gallons of contaminated water flowed into the Susquehanna River. Surrounding communities experienced radiation exposure. Reformers flocked to our cause after that."

Keith shakes his head in indignation. "Last year PG&E pulled the plug on Diablo. The irony is that they abandoned the plant because they were losing money, not because of the human costs."

"We nibble at issues," Deanna says. "In college, we had imagined we could transform the world. All we had to offer was commitment and diligence. Later, minor victories felt like successes."

"Exactly," Keith says. "Then again, it was often one step forward, two steps backwards. We would win a victory against deforestation in one place, and the Interior Department would open vast areas of protected forests to indiscriminate logging in another. We devoted years to lobbying Congress for legislation against air and water pollution, and then the regulations were watered down or ignored. Or the budgets for enforcement were eviscerated. Even Greenpeace International's hard-won victory in 1986 against commercial whaling had been short-lived. A few decades later, Japan simply resumed the practice."

Keith watches the sunset, which is fading like his hopes and dreams for environmental justice. He envisions the multitude of powerful bad actors with unlimited funds to outspend any drive to safeguard the natural universe. "There are endless urgent issues to fight for," he continues. "Carbon gases and ozone depletion. Chemical dumping. Poisonous insecticides. Endangered species. Overfishing. Plastic and oil spills in our oceans. Each battle incites well-endowed special interests determined to squash us." He sneers contemptuously. "They call us tree-huggers while global warming is triggering more powerful hurricanes, floods, droughts, and forest fires everywhere. Our very survival is at risk. It's so overwhelming. And discouraging."

"Did you ever regret devoting yourself to environmental causes?" Rebecca asks. "Or giving up your music career?"

He chews over her first question. "No reservations at all," he says. "It had been hard in the beginning, of course. Prior to Greenpeace, I supported myself as a bartender. Even after joining the organization, it was a while before the group had sufficient funds to pay me anything close to a living wage. Sara and I lived from hand to mouth for years." Keith looks at

Rebecca. "As for my music, it's been integral to everything I do. I became the go-to person for arranging benefit concerts for various Greenpeace crusades. I raised money before that too. The shows helped support the anti-nuclear-power resistance. I had scores of contacts from my Greenwich Village days. I wrote and performed songs for the shows and sang at most of our civil disobedience campaigns."

"You've had a remarkable life," Russell says. "It's a privilege to be your friend." He glances at Deanna, who has her arms crossed over her body to warm herself. Russell slips into the house, returns with a blanket, and covers her. She squeezes his hand.

"Why Greenpeace?" Max inquires. "There are so many ecology groups."

"Eeny meeny miny moe," Keith says with a playful twinkle in his eyes.

"Hmm...Guess you're through with us," Malaika says.

"Okay," Keith relents. "Greenpeace had fit best with my ethical principles. The organization takes a biocentric view of the world. Every species has intrinsic value, equal to humans. And like you, my comrades, the group recognizes that patchwork reform is not sufficient in the long run. That people must ultimately alter the way they live and produce products."

His friends are listening with rapt attention. "At the time, Greenpeace USA was populated by people who came from the same mold as me—as us. Most of them had political experience and insight from years of grassroots activism with diverse movements during the 1960s and 70s. They advocated direct action to achieve their goals but not violence. No destruction of property. I also appreciated that none of the Greenpeace affiliates obtained any money from government sources or big business. Not a cent. They refused to be compromised."

Keith becomes pensive again. "Perhaps, on occasion, we could have been more aggressive, like Earth First! But we stuck to civil disobedience, though periodically Greenpeace did engage in more radical acts of sabotage."

His eyes light up as he recounts one of his favorite events. "In April 1990 we had bolted a steel metal drum holding a Greenpeace activist to the railroad tracks leading to DuPont facilities in California and New Jersey. We were protesting the corporation's production of ozone-depleting chemicals. Boy, did we cause havoc." He halts briefly. "Nonetheless, I mostly conveyed my more militant side through music."

"Play us some of your songs," Rebecca says.

"Perhaps later. I'm too tired now. Besides, it's a Parkinson's 'off' time. My hands are shaking too much."

The six of them sit wordlessly for a while. From the porch, the chefs break the tranquility. "Dinner's ready."

27
Evening: Preserving the Moment

"ANOTHER BANQUET," Russell says, inhaling the yeasty, slightly sweet scent of freshly baked bread. He helps himself to a slice, along with a healthy portion of eggplant lasagna, topped with arugula pesto.

"Please pass the salad," Deanna says. She is determined to forego the calorie-laden main dish that is calling to her with its pungent roasted garlic aroma.

Rebecca eyes Deanna with amusement. "The lasagna is scrumptious," she says. "So is the artichoke soup." In a taunting voice she adds, "It's really creamy."

"Bet you're saving room for dessert," Max chuckles.

Deanna digs into her salad with feigned gusto.

"Here's to us," Malaika says, raising her wine glass. They clink drinks high in the air.

Max turns to Russell. "What was it like teaching during the pandemic?"

"It was a mixed bag. The students craved campus life, and for me, Zoom was a steep learning curve. I made my share of embarrassing mistakes." Russell squirms in his seat. "I couldn't figure out how to use the shared screen to show them points I had previously written on the blackboard. Instead, I prepared small posters with a magic marker and held them up to the monitor. It wasn't until weeks into the semester that an undergrad shyly informed me that the words appeared backward to the class."

He laughs. "Another time, I figured out how to place the kids into separate 'rooms' for discussions but not how to move myself in and out of them. They were totally on their own the first time I tried. And I was constantly having to be reminded to unmute myself. But, for the most part, the students seemed to take my ineptitude in stride. For them I was simply a clumsy old professor who couldn't keep up with the latest technology.

"The whole experience was strange. Some kids would be lying on pillows in bed. Others had roommates in pajamas running around in the background. I did welcome seeing their faces up close although I was uncomfortable staring at my own mug for an hour and a half. Overall, I was relieved to get back into the classroom."

Russell cringes. "Mostly I felt claustrophobic after two semesters at home all day with Beth. I thought we would kill each other." He remembers the constant battles that escalated over time. They were like two tigers defending their territory.

"I wish I could have stayed home," Malaika interjects. "Injustices don't disappear just because of a pandemic. And poor people don't always have a computer. We had to keep the law office open. I mandated masks and kept everyone six feet apart." She gives a sheepish laugh. "Because of my hearing loss, I could barely understand what my clients were saying through their masks. Even with my hearing aids on. It was mortifying."

"Why mortifying?" Rebecca says. "It comes with age." She points to her own nearly invisible hearing aids. "I couldn't follow much of our conversation without these babies."

Max nods. "Me, too. Dependent on them. Too bad there isn't an assistive devise for my cognitive impairment."

Russell turns to him. "Was the pandemic hard on you?"

"Not so much. It occurred way before my memory issues were noticeable. I did have to put several projects on hold for months because of the economic uncertainty. Instead, I worked at home on a building design for a provincial competition."

"Did you win?" Rebecca goads him.

Max grins. "First prize. COVID gave me enough free time to develop my most innovative proposal. It was for a community center complex in Vancouver that included two buildings with fitness rooms, a senior center, multi-purpose spaces, a library, two sports fields, a field track, several parks and playgrounds, an ice-skating rink, and a large indoor pool. I focused on devising the most environmentally responsible and resource-efficient structures possible. It was my proudest accomplishment, and I retired shortly after the complex was completed." He casts a knowing glance at Keith. "The buildings and their surroundings won prizes from Canada's top environmental organizations."

"That's impressive. What a grand way to retire." Keith throws his hands in the air. "I just gave up, became totally disaffected after Trump's election and the pointless spread of COVID. I couldn't relate to the idiocy of the anti-vaxxers. And these same individuals were openly vocalizing their antagonism toward environmental causes, notably climate change. It had been too much for me, so I retired."

He pulls a face as he thinks about his last months at Greenpeace. "Many of us in the movement became depressed. We were holed up at home, like moles, communicating through Zoom. To avoid crowds, direct actions were postponed. At the same time, Trump and his Republican lackeys were taking advantage of the crisis by pushing through one anti-environmental directive after another. It had been a boon for opportunist corporate polluters."

"At least the younger generation seems to have more sense," Rebecca adds. "They're more conscious of global warming."

Keith nods. "Exactly. I'm counting on them to replace old fogies like me."

"My younger union colleagues had seemed overly anxious to trade me in," Rebecca says with a trace of bitterness. "But I have to acknowledge that they performed heroically during the emergency situation." She leans back in the chair. "SEIU staff couldn't afford to burrow in because the healthcare workers we represent were risking their lives every day. They mostly treated those nitwits who had refused the vaccine. The hospitals and nursing homes had been conspicuously understaffed. We were constantly on call to pressure facilities to relieve the overworked caregivers on duty.

"All the same, the contagion turned out to be good for our business," Rebecca says, rolling her eyes. "Nurses, orderlies, aides, what have you, clamored to join the union. It finally occurred to them that they were essential service providers who merited decent pay and benefits. We couldn't sign them up fast enough." Rebecca tenses as she clenches her fist. "So many of our finest direct care workers died from COVID."

Tears well up in Deanna's eyes.

Russell regards her. "What's wrong?"

Everyone stops eating and waits.

Russell squeezes her hand. "What's up?"

Deanna tries to suppress the deeply buried grief that has rushed to the surface. Her emotions feel too raw to share. She is reeling with longing for Sam and peeks at the door as if he would enter at any moment. After a prolonged quiet, she whispers, "Sam died from the Coronavirus." A few tears escape and she dabs them with a napkin. "We had such exciting plans. He intended to retire at the end of the year. We were going to join Doctors Without Borders. Perhaps head to Kenya or Nigeria. We had been anticipating the next phase of our lives. A new adventure. Then the pandemic struck a blow to everything."

She becomes momentarily silent, as if reliving her well-worn grief. "Sam had been one of the first pulmonologists to volunteer. The hospital struggled to find protective equipment, and he distributed what was available to the nurses and assistants first. He was forced to treat patients without even a decent mask. And this was before the vaccine was approved." Deanna manages a weak smile.

"Sam always put others before himself. One day, he came home with a fever and persistent cough. He was overcome with fatigue and collapsed on his bed. Never saw him do that before. He kept insisting that he just needed rest. His breathing became worse, and a few days later I took him to the emergency room, where they put him on a ventilator. After nearly three weeks in intensive care, he died." Deanna appears lost, as if in her own world. "I don't understand why he hadn't been more level-headed about his own safety," she murmurs. "And I should have made sure he had a proper mask."

"You can't blame yourself," Rebecca says. "The government was morally obligated to provide protective gear for every frontline worker."

"You're right," Deanna says. "More victim blaming." Her expression is grim. "I saw so many senseless deaths because of Trump's heartless unwillingness to take charge before the infection spread. At the start, Sam ranted and raved about the administration's incompetence."

A silence engulfs the table. "How long were you and he together?" Rebecca asks.

"It seems like forever—fifty-two years. We met in the Peace Corps, Costa Rica. Then we toughed it out, side by side, in medical school. He had been my lifelong companion through the ups and downs of our lives."

She holds up her glass for more wine, and Russell fills it. "He stood by me during the worst periods of my abortion work. I don't know if I could have handled the vicious attacks without him."

"What was it like?" Malaika says.

"There were some nasty times. I performed abortions part-time for my entire career. At home, I received constant threatening letters accusing me of executing babies. Some said they intended to murder me and my family. We had to set up security cameras. My Twitter and Facebook accounts were filled with hostile, frightening messages. I called the police more than once when protesters at the clinic became violent. Even Sam's practice was endangered. He lost a lot of referrals because of me. His partners were not happy. It definitely left its mark on us."

Max studies Deanna as the harrowing story sinks in around the table. "You're an inspiring woman," he says. "So many abortion doctors are shot or forced into hiding. More than a few gave up. You're dauntless, always have been, even in our college years. And it sounds like you married quite an extraordinary man."

"Sam does sound special," Russell mumbles. "You were lucky to have found him." As he speaks, the words taste rancid, like sour milk. He is caught off guard by feelings of jealousy, self-reproach, resentment, and longing. He had given up the love of his youth, his soulmate, for what? To chase after sex? Keep his so-called freedom? None of his three wives matched Deanna's intellect, savvy, doggedness, and commitment. She is still lovely, he thinks, wrinkles and all. He fixes himself another drink.

Deanna brushes off Russell's disingenuous remark. "Yes, Deanna says, "he was a kind, gentle person. He even tolerated my parents, more than they deserved. And he had served as a buffer between me and them." She stiffens, remembering her mother's perpetual scowl. "I received the most grief about the abortions from my parents. Don't know how it leaked from California to the Bronx, as though they had a direct pipeline to my house. They threatened to disown me. I suspect Mom increased her prayers instead. They harangued me during every visit, but Sam wouldn't give up on them. He kept trying to explain that I was helping desperate people, that, for me, it was a calling. But their heads were stuffed with religious nonsense. They deemed reproductive rights too sacrilegious to even contemplate."

She scans the dinner table. "You should have seen some of my patients. Girls who had been sexually abused, women who were raped, single parents with three or more children, fetuses with severe physical and mental problems, people who didn't want kids." She polishes off her wine. "And it became worse in states where restrictions increasingly kicked in."

"Everything turned bleak and desperate when Trump and his Republican sycophants took over," Malaika chimes in. "The politics of hate and division increased my workload. Too bad it also didn't boost my clients' paychecks. We had untold pro bono cases."

The pressure in Malaika's office had risen to a fever pitch as cases of wrongdoings piled up. She recalls the barrage of calls for help with everything from unlawful evictions and foreclosure notices to wrongful denial of government benefits and police brutality. "We couldn't keep up with the egregious executive orders cascading from the White House. They eased so many antidiscrimination protections that people of color were denied FHA housing loans, food stamps, welfare, Medicaid, even certain educational opportunities. Others suffered too—transgender people, women experiencing sexual harassment and domestic abuse, immigrants subject to deportation, Muslims. . ." Her voice trails off.

Malaika closes her eyes and sighs, taking a moment to calm herself down. "Voter suppression was rampant," she goes on. "And there wasn't much we could do about that on an individual basis. We had a few cases of personal intimidation, which we won. But stricter ID laws, fewer polling sites, longer waiting times, insufficient machines, and excessive voter purging, all aimed at curbing the Black and Latino vote, had to be fought through class action suits. We signed on, of course. And any remedies through Congress were an exercise in futility. Republicans fought us with every available resource in their kit. We were overwhelmed, but the resistance galvanized me, the whole office." She pushes the half-eaten lasagna away and stares at her empty wine glass. "I'm played out."

"Me too," Deanna says.

A devilish smile crosses Rebecca's lips. "I think we need some comfort food." She rises to help the cooks fetch dessert.

"Let's have some music," Max says after dinner, bringing Keith his guitar.

"It's your lucky day. It's 'on-time' for Mr. Parkinson. I feel so good I'm going to try the harmonica. Haven't used that in a long while." Max helps him set everything up.

"Old protest songs again?" Keith asks.

"Of course," the crew shouts in unison.

"For Max," Keith says, as he begins with "Draft Dodger Rag." He moves on to "Blowin' in the Wind," "Bring 'Em Home," and "Universal Soldier." He periodically plays the harmonica, surprising himself with his unaccustomed dexterity.

"Not bad for an old man," Russell says. He turns to Deanna and winks. "And you're still off-key."

"Did you think aging would transform me into Joan Baez?" she retorts. She scrutinizes him. He's nearly bald and stooped over, she tells herself, but he still radiates charm. Deanna shrugs, kicks off her shoes, and curls up on the couch.

Keith performs a few of his own compositions until he is spent. "One more," he says and sings the song again that he wrote for the reunion, picking skillfully improvised breaks. The rendition is met with raucous applause. Rebecca kisses him on the cheek as she helps put away his instruments.

A gentle breeze of affection wafts among them. The music once more arouses a nostalgia for their earlier days together. And the feeling of connection is palpable. They have been linked throughout the decades with gossamer threads, like the strands of a spider's web.

"Enough kumbaya," Max says. "How about a game of charades? Get a bit of competition going. Guys against gals."

"That won't be much of a challenge," Rebecca says, with a sly smile.

"We'll see about that," Russell counters, signaling a V-sign to Max and Keith.

Max retrieves two baskets from the kitchen, along with scraps of paper and pens. "Okay," he says. "Each team jots down ten words or phrases and puts them in the bin."

As they work in their separate corners, the living room is punctuated with sounds of aah! yes! yech! right! ugh!

"We're ready," Russell says, with a smirk.

They roll the dice, and the women win. They go first. Deanna chuckles as she glances at her slip of paper. She pantomimes sports, baseball, World Series, and never.

"The Seattle Mariners," Rebecca yells out.

"How did the two of you know that?" Keith demands.

"My dad was a baseball fan," Deanna says. "He constantly talked baseball until the day he died."

Rebecca sneers at Keith. "And I've followed sports my whole life."

"Okay," Max says. "One point for the women." He realizes that his side is in trouble since they loaded their basket with professional sports terms.

"Our turn," Russell says. He reads, "Watching a romantic comedy," and makes a face. His team barely figures it out in time. They are stumped on *The First Wives Club*, *Wuthering Heights*, and *Pride and Prejudice*. After ten rounds, the women trounce the men, thirteen to seven.

"Another go-around," Keith says.

The following match is closer; the women win eleven to nine.

"Next time we'll have to divide the teams more fairly," Rebecca says smugly.

Russell swats her lightly with his fingertips.

"Charades has been good exercise for the ole brain," Max says. "Noah and Joanna would approve. They're forever pushing crossword puzzles on me."

"To tell the truth," Deanna admits, "the game was fun but a bit taxing on me. My head doesn't work as well as it used to. Sometimes, when I'm in a conversation, I forget ordinary words. They're on the tip of my tongue, but I can't quite retrieve them—makes me feel so stupid."

"I'm not having a great time of it myself these days," Rebecca says. "I'm constantly battling my rebellious brain. After reading a book or watching a movie, I often can't remember the title." She curls her lips in disgust. "Not easy to make recommendations to others."

"Ditto," Russell jumps in. "I'm having a hard time with names, sometimes even with people I know."

"What's my name?" Deanna teases.

Russell scratches his head. "Give me a minute and I'll come up with it."

Keith strains to smile. "My memory is intact right now, but I know Mr. Parkinson will attack the ole noggin sooner or later. That seems to be the usual trajectory. I mostly try to live in the moment. What choice do I have? Do any of us have?"

Malaika laughs. "My eyes and ears have given out." A blush creeps up her neck. "Recently, I asked a bank teller for the balance on my account. I had forgotten to put in my hearing aids and couldn't catch a word, even when she repeated the figure three times. She ended up writing the amount on a piece of paper. You should have seen her face—and everyone else's on the line behind me—as I fumbled through my handbag for glasses."

"Nobody said old age would be easy," Max says. "I just never knew it would be this challenging." He raises his eyebrows. "Johanna surreptitiously tests me to see how far my dementia has advanced thinking I don't realize. In fact, I periodically experiment on myself. It's unnerving not to know for sure."

"I already hear the assisted living facility summoning me," Keith says. "When I get too disabled to care for myself, that's where I'm headed. Don't want to burden Sara any more than necessary."

"Does that scare you?" Max asks.

"A little. Mainly since I could eventually become so incapacitated that I'll end up in a nursing home. I hear they're abhorrent places."

"I can vouch for that," Deanna says. "After Dad died, I brought Mom to California. In due course, her mental and physical condition deteriorated to a point where I couldn't care for her at home anymore. She spent the last years of her life in a nursing home. Not even my difficult mother deserved such squalid conditions. If I didn't visit daily, she would have been forced to lie in bed for a good portion of the day or sit in leaking diapers for hours on end."

Deanna shudders as she dredges up more details from her mother's stay. "You wouldn't believe the tasteless mush they called food. And the overwhelming stench in the air, a mix of stale urine and feces barely masked by disinfectants and ammonia. The place was worse than I ever could have imagined. And it wiped out the assets she and Dad had managed to save."

There is deep anxiety in her eyes. "With Sam gone," she says, "the thought of ending up in a place like that terrifies me. But I'm not going to impose myself on my daughter or grandkids."

Deanna's description of the nursing home triggers a dizzying array of emotions that Malaika struggles to sort out—despair over her imminent role as Darryl's full-time caregiver but also her own prospects as she advances in age. "It's not easy," she finally says, her voice cracking, "having someone dependent on you for their everyday needs. I love Darryl, but I'm overwhelmed by his intensifying disabilities." She stares at the ground. "Of course, I would never put him in an institution."

There is a pregnant hush in the room as everyone envisions the daunting road ahead. "Who is going to take care of me?" Malaika blurts out, glancing around as if seeking answers. "I, too, won't intrude on my children's lives. I'll stay firm about that. But I never actually gave much thought to the reality of nursing homes or the cost. What a horrible way to end one's life. Is that really my future?"

Max narrows his eyes as he gathers his thoughts. "If we live long enough, it could be where we all end up. Living with either of my children is out of the question for me as well. The topic is a hot potato in our family. Both Noah and Johanna are already insisting on taking me in despite my insistence on staying put. When the time comes, I'll go to a residential care facility despite their protests. I understand that they're not as bad in Canada as in the US, though I would loathe living in an institution of any kind."

Russell squirms in his chair. "My kids wouldn't even offer," he says. "And I'm sure Beth would send me to a nursing home at the first sign of need. No way she'd be willing to care for me long-term. She seemed put upon by the limited attention I had required after my two heart attacks. She's not very nurturing." He snickers. "The only thing that would give her pause is the price tag. She loves money, and if I live to a ripe old age, a nursing home would drain our assets." He pauses as if digesting his words. "Why am I staying with her?"

"Why are you?" Rebecca asks. "She doesn't sound like a loving spouse." Rebecca doesn't wait for Russell's response. "Unlike the rest of you, I have neither a partner nor an adult child to rebuff. I'm truly on my own." She smiles cunningly, like a theatre critic ready to ambush a play. "I'd gladly foist myself on my offspring if I had any." She pivots toward Max and Malaika. "Or any of yours, for that matter."

Her voice takes on a serious tone as she recalls the stories she had heard from the union's health workers. "No," she says, "nursing homes aren't pretty. Our aides and nurses constantly gave us appalling accounts of neglect and abuse, even in the so-called better facilities. I'm not sure what I'm going to do when the time comes, but I'm not stepping foot into one of those places."

"I hate being old!" Deanna hisses. "I don't want to brood about who's going to care for me when my head and body stop functioning." She wrinkles her nose. "Or even think about running out of time..."

"Running out of time for what?" Russell probes.

It had been an offhand remark, and Deanna is not quite certain what she had in mind. Her stomach is churning and she feels queasy. She rummages through her brain. Then the answer comes to her. "Time to fight for things I—we—believe in." She is revved up as she rattles off the litany of wrongs in society that should be redressed. "We can't just sit on our duffs agonizing about ourselves."

Russell searches her face. "You certainly have an extensive agenda for a babushka."

She waves him off. "There's work to be done. Lots of work. I, for one, won't rest easy until women have an unequivocal right to an abortion. And that's yet again an uphill battle."

Keith snorts. "Easy for you to say. My tired body demands rest. I'm too old and frail to fight anymore. Probably couldn't even join a protest march for more than a block. My granddaughter is foisting a walker on me, not renewed activism." He crosses his arms, staring into space. Has he let Mr. Parkinson take over his life? Has the disease numbed not only his physical self but also his passion? "I've been languishing," he finally stammers. "There are things I can still do, at least for now."

Words and melodies play in his head as he thinks about the state of the country since Trump's presidency. People who hid their racism are now outspoken, even gaining power. Anti-abortionists have become bolder, enacting restrictive state legislation that not only violates women's rights but democracy itself. A Texas law, which encourages citizens to inform on each other—officially sanctioning vigilantes—particularly rankles him. The electoral system is constantly being manipulated to exclude people of color from voting. Global warming is running amok.

"Yes," Keith acknowledges, "Deanna is dead-on. I want to step up to the plate and do my part again. We can't put the burden entirely on younger generations." He sighs deeply. "I need to get over my resistance to assistive devices. If I can't walk with demonstrators, I'll use a power wheelchair." He feels liberated, as though he has cast off a crushing restraint on his vitality, his drive.

"And I intend to intensify the pace of my protest songs." He pats Deanna's shoulder, giving her a grin. "A ballad about the Supreme Court's devastating abortion decision is already swirling in my brain."

Malaika takes in Keith's newfound resolve and wants a piece of it for herself. She has been so absorbed in self-pity since retirement that she has forgotten who she is—a strong, resilient Black woman. If Keith can be galvanized into action despite his infirmities, then so can she. Malaika recognizes, for the first time, that her emotional atrophy and lack of purpose is self-inflicted. "I shouldn't have let retirement obliterate my sense of self," she says. "I still have a life ahead of me." She sucks in a quick breath. "There are more than a few injustices demanding my attention. And I even have legal skills to offer pro bono. At this point, money is no object."

She smiles playfully at Keith. "People of color also warrant a special song or two from you—Black Lives Matter, police brutality, voting rights."

Max gives Keith a sidelong glance. "I've been remiss as well. Viewed old age as an excuse to settle in, take it easy. Thought I earned the right to rest on my laurels." He adds dryly, "but the planet's problems haven't disappeared merely because we've aged. In fact, they have worsened." While society is going to hell in a hand basket, he has been a bystander. He closed his eyes to the ongoing inequities in Canada, indeed the world, like a tired parent ignoring a sink full of dirty dishes hoping they would wash themselves. "I probably should get involved again too. I'd have to call on Joanna and Noah to assist me, of course. It would be too tricky to do without them."

Max stops to consider what he has said. "No, that would be too much for them. I don't want to be a nuisance. They have busy lives of their own. Just a pipe dream I suppose." He perks up. "But I'll keep sending Keith a steady stream of topics for songs."

Russell winks. "Me, too. Our little troupe will keep Keith busy for years on end."

The six of them erupt in laughter.

"Let's take pictures," Rebecca says. "To preserve the moment."

"Absolutely." Deanna fetches her camera. "Who knows whether we'll be able to do this again anytime soon." She gathers everyone onto the couch. After positioning the Fuji on a ledge, she focuses the lens, presses the self-timer, and runs back to her friends before it flashes. Max sticks out his tongue, and Deanna pokes him in the ribs. In the next shot, Keith puts donkey ears behind Rebecca's head. In subsequent shots, Russell, Rebecca, and Malaika make contorted faces. Finally, Deanna gives up and joins the silliness, stretching her mouth with both index fingers. The six of them chuckle as they shove one another out of the picture.

Rebecca stumbles back to her chair. She feels a sense of peace again as she watches her college friends. We are six old geezers, she muses, giggling and horsing around like teenagers.

Everyone collapses into their seats, still chortling. Russell takes a deep, satisfied breath. "I hear Zoom calling us," he says. "We probably won't be able to convene again for a long while, but we can visit virtually." He leans in. "How about once a month?"

Russell knows that Beth will try to horn in on their conversations and make a scene when he tells her she is not welcome. But the squabbles will be worth it if he can bank on seeing his friends periodically. Especially Deanna.

"I'm not sure I could manage once a month," Keith says drolly. "I'm going to be quite busy composing music for the five of you."

"But you will require an assessment of your masterpieces," Max fires back. "You can play the songs for us on Zoom, and we'll critique them."

"Okay, I'm in. A song per month. You guys always were my best critics. It'll give me motivation to write and play again." He can even hear the harmonica beckoning him.

"As for Moi," Max says, "I'll be at our monthly rendezvous with bells on my toes. That is," he laughs, "if I remember. And you, Deanna?" he asks.

"I don't know. I would have to style my hair and put on fancy clothes, like today." She throws out her arms to draw attention to her sweat suit and headscarf.

"Me, too," Rebecca gushes. "You know how concerned I am with style." She relishes the idea of their companionship, even if it is not in person. Yes, meeting with them on Zoom would go far in combating the isolation she had been experiencing. "I would look forward to a monthly get-together. I have few close friends to complain to or to talk politics with. Instead of throwing a book at the television, I'll save my wrath for you guys."

"Sounds good to me," Malaika says. "I could use an intermittent dose of reassurance, not to mention friends to share my political rantings with." Malaika suspects that she would also benefit from the levity. In their company, she's able to chill out. Since arriving at the reunion, despite some penetrating discussions, she has been in high spirits. Her college pals have allowed her to separate her real feelings from what she thinks she should feel. "Count me in."

"I guess everyone's on board," Russell says. "Monthly kindling to stoke our inner flames."

♀

Deanna sits at the edge of the couch, still giddy. "Someone should make a movie about us, like *The Big Chill*."

"I'd like Jane Fonda to play me," Rebecca says, fluttering her eyelids.

"Kathy Bates would be a better choice," Deanna scoffs.

Rebecca thumbs her nose at her.

"Not many eighty-year-old actresses to portray me," Malaika says.

"How about Diana Ross?" Rebecca says. "Or Pam Grier?"

"Too light-skinned." As soon as she says it, Malaika rebukes herself. Why is she still concerned with the shade of her skin? "Okay, I'll take Ross. At least our hair is similar."

"Keith can compose the score," Rebecca says. "We can also use some of his earlier songs."

"And who exactly would be interested in us six museum pieces?" Max quips. "Luckily, we can't have a funeral scene like in *The Big Chill*. At least not yet."

"Nor could we have Deanna, Rebecca, or Malaika running around seeking a sperm donor from us men," Russell says, straight-faced. "That movie had tons of sexual innuendos too. We seem a bit wanting in that area."

"Speak for yourself," Deanna rejoins with a smirk.

Russell leers at her. "We could have the scene with you crying naked in the shower."

She blushes, throwing him a dirty look.

"What would we do with boxes of running shoes," Rebecca jokes, turning to Deanna.

"We're too boring," Keith concludes, with a glint in his eyes. "Their circle of friends was dealing with betrayals, sacrifices, unresolved issues, and angst. We're a perfectly contented crowd, basking in our golden years."

"Yup, perfectly at peace," Malaika says.

"That's us," Rebecca purrs.

"Well, perhaps eighty is the new forty," Russell deadpans. "And we aging warriors are having mid-life crises."

Everyone bursts into laughter again, but a sudden flash of lightning and an explosion of thunder subdue them. Max counts the interval between the next pair of eruptions; it's less than thirty seconds. "The storm is close," he observes. "I didn't see it coming."

"That's because Rebecca took our phones," Keith says. "And there's no television or newspaper here. That's a change of pace for me."

"Probably for all of us," Rebecca says. "I'm not sure about the rest of you, but I find it a relief. Seems like there's some new catastrophe to worry about every day. I'm savoring our self-imposed oblivion, at least for a few days."

"Yes," agrees Russell. "A reprieve from the real world."

They listen to the storm as the sky darkens and it begins to pour. Rumbles, crackles, and growls are punctuated with bolts of lightning that illuminate a panorama of swaying trees, fallen branches and drooping flowers through the cabin's large windows. Rushing wind randomly knocks on the glass, like a visitor clamoring to come in. The sounds of the storm sing to the friends, reinforcing their sense of coziness and contentment.

28
The Collective

REBECCA PARKS herself on the edge of the bed in her room. She listens to the rat-a-tat of the rain against the windowpane. Otherwise, the cabin is silent. She is alone but not lonely. Prior to the reunion, she had been a solitary leaf floating to the ground only now she feels cushioned, like having a layer of pine needles to soften the landing.

She can't fall asleep and finally gives up. Her head is teeming with the evening's conversation, and she yearns to sort it out. Snippets of comments, wisecracks, and asides blend with impassioned longings, undertones of despondency, hopelessness, and a smattering of optimism. There is also joyfulness in their togetherness, intermingled with levity and even spontaneous outbursts of heartfelt laughter.

The last time she had felt such camaraderie was at MichFest. She first attended the week-long Womyn's Music Festival in 1986, urged on by one of her still-closeted lesbian colleagues. Camping never had been her cup of tea, nor was baring her breasts in public. But the human connections among the hundreds of participants, most of them naked or topless, eventually drew her in. She experienced a sense of solidarity and found the collaborative nature of the event appealing. The women had pitched in to carry out the festival's tasks, from food preparation to garbage disposal. Most participants took pains to chip in and welcome newcomers like her. The air was filled with music from afternoon to evening, like an endless concert.

It was there that Rebecca first met Susan, the facilitator of a queer politics workshop that she had signed up for. Their mutual attraction was evident at the start. The next day Rebecca settled into Susan's tent, where they formed the beginning of a lasting relationship. Thereafter, they took their vacations at MichFest every year until it shut down, nearly thirty years later, after being boycotted by several LGBT groups over its refusal to admit transgender women.

Clothed in warm thoughts of Susan and MichFest, Rebecca returns to bed. But she seesaws between fitful slumber and ruminative musings. Then it comes to her in a flash, like the bolt of lightning illuminating her room, and she awakens with a jolt. If she could embrace the communal spirit among strangers, wouldn't she find even greater pleasure in a partnership with her lifelong women friends? Given their reciprocal, caring relationship, she, Malaika, and Deanna could pool their resources and purchase a large house, share responsibilities, and navigate the ebb and flow of their last stages of life together.

The intensifying wind from the downpour is rattling the windows, stirring up disquiet about the challenges she faces by herself. The three of them, she reflects, are each on their own, but collectively they could weather the uncertainties and frailties of aging as a team. They are all anxious about their future, that is clear, especially the looming specter of spending their final years in a nursing home. In the short-term, they could hire someone to assist Malaika in looking after Darryl, and then a team of caregivers and housekeepers for themselves in the coming years.

Her excitement is almost childlike as she mulls over the possibilities. They had lived jointly for several years in their beloved West Village apartment. They had supported one another emotionally and intellectually with little conflict. Although she was somewhat derelict in her housekeeping chores, she served as their main cook, often concocting sumptuous dinners or rustling up ad hoc creations. These days she throws prepared frozen meals into the microwave. She would relish preparing meals and baking for her friends again. The three women had fared well together, had launched each other into their respective life's work. They had been side by side at the beginning, Rebecca tells herself, so why not at the end?

She falls into a deep, peaceful sleep.

♀

Malaika sips her coffee on the deck, inhaling the fresh scent of the morning, dew drops glistening on the lawn. She realizes that she had never paid much attention to the greenery surrounding her house. Darryl had mowed the lawn and tended to his magnificent flower beds. He was forever fretting over some plant that perished over the winter or a bush that demanded trimming. Her mind had always been elsewhere. He still takes pleasure in the yard but nowadays must direct others to do the weeding, pruning, and mowing. Malaika sighs. She'll soon be in charge of that too.

This weekend has been a much-needed reprieve from the self-indulgent brooding at home. She's been stuck in the past, mourning losses. Malaika suspects that she is too preoccupied with images. She internalized them, took refuge in status symbols to fortify her ego. The walls of her study are lined with awards and press clippings extolling her legal accomplishments. She derives self-esteem through accolades. Here, with her college companions, she is valued as herself, flaws and all.

When she had dropped in on her office shortly after stepping down, she felt like a persona non grata. During the last few days at the cabin, the crew has assured Malaika that she can engage in meaningful work, use her legal skills without the official backing of a law firm. She can blossom, even in retirement. They are spurring her on to a more hopeful future. Malaika is not entirely sure that it will last, that she won't fall back into restlessness and a lost sense of self. But for the moment, she is energized.

Rebecca appears with a mug of steaming coffee. "Good morning," she says, impatient to share her plan. She starts to pace, unsure of how to broach the subject.

"You're spilling coffee. Why don't you sit down?"

She holds her breath, still standing. "I have a proposal."

"A proposal?" Malaika is perplexed by the urgent tone in her voice.

Rebecca grabs Malaika's hands. "Remember how well we got along when you moved in with my family during college? And the camaraderie of our New York apartment?" She grips Malaika's fingers tighter. "I'd like to suggest that the three of us live together again, take care of each other."

Malaika is speechless, her eyes widening in disbelief. Has she misheard? Is she kidding? No, Rebecca doesn't joke about such matters. She decides her friend is sincere but has been carried away by the euphoria of the weekend, like someone hallucinating on drugs.

Deanna hobbles over, eyeing them quizzically. "Why are the two of you so keyed up?"

Malaika throws up her hands. "Rebecca has this cockamamie notion that the three of us should live together."

Rebecca is disheartened by Malaika's perfunctory dismissal of her proposal. She thought it was an inspired idea.

"Hmm," Deanna says. "Interesting. A collective of old female biddies." She hugs Rebecca. "What exactly do you have in mind?"

Rebecca perks up and outlines the plan, emphasizing how they could help one another as they require greater assistance. "Your kids won't have to provide hands-on care," she points out, gazing straight at Deanna and then Malaika. "Instead, their time with you could be more relaxed and natural. Each of us would have a private room, and we might include quarters for your offspring to visit." She gives them a wry look. "Since I never had any children, yours would become mine as well."

A slow smile spreads across Deanna's face. "We could collaborate on political work, like we used to," she says. "We have less energy but far more skills. If we merge our expertise, we could make a hell of an impact." Deanna is invigorated.

Malaika listens askance as they extol the benefits of their group home. They are in never-never land, ignoring reality and practicalities. They reside in different states across the continent. What about their families? What about Darryl? Rebecca and Deanna are complete strangers to him; he wouldn't want to live with them. And her children would be appalled even though they have lives of their own. "Too many complications," she mutters. "Too many complications."

The two women stare at her. "Yes, it would be tricky," Deanna says. "Lots of thorny issues, least of all finding a suitable house. And then there's the location to consider."

"But finances shouldn't be too much of an issue," Rebecca says. "Each of us contributes what we can afford." She waits a while before resuming. "My share would be substantial. Susan had been the only child of a powerful and well-to-do family. She left her entire estate to me. I have no heirs, of course."

"Money is not the problem," Malaika says, a little peeved. "My husband and I are well off." Her shoulders and neck tense up. "I can't just uproot Darryl from his home. Would he even fit in with us? As for me, I'm not ready to start a new life at my age. I would be disoriented, lost."

"We'll find you." Rebecca shoots back and then turns in earnest. "Anyhow, aren't you already lost?"

Malaika is caught off-guard by Rebecca's forthright barb, like a shooter hitting the bull's eye. She's been directionless for so long it feels almost normal. Though she's been drowning in pessimism in recent months, Malaika admits to herself that the picture the women are sketching has its appeal.

Rebecca watches Malaika closely and sensing a bit less resistance takes quick advantage of the opportunity. "We would lend a hand with Darryl, especially when he becomes more incapacitated. There's so much we could accomplish jointly."

Malaika again ruminates on the negatives, her agitation intensifying. The challenges and uncertainties are rippling through her, like a lake suddenly pounded by a strong wind. "Do you really think it's doable?" She is frantically rocking back and forth on the chair. "There are so many questions."

"Of course there are," Rebecca says. "This isn't a decision we can make in one day. But if you're open to the premise, then we can at least explore it." She's aware that it is going to take some coaxing but suspects they might win her over in the end. "In our youth, we thought we could do anything. Maybe we still can."

Malaika starts to speak but can't verbalize what's gnawing at her. Rebecca and Deanna have kindled her spirit. Still, she is too prudent to leap at what seems like a chimera. She clears her throat. "I need time to digest everything."

♀

The men are at the pool, engaged in an animated discussion about Biden. "He's a disaster," Keith says. "Not a forceful leader."

"He's better than Trump. Or any Republican," Russell reminds him.

"How many brain cells did that brilliant observation take?"

"Touché. Nonetheless, we must make sure Trump clones don't take over Congress in the next mid-term election. Voter registration is key, and that's where our efforts should be, like the old days. Too many Trumpian types in our electorate. It's frightening."

Keith staggers over to Russell in exaggerated stumbling movements. "I'm ready to hop on a Freedom bus to the Deep South right now. Take on the white supremacists and their law enforcement allies." He pretends to fend off their beatings with his shaking arms.

"We're not too old to do something," Russell insists.

"I'm grateful to be Canadian," Max interjects. "American society is such a mess. I've heard that over one-fourth of the population is willing to submit to a dictatorial figure and follow his oppressive doctrines." He sneers. "Many of them still believe that Trump won the 2020 election."

The women enter the gate, and Keith waves them over. "We're heading South for voter registration," he tells them. "Want to join us?"

Deanna rolls her eyes. "I thought we were heading to a nursing home," she says. "But please send me pictures." She gives him a smug smile. "Speaking of nursing homes, the girls and I are thinking about moving in with one another."

"What?" Russell says. "You're kidding, right?"

"Nope."

He's flabbergasted. "What are the plans?"

"None yet. We've only broached the subject."

Russell lets her words sink in. The more he thinks about it, the more appealing the idea becomes. He turns to Keith. "Maybe we should horn in on their plans," he says, half-seriously.

Now it's Rebecca's turn to be taken aback. She studies him with a measured look and only then grasps the possibilities. "Interested?" she asks Keith. "You and Sara could have your own room. And we intend to find a big enough place that would accommodate visiting kids and grandkids."

Keith laughs. "I'm going to be too much to handle. Remember, my Parkinson's disease is going to worsen not improve."

"That's the point," Rebecca says. "To take care of each other. I've proposed that we take turns attending to Darryl. We can hire someone as well. I'm suggesting a collective where we would band together for activism but also support one another as we age."

The scheme is tempting to Keith. "I don't know whether Sara would be game," he says, "but it would relieve her of full responsibility for me." He's sure his easygoing but politically motivated wife would fit in with them, possibly thrive.

"You could test new songs on us as you write them. Far better than once a month on Zoom," Rebecca coaxes. Adrenaline is surging through her. The six of them living collectively is even more appealing than her original idea. A commune. It would be unconventional, reawaken the audacity and rebelliousness of their youth.

"Money?" Keith says. "How do we afford this extravagant venture, a house with an untold number of rooms? Environmental activism hadn't exactly been a lucrative career. Sara and I are not wealthy."

"I am," Rebecca says. "We can pay for everything Marx style: 'From each according to his ability, to each according to his needs'...Or *her* ability and needs," she corrects herself.

"Max?" she says. "What do you think?"

"Don't know. This is a bolt from the blue. Such an enterprise would be life-changing—certainly not something I would do lightly." He scrambles to find the least offensive words before resuming. He lowers his eyes and whispers, "It would be a curveball for my daughter and son. I haven't told them very much about the five of you. They're bewildered as to why I even came to this reunion."

They look at him, and he shrugs. "I had left my life in the United States behind me," he says, staring at the floor. "It was the only way I could handle abandoning everyone and everything."

"Well, it's time to reclaim us," Rebecca retorts.

He smiles at her. "You haven't changed a bit." He pauses. "And I'm glad of that."

"You'll consider our proposition, then?"

"I'm a Canadian citizen and would never give that up. And there's healthcare to consider. More importantly, Noah and Johanna would be devastated. I could never keep house with you full-time."

Russell is growing more interested in pushing the plan forward. "You could spend several months with them on a regular basis, which would also safeguard your Canadian citizenship and medical insurance. The rest of the year with us."

Deanna gives Russell a bemused look. "Your enthusiasm seems to be rising. Don't you have to sound out your wife?" She hesitates. "Besides, I'm not sure we would get along with Beth. Nor she with us. At least from the way you describe her."

"I would leave her," he says in an impassive voice. "It's time." He has no appetite for having his wife participate. He views this as an opportunity for them to separate, something he's been afraid to carry through for too long. The prospect of sharing a house with his friends would give him an incentive to move on, not worry so much about the future. In fact, the thought of a joint life with Deanna in his old age uplifts him. It would lighten his days to hear her contagious laugh. It hasn't changed in over sixty years.

"Divorcing Beth would be a big step," Malaika cautions.

"Yes, of course. But whether this housing experiment works out or not, I'm convinced that I should. I've been reminded this weekend about the importance of mutual trust and respect. I don't want to live the rest of my life battling with a partner." Russell closes his eyes. "I hope Allison is supportive—the only one of my kids who cares about me."

"We'll help," Rebecca says. "And facilitate negotiations with the rest of your brood. We'll lure them in with our loving, unconventional family. Maybe they will see you as we do. At least we can try."

Malaika glances around and shakes her head. "Everyone's talking about this so-called cooperative as a fait accompli. I'm still having trouble assimilating the plan, not to mention convincing my husband and kids of its advantages for me...and them. You guys have always been impulsive. We need to sort things out slowly and deliberately to avoid driving into a ditch."

"But not too slowly," Rebecca says. "We're not getting any younger." She puts her hands on her hips. "Obviously we each have to mull it over at home. But it would behoove us to brainstorm a bit more while we're here. Set the groundwork. Then we can talk further on Zoom."

"Okay," Malaika grumbles. "After dinner. But for now, I'm taking a nap."

"Me, too, Rebecca says.

♀

While Malaika and Rebecca sleep, Deanna takes a long swim, easily falling into a steady rhythm with a breaststroke. As she glides back and forth across the pool, she ponders the gang's potential communal project. In many ways, it makes sense. At her age, she is vulnerable to a host of unforeseen accidents and ailments. She will have to brave them alone. Even if she relocates near her daughter and two grandchildren, she wouldn't want them to become responsible for every health setback. Already her knee is deteriorating, and she will have to have replacement surgery. She's unsure who will assist her during the months of recovery. It would be comforting to have friends close at hand.

Regardless, the house in Stanford is too large for an eighty-year-old to manage. It would be reassuring to shop, cook, and clean with other folks. What's more, there would be built-in company. The six of them never seem to bore one another. Even when they are sitting in silence, she feels at ease.

Her pro-choice activism has been rewarding. She's linked up with legions of women in battling hardcore anti-abortion forces. Nonetheless, Deanna senses that the younger generation, though they respect her extensive credentials with the movement, views her as a political has-been. She often feels alone at events. For Deanna, Roe v Wade had been groundbreaking and although she is equally outraged as them at its reversal and determined to chart a way forward, she is not quite as bright-eyed and bushy-tailed at rallies as she once was. The long-distance marches and hours of speeches, while inspiring, are taxing. The feisty younger women, with their catchy signs, whizz by her with a zeal that takes her breath away. She would feel so much less conspicuous striding alongside Malaika and Rebecca at their own pace, allowing themselves frequent rests. Perhaps the guys would join them. Singing and clapping with the gang would go a long way in detracting from the agony of standing on her feet for hours on end.

As she swims, Deanna considers whether their proposed commune could work. The upsides prevail, no matter how much she twists and turns the arguments. Moving in with each other would be a momentous step for all of them, but she is ready for a serious dialogue on its prospects. She floats on her back, peering at the sky. Clouds are slowly rolling in but the sun is still sending waves of warmth over her. There is a soothing quiet in the air, interrupted only by the steady, low hum of the pool's pump. The earlier cacophony of chirping, whistling and croaking birds has wound down to a muted drone.

She steps out of the pool and towels herself. Something is gnawing at her. She must talk to Russell before the six of them meet that evening. After changing clothes, she seeks him out.

"Hi," he says.

"Can we take a short walk?"

"Sure." Russell is pleased but surprised. He and Deanna haven't been alone since they arrived.

They amble down a nearby path that leads to the edge of the forest. Despite her cane, she stumbles on the rocky trail. Russell takes her arm. He has the urge to hold her close but restrains himself.

Deanna stops short and turns to him. "If our communal plan actually pans out," she begins, "you and I have to clarify our relationship."

"How so?" Russell is mystified.

"I love you as a dear friend. But only as a friend. I have no intention of entering a romantic relationship with you. Ever. I need an understanding between us right from the start. You can't leave your wife with the false notion that you and I will become a couple."

Russell is startled by her terse, straightforward warning. He shouldn't have been—she never did mince words. "So, you intend to sleep around." He smirks. "Hot and cold running men. . ."

She cuts him off, miffed. "I'm serious. We had settled into a satisfying rapport in college, and I expect our relationship to remain that way. We must straighten this out before we go any further into this venture."

Russell is disappointed and knows that it would take a Herculean effort to change headstrong Deanna's mind. Nonetheless, he takes her hand and squeezes it. "I will respect that. Just spending my last years with you and the others would give me immense pleasure. I'm fairly certain that I want in. But first I must chew over a few concerns, especially financial ones. Beth is going to try to extort a bundle from me."

"I just hope you stick to your word about us," Deanna says. "I don't want that hovering over my shoulder." She's not convinced Russell will follow through on his promise. She can feel his neediness, laced with desire. After Sam's death, Deanna had forsworn romantic entanglements. I'm eighty years old, she reminds herself. Carnal pleasures are for the young. She had her fill. And yet she is feeling a sexual appetite inadvertently bubbling within her. She brushes it aside. She's not going to pair up with Russell or anyone else for that matter. Sam had fulfilled that aspect of her life; he will remain her last lover. Deanna and Russell walk back to the cabin silently, lost in their own thoughts.

♀

Malaika wakes up groggy and grabs a cup of coffee. Usually a nap recharges her, but today, disturbing dreams interfered with her sleep. As the caffeine takes effect, she is more alert but still disconcerted by the nightmare that seemed far too real.

It began with an image of herself lying in a coffin, surrounded by five ghosts who, one by one, recited her lifelong failings. She was motionless, mortified. Then they demanded that she summon Darryl, their children, and grandkids to the funeral, and ordered Malaika to deliver her own service. She became frantic; what could or should she say about herself? She started sobbing, seemingly draining her tear ducts of water. Gradually, the ghosts transformed into her five companions, and they assured her that they would deliver the eulogy instead and acknowledge her noble and generous heart. As they were sprinkling purple glitter into her coffin, she had woken up with a start.

Malaika sits on the porch steps, puzzling over the dream. She reflexively rubs her eyes, as though the tiny, sparkling particles had actually fallen into them. Deanna and Russell's approach ends her spooky musing.

"What are the two of you scheming?" she says.

"Preliminary talk before tonight's discussion," Deanna says. "Straightening out a few things."

"Like the fact that she won't sleep with me," Russell interjects with a mischievous chuckle.

Deanna bats him on the arm with her cane.

It starts to rain again, a drizzle that quickly mushrooms into a downpour. The three of them dash into the cabin. Keith, Max, and Rebecca are sitting at the dining room table playing rummy.

"I'm in the lead." Rebecca gloats as she lays down another winning hand.

Russell heads to the game room and retrieves Trivial Pursuit. "Anyone in the mood?"

"Absolutely," Keith says.

"Me, too," Rebecca says, gathering up the cards.

"Ditto." Trivial Pursuit is one of Deanna's favorite pastimes.

Max is somewhat hesitant, concerned that his memory will betray him. "I'll watch."

Malaika also pulls out. "I need time by myself." She curls up on the couch with a book.

They divide into teams by drawing lots. It ends up males against females, a division that Keith wanted to avoid. "Okay, the gender battle is on," he groans.

As usual, the competition escalates, like a wildfire. Russell's retentive memory serves him well, especially in the history and literature categories. Keith has an edge in entertainment, Rebecca trounces them in sports and geography, and Deanna has the advantage in science. They are neck and neck, applauding and cursing each other. The rivalry is intense, but Russell and Keith prevail.

"Lucky break," Rebecca says, folding her arms across her chest.

"Sore loser," Max says from the sidelines.

Rebecca calls for another round.

This time, each of them concentrates even harder as the pressure builds. Rebecca's heart is pounding as she wracks her brain for answers. Russell is sweating. The game again is close, but for a second time Rebecca and Deanna are defeated.

"I need a drink," Rebecca declares, obviously irritated. She hates being bested by anyone, most of all by the guys in her old crowd.

♀

Malaika heads upstairs to take a shower. She is having trouble concentrating; her attention keeps drifting to the upcoming discussion. As warm water streams over her body, she starts to cry. She feels overwhelmed, at once confused and hopeful. The gang has unrealistic expectations, Malaika admonishes herself, yet their very presence reassures her. The thought of talking over the proposed commune lifts her spirits. Yet she is sure the whole thing is mostly crazy talk. She is so dazed that she can't even wade through her own feelings, but she must. She lifts her face to the gushing water and resolves not to lose sight of what she wants before anyone else weighs in, including her family.

She joins the others, still bemused. Max hands her a glass of red wine, which she sips gratefully. Deanna and Russell bring in the hors d'oeuvres.

Dinner is a festive occasion as they deliberate about their weekend and the sense of esprit de corps, clicking glasses of Champagne. They recall joyful moments as youths, butting in on each other with stories. Their exuberance is tempered only by the somber realization that this is their last night together, a lingering whiff of melancholy hanging in the air.

The cooks bring in a scrumptious dish of mushroom-baked ziti with ricotta and spinach along with a salad, which the group digs into with gusto. They especially gorge on the chocolate key lime pie, which tastes bittersweet, like their evening. Even Deanna throws caution to the winds and enjoys a large portion.

The house becomes wrapped in twilight as the meal crawls along. The dining room window is ablaze with an amalgam of hues—fuchsia and lilac clouds hover over a pink, rose and blazing, orange-streaked sky. The gang sinks into a sense of contentment as they sift through memories that gently fold into the present, like ingredients blended into a luscious cake. The dazzling panorama fades into darkness as they clear the table.

♀

After dinner, Rebecca doesn't mess around. "Let's go into the living room," she directs them. "It's time to put our heads together and think about our new home." She is anxious to begin their deliberations and intends to subtly drop in irresistible incentives to convince anyone who is ambivalent. "Let's focus on the big picture. We can leave any pesky details for Zoom meetings."

"Ah, but the devil is in the details," Keith jokes.

"Yes. And I have a few to discuss before we proceed," Max says. "First of all, we'll never find a house that meets our specifications. We'd have to build it. The bedrooms, dining room, living room, and kitchen would have to be on the ground floor to accommodate our present and future disabilities. We'll need wheelchair access and should probably have separate bathrooms for each of us. The rest of the quarters—for care assistants, visiting kids and grandkids, and a playroom—could be on the second and third floors. We may want additional spaces ..." He hesitates mid-sentence, his mind racing through the options. "Perhaps it would be better to have a one-story house and separate cabins for guests and aides. That would require lots of acreage."

He shakes his head at the complexity of it all. "I guess the exact style could be determined during later negotiations." Max gazes around the room. "At any rate, I volunteer to design our humble abode."

Everyone claps and hoots approval. "Lucky us," Deanna says, "having a talented architect in our midst."

"As for the blueprint," Max continues, "we must minimize our environmental footprint, even though we require a sizable place. We'll use solar and geothermal power where feasible; heavy insulation; energy-efficient building materials, windows, lighting, and appliances; and whatever else pushes the boundaries of sustainability."

Rebecca beams, her face flushed. "So, you're going to join our household?"

"I haven't decided," Max says, "but I'll be your architect regardless."

"It wouldn't be the same without you," Rebecca says. "But I understand. You have other people to consult." Despite what she says, Rebecca is frustrated with Max. He is eighty years old and should be able to determine where and with whom he lives without permission from his children. Rebecca taps her fingers on the table, aware that she is the only one without any kin to confer with. She's impatient for Max—indeed for all of them—to make up their minds.

Deanna laces her fingers together and leans in. "I'd like to suggest building a swimming pool on the property. It would be great exercise for everyone."

Rebecca raises an eyebrow.

"Except for Rebecca," Deanna says. "She can watch us."

The others nod approval.

"Lots of bookshelves," Russell suggests. "What a collection we would have."

"And a fireplace," Malaika inserts. "That would make it cozier." The whole enterprise is more and more inviting to her as they kick around its layout. She'd not only get assistance with Daryl but would have close allies around her when he dies. His approaching death is finally sinking in, especially her loneliness in its wake. The place that they are sketching out is promising; she envisions nights by a fireplace debating current events and the latest books.

"A large porch as well," Keith teases, "for the six rocking chairs overlooking our estate." He, too, is becoming more convinced that living with his friends would be a sensible choice for Sara and him. Nonetheless, he is mindful of the huge cost of their plan. He has always been parsimonious, preferring a simple lifestyle. For many years, he had given up his car and mostly traveled by bicycle or mass transit. The gang is visualizing an opulent country manor with all of the trimmings. He's not even sure he is willing to let them subsidize him; he and Sara are obviously the ones with the fewest resources.

Keith takes a deep breath. "The plan is too rich for me. My wife and I can't afford anything near what we are discussing."

"Put that out of your mind," Rebecca says. "Each person or couple will put in what they can. I've inherited sufficient resources to fund the rest. I would consider it a privilege to share the inheritance with my comrades as a part of living my politics. In any case, listening to your music would be worth the price of admission alone."

Keith presses one hand against his heart and blows Rebecca a kiss with the other.

"We should keep in mind," Max reminds them, "that it will be a complex, challenging road. We'll require a great deal of assistance. This will be decidedly different from my previous experience living in a commune. Then, I was young, healthy, and hardy." He recalls those years, living intimately with people he hadn't previously known. Even so, it had been a congenial time, hard work comingled with a sense of community. In this situation, it might work out even better since they have a deep, abiding bond.

"Of course, we'll require outside support," Rebecca snaps. "That's the point—to help us live life to the fullest as we age. This is an elder-care project as much as anything else."

"And we can combine our strengths," Deanna says. "We won't be living off the land, as Max did during his earlier years. But we can cook together." She smiles at Rebecca. "I anoint you chief chef. As for me, I'll direct the landscaping. I had given up gardening in California but now feel motivated... it would be for us." She giggles. "I promise you, my dear friends, a rose garden."

"Don't forget roses have thorns," Russell says, his eyes twinkling.

"I'll plan the menus too," Rebecca says, interrupting him. "Make sure we have a healthy diet. Lots of vegetarian meals. That certainly would benefit Russell. Prevent him from having another heart attack. I've been a vegetarian for over forty years." She pats her stomach. "A tad rotund, but I'm as fit as a fiddle, even without exercising."

Russell turns sheepish. "We don't eat very well at home, I have to admit. Beth and I dine out much more than we should. Rich food. Neither of us likes to cook."

Deanna shakes her head. "We'll take care of you."

He nods, his eyes glowing. "I'll paint the place. Whatever colors the women decide on." He winks at them. "I'll also serve as the all-purpose handyman. I'm fairly skilled at repairs or at least in diagnosing problems."

The others cheer, but Deanna looks skeptical.

"There's a lot you don't know about me," Russell says flatly.

"And I offer my expertise as a lawyer," Malaika says with a shy smile. More whoops of approval. She goes on, "I can do the legal work for buying land, constructing the house, and making financial arrangements among us. Like Max, I volunteer whether or not I move in."

Rebecca winces. "We need you." She stares straight at Malaika. "And you need us. We can't save each other from old age, but collectively we can ease its progression and enhance our lives."

A prolonged hush settles over the room.

"Anything else for now?" Max asks. "We'll have lots of particulars to discuss in the coming months."

"How about a name for our abode," Rebecca says.

"Wrinkled Rebels," Keith pipes up.

His pals give him a thumbs-up.

29
Leave-taking

Max had set his clock for 6 am to allow ample time to reach the airport. He's looking forward to navigating the trip, again on his own. The weekend has given him even more resolve to extricate himself from his children's grip on his everyday affairs. At times he requires assistance, but their hold on him is generating even more dependency. He has carefully mapped his way, leaving nothing to chance. He will splurge; he intends to take a taxi straight from the cabin to the airport. He's too old to scrimp on himself. Max is a bit irked that Rebecca, in her usual bossy fashion, refused to relinquish their cell phones yesterday. He'll have to call the cab this morning after he finishes packing.

He throws his belongings into the suitcase helter-skelter, resolving to sort them out at home. He reaches into his pocket to reassure himself that the carefully placed airline ticket has not abandoned him. After looking around the room to check that he has not forgotten anything, he heads downstairs to the kitchen.

Nobody is around. He makes a pot of coffee and pours himself a cup. He sits down at the small, round table and stares at the basket full of cell phones that Rebecca placed there after the crew retreated to their rooms last night. The devices are contentedly ensconced, seemingly as reluctant to leave as their owners. After plucking his out, he discovers that the battery is dead. Of course. So much for careful planning. He brings it up to his room, plugs in the charger, and returns to the kitchen. It's already six-thirty, and he has yet to make arrangements for his ride.

Russell appears and grabs his phone. "Rebecca surely knows how to inconvenience everybody. What am I supposed to do with a dead cell phone? Luckily, I scheduled a car in advance."

"Well, I didn't."

"Catch a ride with me. I'll take you to the bus."

"Actually, I'm heading directly to the airport. My phone should have a charge soon. Thanks anyway."

Russell sips his coffee. "Do you want breakfast? The cooks are gone, but they left rolls, pastries, and bagels."

"Too restless to eat. I'm anxious to get going."

"Did I hear food?" Rebecca says, as she walks through the door. She snatches a cinnamon roll. "Yum." She is determined to repress her burning sense of loss, like a mother whose children are leaving the nest.

The others join them. There is an elegiac ambience fused with equal measures of edginess and anticipation. They engage in chitchat, avoiding sappiness, everyone absorbed in their own musings. Reality awaits them, their willful kin who might challenge their plans.

Malaika slips out of the cabin. Dragging her luggage behind her, she finds her rented Honda patiently waiting for her. She is dressed as she was when she arrived, including the head wrap, as though her world is back to normal. But it's not. For the third night in a row, she slept well, unlike the insomnia she endures at home. Except for the one disturbing nightmare, Malaika feels rested for the first time in a long while. It has improved her concentration and memory not to mention her overall sense of well-being. Even her self-esteem has resurfaced, and she is ready to face the future with more confidence, whatever the outcome of their proposed living arrangements.

She is still a little leery of approaching her family. Malaika sizes up the situation. Because Darryl is more concerned with her happiness than anything else, he might go along with the plan. She will be on more treacherous ground with their four children and seven grandchildren. They, too, want what is best for her but will be put off, perhaps even offended, by its unconventionality. Her brood views themselves as dignified, part of the upper crust. Although she had drummed into them an awareness of injustices and an obligation to folks less well-off than themselves, they had been born with a silver spoon in their mouths—unlike her—and are wary of anything that might compromise their standing in the community.

Nevertheless, despite their hoity-toity demeanor and stylish attire, they are committed to their Black identity. Having experienced discrimination to varying degrees, they are fully aware that their financial and educational status is not protection against racial profiling or police brutality. Kayla, in particular, armed her children with defensive tactics when confronted by cops. To her dismay, the youngest ignored the warnings and, when stopped for running a red light, had behaved insolently; Kayla had to retrieve the injured Damien from jail.

The entire family, each in their own way, is engaged in the Black Lives Matter Movement. None of them will take the idea of her moving in with an all-white crowd lightly, even if they are her oldest friends. Yes, they had encouraged her to attend the reunion. Still, they will view Malaika's joining them permanently as turning a one-time indulgence in a cherry-topped sundae into an everyday meal.

While walking back to the cabin to rejoin her companions, Malaika mulls over her children's inheritance. She and Darryl have considerable assets, and their kids will want to know how much of the money they intend to leave them. Since she doesn't know what she'll be expected to contribute to the collective, much less how much to reserve for her family, she's stumped as to what she will tell them.

♀

As Malaika approaches the house, she hears the grating sound of tires kicking up stones and the muffled moan of an engine that is becoming louder. Russell is standing on the porch, glancing down the gravel road, looking irritated.

"It's probably my ride," he informs her, his face tight. "Two hours early." He's not quite ready to leave his friends, especially so abruptly. He opens his mouth for the expletive that is ready to erupt but shrugs instead.

A silver Toyota pulls up to the cabin but instead of a chauffeur, a tall female and male emerge from the vehicle. Russell does a double take and stares at the man. Malaika, too, can't take her eyes off him. He's a clone of the young Max.

The two figures visibly stiffen, like deer caught in headlights. They are at a standstill and the only sound is the faint chirping of early birds.

"We're looking for our father," the woman eventually says, mustering a polite smile.

"I know." Russell is still gawking at the clone of the young Max. The only difference is the hair, also blond but neatly cut. "I'm Russell."

"And I'm Malaika."

The newcomers are smartly dressed. Noah has on crisp jeans, a wheat tweed sports jacket, and shiny brown loafers. Johanna is wearing a demure long gray shirt dress, matching open front crop blazer, and black shoes with sensible heels. She has blonde hair like her brother, hers cascading to the shoulders. She wears no makeup but has naturally long, dark lashes that accentuate her pale blue eyes.

"Please come in," Russell says. "Join us for breakfast."

"We already ate," Noah says, his voice flat. Remembering his Canadian manners, he abruptly adds, "thank you anyway."

Rebecca's eyes widen as they walk in. For once, she is speechless.

"Well, well," Max says, embracing his kids. "Look what the cat's dragged in." Though his heart swells with love for them, their coming to fetch him is an affront to his dignity. He is struggling to maintain his independence, cope with his cognitive decline, but they persist in coddling him. They are so overbearing, he muses, that they won't even let him take the trip home by himself. He doubles down on his earlier resolve, assuring himself that this will be the last time. From now on, or at least until he has full-blown dementia, his decisions will be his own. Then they—or anyone else for that matter—can do as they like with him.

Pivoting toward his companions, Max says, "You've met Russell and Malaika. I'd like to introduce you to the rest of the crowd: Rebecca, Deanna, Keith."

The siblings shake hands all around, a smile plastered on Johanna's face. For the second time, she checks her watch. "It's getting late, Pop."

Rebecca touches Max on the arm, not prepared for him to depart just yet, her fingers lingering. Johanna purses her lips and exchanges a glance with her brother.

Max senses that everything about his friends antagonizes his children. It strikes him that they are jealous, intuitively discerning his fierce attachment to these aging Americans. He should not have withheld his past from them; perhaps then they would not be taken so unawares. He had shielded his offspring from his upbringing in the States, the pieces of him that belong to what they dismissively call "down there." His estranged parents and brothers were strangers to them, just like his cherished Becca and the rest of the clan.

Rebecca feels unnerved under the watchful eyes of Max's children. She views herself through their lenses, a short, scruffy old hag dressed in a rumpled T-shirt and worn-out jeans. Mortified, she almost feels undressed. She pats her frizzy hair, glaring at them.

"Max, before you leave," she says, "I have something for you. Wait a sec." Rebecca returns momentarily with six purple mugs wrapped in newspaper. After tearing the first one open, she hands it to him. The inscription reads, "Max, Reunion Weekend, June 5, 2025." She flashes a smug smile at Johanna and Noah. She envisions the cup hanging proudly with the other five in their future collective home. They will serve as a reminder of where and how their plan was first conceived.

The mood has turned tense, especially since Rebecca, Max suspects, is unconsciously—or perhaps consciously—egging his children on. But they will cork their emotions like a half-full bottle of wine, to nip on later, privately. They are thoroughly Canadian, mild-mannered and undemonstrative, at least with outsiders, always maintaining a public face.

Americans, Max thinks, still imagine that they live in the Wild West, ready to shoot anyone who looks at them crooked. Rebecca is simmering, ready to boil over, and he doesn't want to deal with any of this drama anymore. They are like cougars fighting over their territory, only in this instance the territory is him. He exhales, letting his exasperation drift away.

"Let's get this show on the road. Noah, please grab my baggage from upstairs." He's tired of the tug of war and shuts down, letting his family lead the way. He worries that this is not a great start for any dialogue with Noah and Johanna about the communal housing project.

The friends walk them to the car and, with a quick wave, Noah and Johanna get in. Max hangs back, taking a mental picture of his pals. He hugs each one in turn. Rebecca holds onto him, whispering, "We'll be waiting for you." He reluctantly pulls away and decamps with his children.

♀

"Bitch," Rebecca mutters under her breath as they wave goodbye to Max and his family. "She's probably just like her mother."

"Careful," Deanna cautions. "We'll need to win her over if we want our Max to join us."

Rebecca nods absently. Still chafing, she turns to Russell. "Guess your brood isn't coming to call for you."

"Guess not," he says with a hurt look in his eyes.

"Sorry, ole friend," Rebecca murmurs, linking her arm through his. "That was cruel." She tends to let her mean streak slip out whenever she feels slighted. Only it's often aimed at a person close to her, a non-offending party, as Susan used to remind her. "Stop lashing out on me," she would implore, "just because someone else has hurt you." It was a failing

Rebecca could never quite get under control. She didn't mean to offend Russell and wishes her words could fade away like waves washing over footprints in the sand. Her face crumbles. "Sorry," she repeats, forcing a weak smile.

They walk back to the house, Rebecca still arm-in-arm with Russell. He brews a fresh pot of coffee. Anxiously nibbling on the remains of breakfast, he imagines his reception at home. Beth will greet him, arms folded across her chest, demanding details of the weekend. He wants to tuck the experience away for himself, not share any of it with her; his wife will attempt to spoil the trip with sarcasm and acerbic remarks.

He is relieved that he has decided on the divorce. It's a huge weight lifted off his shoulders, as if he had been toting around a heavy sack of negativity. He is done with the unbearable tension that pervades his household. Beth sucks so much oxygen out of a room that he can hardly breathe. But why wait and expose himself to her cheap shots? Perhaps he should just walk in and announce immediately that he is leaving her.

He berates himself for the hundredth time. How can someone as successful as he, who has climbed the academic ladder with brainpower, imagination, and expertise, be so damned foolish in his personal decisions? Three strikes and you're out, he grumbles to himself, as he reflects on his failed marriages. Can you renounce one life and start over at eighty years old? He rubs the bald spot on his head. Can he trust himself to start over? Perhaps he does lack emotional intelligence, as Deanna has repeatedly told him this weekend.

He obsesses yet again about money. Beth will not let him go easily. There will be months if not years of legal bickering as she pulls out all stops to take off with their resources. He must salvage half of them. If he moves in with the gang, he aims to chip in his fair share and not let Rebecca bear the brunt of the expenses.

Russell's face clouds as he agonizes over the challenges awaiting him. He promises himself that he will not resort to hitting the bottle again, no matter what he is forced to contend with. He might consider attending an AA meeting or two, just to check it out.

He goes to the window for the third time to look for his ride. Nothing yet. Now he frets over whether his driver will come. Maybe he should call.

"You're such a nervous Nellie," Malaika says. "If he doesn't show up, you can ride with me. I've decided to visit Shanice again in the city before I head back to DC."

Just as her words settle, a vehicle approaches.

"That's for me," Russell says.

"Well, it's surely not for me," Deanna deadpans. "I don't run around in chauffeured cars."

Russell draws a breath, smarting. "Both you and Rebecca seem to have it in for me this morning. I have enough hostility coming my way at home. Do I really have to take it from my friends?"

Deanna reaches out and strokes his hand. "We're all tense. I'm sorry."

Appeased, Russell smiles at her. Like Max, he is reluctant to leave. At length, he gathers his bags and heads to the car, the rest of the group in tow. His eyes dance from one person to the other, coaxing his lips into a broad smile.

He embraces Rebecca first. "You've really succeeded in pulling this off. Thanks for such a perfect weekend. You are as amazing as ever."

Folding his arms around Malaika, he says, "I've always admired your vitality and spunk. We'll help rekindle it. I promise."

Next, he holds out his hand to Keith but pulls him into a bear hug instead. "You hang in there, bro."

He locks eyes with Deanna and cradles her face with his hands. "You will be special to me forever. No matter what happens."

Russell climbs into the back seat, blows them a kiss, and calls out, "See you soon on Zoom."

As the limo rushes off, he wonders if their elder-care commune could possibly work out.

♀

Before long, Keith's Prius pulls up with Jenna at the wheel. She hops out and sprints to the cabin before anyone can greet her. The four friends are standing at the open door. "I'm here, Poppy!" she says, looping her arms around Keith's neck.

"Such fanfare." Keith gazes down at his radiant granddaughter.

Jenna steals a glimpse around the house. "Where's the rest of the clan?"

"Only us girls and your grandfather are left," Rebecca says. "The others have already gone home." She gives her a shy smile. "Are you hungry?"

"Starving," Jenna says.

Rebecca motions for the group to move into the dining room. "I'll make lunch. There's still plenty of food in the fridge."

Keith knows that Jenna eats like a bird and is just scheming to learn more about the women. "So, what do you want to know about the weekend?" he asks her. "Feel free. My friends are not shrinking violets."

A crimson flush creeps across her face. "Am I that transparent?"

"Yup."

The three friends exchange glances. There is a silence as each person gathers her thoughts. "It was like time stood still,"

Deanna eventually says. "After so many decades, we still fit well together."

"We found support and inspiration from each other," Malaika adds. "Just like when we were young." She flashes a look of affection at her companions. "They make me feel alive again."

"And they took good care of me." Keith says. "Just like you instructed. Even encouraged me to play the guitar." He presses his granddaughter's hand as he considers his next words. "We're kicking around the idea of an elder commune, a house for the six of us and our spouses." He gives her a measured look. "I'm going to be too much for your grandma to handle alone. If our collective pans out, she would have assistance."

"But it's not just for elder care," Rebecca says. "We have goals for the future." She stares directly at Jenna from across the table. "We intend to work for social justice. To make this a better world for your generation and your children."

"You would always be welcome at our home," Deanna says. "We intend to have accommodations for our families."

Jenna is surprised, not opposed to the idea but full of questions. She hungers for more morsels about them, the trajectory of their lives. And the men in their circle. Jenna is eager to delve into their long-ago experiences like a prospector digging for gold. And their enduring friendship. What is the glue that holds them together after so many decades? As they eat lunch, she showers them with questions, in quick succession—about the collective but also about the weekend, their lasting bond, their histories. Each new query leads to another as she feasts on their stories.

Jenna is close to both of her grandparents but realizes that she has never really listened to their tales, really listened. Now she pays full attention, truly hearing what these awe-inspiring women are telling her. At first blush, she underestimated her grandfather's friends and their place in his life. She was laser focused on the creases on their faces and necks, liver spots, balding hairlines, limps, and ambulatory weaknesses. They seemed like a bunch of dotards. Throughout her childhood, Poppy had regaled her with anecdotes about their earlier political escapades. Their demeaner just didn't fit in with those narratives. Now, she takes in the glint in their eyes, strength of character, and keen intelligence behind their aging façades.

She appreciates how these old-timers have brought out her grandfather's vitality. He appears younger-looking, more spirited than before the weekend. His face has more color. She envisions how they could strengthen each other, provide spiritual fellowship, comity, and affection well into their advanced years. She had been momentarily disconcerted by their plans but at this point recognizes the promise.

Midday turns to late afternoon, and Keith gives his granddaughter a weary glance. "Time to go," he says. "We have a long trip ahead of us."

"I exhausted you," she says apologetically. She rises from the table and places her hands on his shoulders. "If you need my help convincing Mom and Grandma about the collective," she says, "count me in." Jenna smiles at the others. "I intend to drop by so often you may need an exterminator to get rid of me." She turns back to her grandfather. "I want to hear more details on our way home."

"I, for one, intend to sleep," Keith warns her.

Jenna links her arm with his as they head to the car, supporting him securely. The women, who have fetched his luggage and guitar, begin singing the song that Keith wrote for them, and he joins in. Deanna, as usual, is blithely oblivious that she is off-key.

"No long faces," Keith insists as they embrace him. "This is not the end for us." Keith hums "When I'm Sixty-Four" as Jenna helps him into the Prius.

Once the vehicle is out of sight, Rebecca, Malaika, and Deanna regard each other. "Our third degree is over," Rebecca says.

"She's just checking us out," Malaika says. "Making sure Keith will be in good hands."

"I think Jenna is adorable." Deanna chuckles. "Less off-putting than Max's progeny."

"For sure. Little snobs, those two." Rebecca is still steaming at the way Max let his children push him around, at how he didn't stand up for himself or, for that matter, her.

Malaika glances at her watch. "It's time for me to go. Shanice will have dinner waiting for me."

The three women form a small circle, holding hands, their bony, veined fingers gripping firmly. Malaika leans in, gives a quick kiss to each of them, then folds herself into the car. She grabs a last look at her two pals in the rearview mirror before heading off. She can now allow herself to concentrate on her family and the realities of the future. A fusillade of options, opinions, stumbling blocks and decisions dart through her mind, like fireworks. Her lips start to quiver, and she chokes back a sob as tears spill down her cheeks. She's counting on guidance from Shanice but knows that, ultimately, she must take charge of her own life. Like she always has done.

♀

"And then there were two," Deanna and Rebecca blurt out in unison, their laughter blunting the ache from Malaika's departure.

As they lumber back to the house, Deanna flinches. She is limping badly, even with the cane. "The ole knee is deteriorating fast."

"Get it replaced! What are you waiting for?"

"Recovery could take at least six months. Who's going to take care of me?"

Rebecca stares at her dumbfounded. "What the hell are children for? You're going to visit your daughter tomorrow. Why not just stay for the surgery?"

Deanna bites her lower lip as she wrestles with the suggestion. "Angela has a busy law practice," she says. "Her husband, Cornell, is New Jersey's attorney general. I don't want to impose on them."

"Oh my god. Stop acting like a martyr. That's for Jewish mothers. Angela's your daughter. The least she can do is tend to you while you recuperate."

"And my obligations in California? Can I just abandon those?" Deanna combs through the commitments that suddenly press on her like a computer teeming with unread emails.

Rebecca points to Deanna's cane. "A walker is next. Then a wheelchair. What can be so important that you'll give up your mobility altogether?"

"Okay. I'll talk it over with Angela. But please stop browbeating me."

Rebecca eyes turn sullen, like a Basset Hound. "I only have your best interests at heart."

"I know, I know." Deanna's expression softens. "I'm just anxious about my visit with them. It's been such a long while. Like Malaika, I haven't exactly been June Cleaver as a parent or what she surely would have been as a grandmother."

Deanna sits down on the couch next to Rebecca and sighs. "Other grandmothers dote on their grandchildren. Since Sam's death, mine have had to make do with Zoom chats and presents from afar. They're growing up without me."

She pinches her mouth. "I've blamed our lack of in-person contact on Angela's unwillingness to make time to visit me. And the geographical distance between us. Then there's my assorted obligations. Arthritis became yet another excuse for not traveling to New Jersey. I've faulted everyone and everything besides myself. But the responsibility is mine. I let Sam's death alienate me from the family. She wallows for a moment in regret. "In the end," she continues, "Angela and the grandkids have been deprived of a close connection with me, and I with them."

Rebecca clutches her arm. "Now is your chance," she says. "Stay for six months and get to know them. Maybe by then we'll have concrete plans for our collective. At that point you can move East permanently."

Deanna envisions her three grandchildren and their chirpy "Hi, Nana," over the internet. At fifteen, Trayvon is a star basketball player in high school. If he's averse to a cuddle or two, at least she can go to his games and cheer him on. The two youngest, Asia and Tiara, may still be agreeable to snuggling and bedtime stories.

Slowly, the truth sinks in: she's not only been camouflaging her loneliness with endless hustle and bustle but also the steady deterioration of her knee through pain killers. Voila! If the ache is gone, the atrophy disappears. Yet again she has succumbed to smokescreens. As a physician, she should know better. She yearns to walk freely again, play pickle ball, keep herself physically active—not fall headlong into the incapacities of old age without giving it the old college try. She thinks about the glorious hours of swimming this weekend and how it energized her whole being.

Deanna meets Rebecca's gaze. "You win. If it's amenable to Angela and Cornell, I'll stick around for the surgery and convalescence—but only if you visit. New Jersey is not that far from Baltimore."

"Aunt Rebecca will be a regular guest," she says drolly. "After all, I should get acquainted with the motley kin of my future housemates."

Deanna shakes her head. "You'll never change." She surveys the now-empty great room before turning to face Rebecca. "It's truly been a life-changing weekend." She would like to say more but can't find the words. Eventually, a simple "thank you" leaks out, having to suffice. They acknowledge her imminent departure with a squeeze of their hands.

Deanna gathers her belongings, and Rebecca carries the suitcase outside as they wait for the taxi. She will catch a Trailways bus from New Paltz to Paramus. During the one-hour bus ride, finally alone, she intends to absorb the full implications of their get-together and possible shared future.

After relinquishing her cane to the adjacent seat, Deanna struggles into the back of the cab, moaning in agony.

She stares at Rebecca.

"What?" Rebecca says.

"My mug."

"Yes, of course." Rebecca hurries off to retrieve the prized memento. She hesitates for a moment, then fills the cup with water and drops two Tylenol into her palm. She hustles back to the taxi, the liquid splashing. Deanna shoots her a grateful look as she pops the pills into her mouth. She offers a weary wave, tilts back her head, and closes her eyes as the cab speeds away.

♀

And then there is one, Rebecca mouths to the rustling trees as she settles on the porch swing. She's not in a hurry to leave;

tomorrow morning will do. After all, she has nobody to return to. Each of the others will confront a mixed bag of family dynamics, an indeterminate tapestry of devotion, disquiet, affection, outrage, tenderness, and alarm. They will negotiate and wrangle with loved ones who may resist any break from the status quo. A consistent life, no matter how unsatisfying, is often preferred to untidiness. She and her friends are tampering with the known. Their proposed collective threatens to make gigantic waves throwing their respective families off course, like a ship tossing helplessly in a violent storm.

She, on the other hand, can make the transition seamlessly, throw on a new life as effortlessly as a bathrobe. There is no contentious spouse, no children or grandkids, no bitter siblings to obstruct her decisions, including the disposition of her inheritance. She's in charge of her life. Rebecca smiles sadly. There's no one else.

She looks up at the mountains. The sun has slipped away, creating golden tones of orange and pink in its wake. She picks up the remaining mug from the box and holds it up to the fading light: Rebecca, Reunion Weekend, June 5, 2025. She vacillated between "Becca" and "Rebecca" but ultimately decided that Max's pet name for her was between them alone.

She reflects on the two loves of her life and wonders whether she could have interwoven them through a baby. In different circumstances, Max could have donated his sperm, creating the child that she and Susan longed for. Would it have resembled her handsome Max? Or look more like her?

If only, if only. She dismisses the notion. Rebecca does not like to second-guess the past. She has never had much patience for people who obsess over every step they take, who wonder if there could have been a better way. She learned that from her beloved father. She can hear him scoffing, "Would have, could have, should have. What nonsense! Move on." So, she always forged ahead. Susan once had bought her a T-shirt that said, "Just Do It!" She still has it somewhere, tucked in a drawer.

The future is too overwhelming to fixate on what could have been. For once, she's not in control. She has no idea whether her vision of their shared household will come to fruition. The uncertainty has given rise to an uncomfortable sense that she is free-falling without a parachute, fully dependent on her comrades and their unpredictable families. That's not her usual modus operandi. Although she is confident in the rationale for their future arrangement—as certain as she had been in organizing workers and bargaining with their employers—at this point, she can only await their individual decisions.

And the best laid plans often go awry. She wrinkles her brow. Their proposed commune is an experiment without a blueprint. They will be improvising every step of the way. Where should they reside that would suit each of them? Will they really be able to take care of one another in their very old age, even with help? Is it just too massive an enterprise? Legal considerations, financial matters, and logistics reverberate through her head like the roar of a massive waterfall against the rocks.

Despite the loving bond that she and her friends share, Rebecca concedes that their surrogate family could experience similar dynamics as biological ones; it could nourish them with comfort and support but also engender misunderstandings and even discord. But in her estimation, the joy and mutual benefits would by far outweigh any drawbacks. This weekend has made clear that even after decades apart, they still speak the same language.

Rebecca swings gently, listening to the quiet surrounding her.

Acknowledgements

To the best of my ability, I have endeavored to accurately portray the historical events of the 1960s and 1970s in which my characters participated as well as the actual settings in certain places during those years, such as the City College of New York. However, the plot and principal players in *Wrinkled Rebels* are all fictional.

I would like to thank Jessica Bell and Amie McCracken at Vine Leaves Press for believing in the book and bringing it into the world. I could not imagine the novel in better hands. I am appreciative of the contributions of my developmental editor, Melissa Slayton, the rest of the Vine Leaves team around the world, and the press's uplifting, motivating community of writers on Facebook for keeping me going during the years prior to publication.

As always, my deepest gratitude and affection go to my spouse, George, for being my first reader and critic. I couldn't have written this book without his ongoing encouragement and unstinting support.

My heartfelt thanks to the enthusiasm and helpful critiques from early readers of the story: my good friends Janice and Anna and cousins Sharon and Carol. And to my forever friends from my undergraduate years at City College who contributed, if indirectly, to this novel: Bobby, ViviAnn, Billy, Bruce, and David. Thanks to other special friends who have offered me emotional sustenance over the years: Betty, Sandy, Phyllis, Marilyn, and Judy.

I am indebted to feminist and political activist Jo Freeman for ferreting out some factual errors and suggesting valuable additions.

I especially appreciate my daughter, Alix, who has provided me with affection, inspiration, and laughter; her steadfast belief in me and my work helps keep me writing. Two precious grandchildren, Zinn and Gray, fill my world with love.

Finally, I want to thank the many 1960s and 1970s political activists whose stories have contributed immeasurably to this novel.

Vine Leaves Press

Enjoyed this book?
Go to *vineleavespress.com* to find more.
Subscribe to our newsletter: